THE BEAUTIFUL ROOM IS EMPTY

EDMUND WHITE

THE
.BEAUTIFUL
.ROOM
. IS EMPTY

ALFRED A. KNOPF   NEW YORK   1988

THIS IS A BORZOI BOOK
PUBLISHED BY ALFRED A. KNOPF, INC.

Library of Congress Cataloging-in-Publication Data
White, Edmund, [date]
The beautiful room is empty.
I. Title.
PS3573.H463B43   1988   813'.54   87-40495
ISBN 0-394-56444-8

Manufactured in the United States of America

FIRST EDITION

To Stanley Redfern

"Ah! Do you have to be sensual to be human?"
"Certainly, Madame. Pity is in the guts, just as tenderness is on the skin."

Anatole France, The Red Lily

Sometimes I have the feeling that we're in one room with two opposite doors and each of us holds the handle of one door, one of us flicks an eyelash and the other is already behind his door, and now the first one has but to utter a word and immediately the second one has closed his door behind him and can no longer be seen. He's sure to open the door again for it's a room which perhaps one cannot leave. If only the first one were not precisely like the second, if he were calm, if he would only pretend not to look at the other, if he would slowly set the room in order as though it were a room like any other; but instead he does exactly the same as the other at his door, sometimes even both are behind the doors and the beautiful room is empty.

Franz Kafka,
in a letter to Milena Jesenská

THE BEAUTIFUL ROOM IS EMPTY

ONE

. . . .

I met Maria during my next-to-last year in prep school. She was studying painting at the art academy just across the street from my school, Eton, and she was seven years older than I, but she scarcely seemed to notice the difference. I see her even now striding along in black pants and a man's white shirt spotted with paint, her hair slicked back behind her ears, squinting into the faint winter sunlight. She's wearing white sneakers, also spattered with paint, a sailor's pea coat and no makeup, although her eyebrows have been slightly plucked. She looks very scrubbed and German but also faintly glamorous; the glamour clings to her like the smell of Gitanes in wool. Is it the hard defiance in her eyes or just the slicked-back hair with its suggestion of the high-school bad girl that lends her this dangerous aura?

It's terribly cold, snow is excitingly in the air like the promise of Christmas, we're hurrying up the steps leading to the academy's museum, and she has a cigarette dangling from her small blue hand purely for ornamental effect, since she doesn't know how to inhale.

It must be Sunday because there are two middle-aged

ladies out for the day from the big ugly city nearby, bundled up in old furs and posing on the steps for a man who is swaddled in a car coat. He's signaling the ladies to squeeze together, now he's inviting them to smile, now he's adjusting the focus and about to snap—when Maria sails between him and his subjects muttering to me, "Don't worry about this guy. Believe me, he's not exactly an artist."

I remember that moment because it was so out of character for Maria. In the 1950s in the Midwest there were very few culture vultures, the Abstract Expressionists were still beleaguered, and those ladies and the photographer were about to go into the school museum to look at the student show and, no doubt, have a good laugh. "Is that a Ferris wheel? A nose? Or did someone just toss his cookies?" they'd ask. The real cards would wonder if the painting had been hung upside down by mistake.

Things were simpler, clearer then. On one side were the painters, a few taunted, poor, scrawny kids, and on the other the philistines, the fat-cat majority. Certainly the painters felt justified at striking back at what they called the "boor-zhwah-zee," but Maria hated all sorts of cruelty, especially to other women and to animals. A little bit later, just a year or two later, and she'd never have insulted that Sunday photographer. She'd have said, "Who knows, maybe he's a genius in disguise. After all, Rousseau was just a Sunday painter." She thought some sort of second American Revolution would have to break out to equalize the wealth, but she prayed it would be bloodless.

A bearded sculptor in his early twenties named Ivan, who dutifully molded and cast big bronze insects, though he far preferred living the life of the artist to making art, had discovered me in the Eton barbershop. The art academy was side by side with the boys' school, but the students and teachers of the two institutions never mixed, although a few of the poorer artists worked in the Eton kitchen. The barber-shop, the kitchen, the Saturday-night movies when everyone sat on folding chairs on the basketball court of the boys' gymnasium—those were the only places where the two populations might have spoken to each other, though they never did.

I did. I spoke to Ivan. I don't know what I said, but he invited me to his studio. He thought I was precocious for some reason; maybe he just picked up on my eagerness to gnaw off the restraints. Through him I met other painters and sculptors, including Maria.

In the long winter afternoons when the skies would turn as cold and silvery as fish scales, I'd sit in the painters' studios and smell the espresso cooking down in nickel-coated pots on hot plates and try to find in their work what they'd secreted there. At first I'd struggle to see things, guess at what was being masked by all that fudge-thick impasto, that haze of flung drops, but I discovered very quickly how "bourgeois" my interpretations—or any interpretations—seemed to the artists. I also learned to say "painter" not "artist."

I was so eager to please (an extension of the high-school urge to Be Popular) that after only a few hasty observations of how the painters responded to each other's work, I'd mastered their technique. I, too, would sit on a high wood stool, itself piebald with spattered paint, and look and look without saying a word. That was the trick: say nothing, show nothing. A senile radio would be muttering to itself. The smell of oil paint and turpentine (for acrylics had not yet been introduced) stung my eyes and made my nose run. Windows climbed one wall, floor to ceiling, and through them I could see the silver-lined gray clouds boiling and descending like a deity about to abduct an extremely willing shepherd.

I looked and looked at the painting, trying to figure out what was there to be seen. Was it a sort of chess problem to be solved, a visual riddle, or was it a cat's cradle of tensions (I'd heard someone talking about "push" and "pull")? Or was I being too "intellectual" (a fault, as I'd gathered)? Should I regard the painting as a spiritual X-ray, a glimpse into the painter's unconscious ecstasy or agony? Or was it something like a football field on which conflicting teams of thoughts and feelings had skirmished and left this muddy aftermath of the action (for people spoke of "action painting")?

The painters themselves weren't quite sure, I realize now. After all, they were students in a provincial school and had nothing to go on beyond occasional visits to New York and perusals of stylishly inscrutable art magazines in which the celebrated genius of the moment intimidated everyone with grim whimsies ("If a bull wants to sit down in my arena, let him!" a gaunt young art widow, herself a painter, had recklessly declared).

One of the student painters I met compared his work to jazz and I dutifully looked at his canvases while listening to the newest bop, those cool blue blips and pop-eyed blasts, muted ballads or zany calisthenics. Another guy, a smilingly ironic man who seemed to be Maria's lover, said, "It's a dance. I mean, you know, it's when, you know, the painter moves toward the easel, like, and that is the real painting, you see, kind of like that."

No matter what people said or showed me, I just nodded, wisely. If I did venture an opinion, I replaced my native glibness with a slow groping after simple yet oblique words. Groping was taken as proof of sincerity.

But for me the encounter with these men and women and their efforts to explain themselves, with their proud poverty and shared solitude, gave me a view of a bohemian world in which people pursued goals that my father would have despised if he'd ever heard of them. After the stolidity of my childhood—the affluent Midwest of new Cadillacs, Negro maids, and wineless six-o'clock dinners—the sheer effrontery of these painters staying up all night and stretching canvas tight as drumheads, then thumping them with brushes, crayons, charcoal, finally smearing the whole mess away with rags—that thrilled my timid heart. "Common sense" was the name my father and his friends gave their smugness. They worked long hours, saved their money, minded their own business, and furnished their big houses with wall-to-wall carpeting and heavy, store-bought furniture. The sheer weight of their breakfronts and breakfasts, of their wool suits and wooly ideas kept them safely earthbound. But here were these kids, also Midwesterners, who'd left their Wisconsin dairy farms or Indiana milltowns and the chance to take up solid jobs with a future, in order to come here, to puzzle over French novels, listen to Gregorian chants, cut their own hair, work menial jobs, and stab and daub all night at scary, childlike paintings.

During that first Michigan winter, I scarcely knew Maria. She crept up on me like the sun, at first just a silvering of the hard pond, a gleam shot through icicles, but at last a patch of blue quarried out of gray cloud.

Ivan, the sculptor who'd discovered me, gave me a weird surrealist book to read, *The Songs of Maldoror* by the Count of Lautréamont. I remember I was most impressed by the biographical note that said the author had been not a count at all but a penniless Uruguayan who'd committed suicide in Paris at the age of twenty-four in 1870. I'd sit in Ivan's studio and read to him from this upsetting book about a long talking hair from a whore's head or a man who'd coupled in the sea with a shark. I remember a line that said, "I'm like a dog with its love for the infinite."

Ivan had a bushy, black beard but baby-smooth fore-arms and chest. He was short, stocky, friendly. Even in the coldest weather he wore nothing but a blue denim jacket, a red wool scarf, and a leather hat—not a cap but a proper hat fashioned out of rain-stained leather. He smoked sweet, cheap tobacco in a pipe that dipped and then curved up like a pipe under the sink. He liked red wine from gallon jugs and he drank it out of paper cups. And he liked *Maldoror*—so much, indeed, that he felt no need to seek another book. It was his book, as the Bible was his father's. I'd read it out loud and he'd sip wine from his cup and laugh, showing big white teeth outlined with tobacco stain; particularly good passages would cause him to drum the arms of his chair, hiss, and bounce up and down with the sort of bloodthirsty glee more usual in wrestling fans than readers. He never talked about women, although I gathered he was sunnily sexual with several of them.

Through him I met Paul, my first genius. He was a tall scarecrow leaking straw, the pale, uneven sheaves of his hair. His glasses were round, black, an anarchist's glasses, but his eyes were those of a nihilist without a program. He was the best painter at the school. Everyone, even the teachers, nervously acknowledged his superiority, and that distinction hovered around him, except Paul was indifferent to it. When I say he was a nihilist, I mean only at the core; on the surface he was scrupulously attentive to every detail, especially if it concerned someone else. He was so little at home in the world that each of its rituals (shaking hands, buttoning a coat, taking a step) required his concentration. He showed a minute interest in other people, tried to understand what they were up to, and the effect was strange, even comical, for his intelligence was so great that it attributed seriousness and ingenuity to whatever it studied—often more than was, in fact, there, so that when he cautiously discussed Ivan's bronze insects, they climbed a rung up the evolutionary ladder. Ivan would grin and nod and drum the chair arms with pleasure.

Since Ivan believed the best art was the least conscious, it didn't distress him that he'd never considered any of the intentions Paul ascribed to him.

I can remember visiting Paul in his studio on a cold winter day that had only brightened for an instant before paling, like a deep sleeper who turns over just once. The street outside the studio was lined with cars buried under snow. Each studio windowpane was frosted along its edges. Paul paced around his cubicle and made coffee for me with the same bemused attentiveness he devoted to everything. He wasn't big, but the effect was of Gulliver among the Lilliputians. Morally, too, because he gave the impression of being superior to everyone. Not that he was arrogant. On the contrary, his very patience and humility attested to the care he had to bring to the strange expectations of other people. We both sat and looked and looked at his latest painting, which I admitted to myself I would have considered a fraud if I'd seen it a month earlier, before I knew Paul and his reputation, before I'd felt his force. Now I considered his painting to be heroic, an unlikely war waged by this most diffident of men. Ivan suggested that someone should steal Paul's paintings away from him, since, to save money, he kept painting one masterpiece over another and his whole oeuvre could be found on one thick canvas. Paul laughed at Ivan and said, "It's student work. I'm just a student."

At that age (I must have been seventeen) I had no way of classifying or dismissing this encounter. I couldn't say, as, horribly, I might have said later, "He's a vigorous but undisciplined abstractionist who's slightly provincial." I was so young that I attributed the successes of a whole school to this single marginal member. And I liked him because I felt he liked me, no matter how remotely. Perhaps his remoteness was precisely what I trusted. I brought him some of the poetry I was writing, or rather my verse translations of Book IV of the *Aeneid* that we were working on in Latin class, and Paul said my version sounded like Milton.

"Is that good?" I asked.

"Very good," he said. "It's so big and full and extravagant."

Every afternoon, from three to five, when the other boys were either playing sports or attending study hall, I'd dart across Academy Row to the art academy. I was probably breaking a rule, but it had never been formulated because no student had ever wanted to infringe it before. I had to wear a coat and tie as the prep school required, but the bohemian painters in their coveralls and work shirts forgave me that; they saw me as a prisoner of a "bourgeois" system I'd soon be escaping.

On Saturday nights, when the boys' school, the girls' school, and the art academy convened in the gymnasium for a movie, I filed in with the other boys—but then broke away and, wearing my Brooks Brothers suit, sat in the midst of all those beards and peasant shawls. I sat there blushing because I was afraid to lose my prep school friends—I was a fearful, conservative boy.

A decade later in America, art became a national pastime, and museum-going a cheap weekend date, a sort of Sunday drive without the car, but in the mid-fifties my painters were far from acceptable. That was a time and place where there was little consumption of culture and no dissent, not in appearance, belief, or behavior. There were very few foreign movies, no amused stories in the press about the hijinks of the avant-garde. Everyone ate the same food, wore the same clothes, and people decided whether they were Democrats or Republicans. The three most heinous crimes known to man were Communism, heroin addiction, and homosexuality. Boys played sports, girls planned their trousseaus, parents and children alike read comic strips in the paper and shared a chuckle. Of course there were the motorcycle-riding, hell-raising, hooky-playing "hoods," but our school didn't have any of those.

It felt, at least to me, like a big gray country of families on drowsy holiday, all stuffed in one oversized car and discussing the mileage they were getting and the next restroom stop they'd be making, a country where no one else was like me—or worse, where there was no question of talking about the self and its discontent, isolation, self-hatred, and burning ambition for sex and power.

And yet here were these painters and potters and sculptors. Not just the odd, tormented weirdo I'd known before, the prissy teacher's pet, the scrawny organ student sneaking into chapel to rehearse, the wimp lurking around after shop to make something pretty for his grandmother—no, here the freaks had banded together, they passed the communal wine cup in the movie's flickering darkness, they snorted when the hero on the screen pledged to defend America and all it stands for.

They seemed to have bought the right to eccentricity by working very hard. That was the American part. They'd wear layers and layers of sweaters, fleece-lined boots, hats and babushkas, mittens with the fingers missing, and they'd stamp their feet against the cold as they labored late into the night. The wind slipped in through rattling skylights and cold seeped up off stone floors; even at noon the sky never rivaled in brightness the humming neon tubes above them, while their vats of clay grew crystals and the nails they drove into boards seared cold into their naked fingers—but they worked on and on, staring at these big nightmare cakes they never finished icing.

I didn't have an appointment with Ivan or Paul. I was wearing nothing but khakis and a sports coat despite the freezing winter winds. I darted across Academy Row, skipping stylistic centuries as I left the fake gothic battlements of the boys' school for the unadorned, 1930s modernism of the art school. No cars were moving down the road. Everything was silent. Rain had pockmarked the snow before last night's freeze set in.

In the studio building the radiators knocked slowly and constantly. In each cell someone was working. Here and there the odor of cigarettes or coffee scorched through the blanket smell of oil paint. An atmosphere prevailed of intellectual and manual labor, of frustrated but hopeful solitude—something serious, unrebukable. That was when I had my first look at Maria. I didn't yet know who she was. I just glanced into a studio and saw her there, paintbrush in hand, eyes closed, waltzing slowly around the room. The radio was playing the waltz from *Der Rosenkavalier*.

Paul greeted me with his Martian approximation of a smile but no handshake.

"Am I disturbing you?" I asked.

"No," he said, cocking his head to one side as though to test the accuracy of his reply.

And that was that. He pointed to a canvas-backed director's chair. I slid into it. He pressed a cup of coffee into my cold hands. Then he regained his high stool and we both looked and looked at his painting. People say that painting is an instantaneous not a temporal art, but for me the contemplation of Paul's work unfolded thickly in time. What does he want me to say? What words of mine would please him, even help him? Should I say nothing? Those were the social questions that alternated with my slighter but quite real curiosity about his work.

Then I'd sneak a glance at him, at his powerful jaw propped up by his hand as though its very weight solicited support, at his smudged glasses, at the tiny spume of blond hair on his Adam's apple that the razor had missed for several days. I tried to imagine kissing those dry lips, wrapping my arms around that tall skinny body, but I couldn't thread that particular loop of film through the projector. As half-consciously I inched toward my desires for men, I clung to my official goal of stifling these desires. I wanted to be a heterosexual—perhaps with a bohemian girl? Back to Paul's canvas and its lipstick colors crosshatched by charcoal stabs, scene of a crime not yet committed.

I feared Paul attributed powers of observation to me that weren't there. We listened to an old scratchy recording of a Bach unaccompanied cello suite. The music, so spare, so passionate, seemed at any moment about to break into speech. It cut with precision into the big soft folds of time that nearly smothered us.

In this studio with the bluish light reflected off the late-afternoon snow and the sound of outdoor voices traveling easily as over water, I felt a new form of comfort. Paul was beside me, blinking and thinking, a bird on spindly legs regarding his own gaudily cerebral paintings. A year before I'd wanted to be a Buddhist monk, but now I thought I'd prefer to be an artist of some sort. I wondered what Paul was thinking. Was he busily proposing and rejecting solutions, or was he staring into a void of indecision, of fear about going on with the work? I couldn't tell, since he did not like to talk.

His silences were enough like my father's to fill me with grave anticipation. But he himself was completely different— as thin as my father was fat, as deferential as my father was overbearing, as open to new ideas as my father was closed.

On the particle-board partition that separated his cubicle from the next, Paul had thumbtacked things that might inspire him: a reproduction from *Time* of an Arshile Gorky drawing; a *National Geographic* photo of neon-bright tropical fish darting through dun-colored fans of coral; a pencil sketch he had scrawled on a paper place mat from Howard Johnson's.

I glanced at my watch and realized I had to hurry back to school for the ringing of the next bell—I was on waiter duty at supper time. "How wonderful it must be to have long hours of freedom," I said.

Behind the glinting, anarchist's glasses Paul's eyes looked exhausted: "Someday you'll have more freedom than you'll want." I could see his freedom was glued to him like a leech. Every day he looked thinner, older, more fragile, almost like someone recently dead who appears in our dreams, unshaved and reproachful.

At the party in Jim Coburn's studio (he made stained glass) I started talking to Maria. I'd never before been to a grown-up party as a grown-up and I'm sure I took it more seriously than anyone else there—I must be the only one alive who still remembers that casual event, a birthday drink in the middle of the afternoon.

Maria was wearing a man's shirt of white Oxford cloth; the button-down collar was unbuttoned and tipped up in back, so that it framed her long pale neck. In the hollow of her neck there was a smudge of red paint, just where a grandmother in a play might have worn a cameo on a black ribbon.

She was talking to a young man who seemed all hair, a haystack of hair; his shoulder-length hair merged into a russet-highlighted beard, which in turn seemed to grow into his brown poncho, to be its father. Maria was wielding a cigarette unconvincingly, sipping wine, and squinting. But when I glanced back a moment later, she was wide-eyed and laughing. Her smile looked so clean, as white as the whites of her eyes. She was really laughing in an almost soundless quake, but her eyes were blind with tears of amusement. When Ivan introduced us, she wiped away the tears and dialed down the brilliance of her smile.

"You're the one!" she said, very kindly. "Everyone's talking about the Boy Who Dared to Cross the Street." And she laughed in the softest, most reassuring way to invite me to see myself as a droll rebel. "Let me get you some more wine," she said, and a second later she was pushing past dangling panels of colored glass.

We found ourselves in her dormitory room. Like everything else in the art academy, her room had a distinctive odor I've never encountered since except once, recently, in the Chanel boutique of a Paris department store. I almost asked the saleswoman what the smell could be, but the most important things in our intimate lives can't be discussed with strangers, except in books.

I was flushed from the wine, which, like an old-fashioned movie director, had edited out the entrances and exits and now was tracing a halo around the starlet's profile. Everything in the common room had been chosen by the great Finnish architect who'd built the school, from the molded blond plywood chair I was sitting in to the unbleached muslin curtains. Outside, saltimbanques of snow were leaping up and flipping backward.

That first visit I noticed several things about Maria that don't usually go together—her hard intellectual zeal, for she was telling me about John Dewey's *Art and Experience*, and her motherly kindness and love of coziness, for she'd tucked a down comforter over my legs, something she called a "bleemo" and that years later I realized must be a funny German-American pronunciation of *plumeau*. She did have a sharp way of arguing ideas, of saying "Nonsense!" or "What rubbish!" which reminded me of our English exchange student, who, despite his shingles and shyness, was intellectually combative. Of course, Maria was sufficiently American to smile every time she called me a "total idiot."

She worried I might find her room drafty.

"You should try *our* dorms," I said. "Deep freeze. Their tribute to Merrie Olde England."

She poured out a cup of tea to sober me up for my return to school. "I picture your school as far more decadent than ours."

"No such luck," I said.

Because they were both men, I was more drawn to Ivan and Paul than to Maria, at least at first. I was always trying to figure out their schedules, to find them in, to visit them without troubling them. I spaced out my visits.

When I ran into Maria a week later, she was standing beside a broken-down old station wagon and talking to a tall woman in coveralls. When introduced, the woman shook my hand with a hot hand she drew out of a rawhide workman's glove.

Maria invited me to climb in beside her and drive into town. During my three years at school I'd been downtown only twice; it was strictly against the rules.

It was snowing. The wipers slowly and noisily creaked against the dirty windows. We peered out of the portholes they cleared as the car crept down suburban lanes past the distant yellow lights of mansions. The bald tires slid on the ice. Maria said, "Shit," and flashed me a tiny smile at her daring, for young ladies did not say such words. Nor did anyone in that rich Detroit suburb, the home of the "automobility," drive a ten-year-old station wagon with a rusting fender and just one new door, which was painted a different color. Everything was cozy inside the car, with its blasting heat, its tinny radio, and, in the back, a can of turpentine and the rack for paintings. Outside, the snow was draping the luxuriant black pines in white.

Away from her school and mine, we both relaxed. I

imagined she no longer had to observe everything with the exhausting attention of someone always expected to have an aesthetic opinion. Nor did she have to behave with that deliberateness required of someone who lives in a small society where no rules are explicit but every action may be setting a precedent. After all, the art academy students were all free to do exactly as they pleased, a terrible responsibility, and even their teachers were painters with odd personal habits, including the urge to be alone. Here were sixty young people, men and women, some of them away from their rural, religious homes for the first time, and they were all expected to paint great paintings, move nearly wordlessly into and out of each other's austere single beds, listen to Bach or Charlie Parker, and wear strange clothing that ostracized them from the prep school boys as well as from the furred gentry of the adjacent estates.

In town Maria and I felt better. At least I did. The streets had been cleared, traffic lights lidded in snow burned like mad eyes, Christmas shoppers submitted to their forced labor, there were other cars cruising around as old and dirty as ours, everyone seemed busy and indifferent—the rich anonymity of the city. Maria invited me for a hamburger, not at the fancy Petite Auberge where "half-pounders" were loaded with melting Roquefort, but, as she said, "At that adorable greasy spoon." From my mother I'd learned that "nice" people should always frequent "nice" places, but here was Maria, certifiably nice, who relished the diner, twirled on the metal stool like a bobby-soxer, and punched out tunes on the jukebox. "Don't you just love the Everly Brothers?" she asked.

I shrugged, but I think in that one remark Maria changed my way of seeing things. My father was rich in his remote but solid way, and my mother, divorced from him ten years earlier, was poor in her flamboyant way, squandering money on clothes and economizing on food. They each disapproved of each other; my father especially disapproved of my mother; the net effect was to confuse me. I never felt right in any setting. That I also feared I might be some sort of pansy only made me feel all the more weird.

I wanted to escape my childhood world and be superior to it. I'd read about Oscar Wilde. Wilde made brilliant repartee, but not in a void. People had listened, remembered his words. I, on the other hand, quoting Wilde, had said of the recently widowed mother of one of my junior-high-school friends, "I hear her hair has turned quite gold with grief," and Kathy Becker, the class sweetheart who always wore baby blue cashmere, shook her head and said, "I feel sorry for you—you're sick." That Wilde was broken and Rimbaud driven into exile only seemed the reasonable price society demanded for such splashy transgressions.

The lurid decadence of nineteenth-century Europe, with its mauve glasses and moth-eaten velvets, its melancholy lords and suitably untouchable ladies—that was a world I pined after, not this Detroit of behemoth cars, beetling their way through snow, these peppy renditions of novelty songs (Rosemary Clooney singing "If I'd Knowed You Was A-Comin' I'd've Baked a Cake"). I felt a real nausea whenever I faced America's frumpy cuteness, the Red Nosed Reindeer stamped out of dirty white plastic, the Hit Parade singers on TV dressed up to look like little kids, grown women in nylon Gretchen braids.

But Maria turned this dross to gold by touching it, by holding it out and looking at it. She suggested it was sufficiently distant from her to appreciate.

Rather startled, I said, "You mean you actually like this music?"

"Little snob," she laughed, her eyes tearing in some paradox of affection I couldn't quite understand, "such a snob," and she kissed me on the cheek as if I were some wonderfully stuffy old man. Her flat-chested torso shook soundlessly. With the back of her hand she slowly nudged the tears out of her eyes.

And then I did relax. I cautiously admitted to myself that I liked this tiled restaurant and the teenage cook with the paper hat perched on his greased-back hair. I liked the idle pleasure of sitting over a third coffee with a friend, saying whatever came into my head, then lapsing back into a daydream, listening to snow chains on the street outside. Maria and I decided to collaborate on a best-seller. We took turns elaborating a plot about riches in Detroit, romance in Rio, broken heart in Paris, drug addiction in New York. We'd both burst into a new episode at the same time, laugh, insist the other one speak first. Maria deleted anything highbrow or arty. "We want this one to sell," she said.

Until now I'd divided the world into either philistines or aesthetes. The pretensions of the aesthetes convinced no one, me least of all, since most of the jocks who attracted me were philistines. Or perhaps I felt that over here, in America, the aesthetes were weakened, languishing, having strayed too far from the mother ship of Europe. At the same time, I never doubted that the *Hammerklavier* sonata was superior to "Kitten on the Keys."

But here was Maria with her smiling impertinence, suggesting that we aesthetes of course lived for high art, but (come on, admit it) we also loved wild rides in jalopies, heavy petting, window shopping, followed by a really greasy burger, cherry Coke, and chocolate cream pie. "Try not to hate your own country, Dumpling," she said, no longer laughing, but as though she were telling me to bundle up against the cold.

She had a way of making a visit to her room or studio at once physically enervating and mentally bracing, for at the same time that she was making hot chocolate on her hot plate or tilting the lampshade to screen the glare she was also challenging all my views. Although I was an atheist, I was a mild sort of unbeliever, looking back with reluctance at those brocaded chasubles and smoky censers, but Maria despised all churches with the wrath of a Savonarola. At the boys' school we had to say grace before supper, and Maria thought this custom outrageous.

"I just go through the motions out of respect."

"Respect?" she snapped. "Why respect mindless superstition? I refuse to go along with grace at family meals."

And yet she loved her mother, who never argued with her brilliant daughter but just murmured soothing things: "If there is a Lord, I'm sure He loves you, what with all the good you do, I never saw the like. Did you try Aunt Sarah's pickled watermelon rind?"

Maria was equally uncompromising about the revolution that was coming and the benefits Communism would bring to all of humanity. If I mentioned the imprisonment of dissidents, she'd say scornfully, "Do you seriously think the civil liberties of a few individuals outweigh the right of millions of ordinary people to feed and educate their children? And not just their boys, their girls too. There are so many women doctors and women party members in Russia. Anyway, it's a brand-new experiment, not even forty years old. Of course, they can't change Russia overnight, after centuries of czarist oppression." She really talked that way. Before she'd come to the art academy she'd been at the University of Chicago.

When I asked Maria how she liked social realism in painting, she said, "But we know so little about their painting, we're told it's nothing but banal magazine illustration, but have we seen their best work? What if it is bad art, so what, if that's what the people like? I worked on that socialist paper in Iowa City last summer and we learned that factory workers and farmhands like illustrations precisely to the degree they are realistic. Anything the least bit abstract they loathed."

"But what about your own painting?" I asked.

"I'd be willing to burn every painting ever painted to feed one person in India. Or Mississippi."

"Then why do you keep on painting?"

"I tell myself," she said, lowering her eyes and laughing, "that I'm painting for the masses a hundred years from now. Too crazy. I don't know why. Perhaps I'll stop."

Maria's political conscience struck me as admirable but superfluous, like some unusually harsh act of religious penance. I myself embraced the worm's-eye view of the world. I thought no one would stick by me in a pinch. I owed nothing to anyone. My drive to ingratiate myself with other people was scarcely a moral urge, but rather the reverse, since I'd betray anyone or any principle to win the approval of whoever happened to be next to me at the moment. Although I had scarcely acted on my sexual impulses, I knew that if they were discovered I'd be an outcast, no matter in which society. When I repeated Maria's socialist doctrines to the kids at my school, it was only to thrill them, to demonstrate my Christian willingness to sacrifice my comfort for the betterment of mankind. My socialist posturing was also a way of social climbing, since I always included my father among the capitalists I was determined to dethrone, whereas he was just a small entrepreneur.

Not that I was selfish. I never hoarded candy or dollars or ideas; in fact I anxiously gave them away to buy off hostility or to bribe affection. Far from being indifferent to suffering, I winced so much at the sight of pain that I couldn't sit through a horror movie. The only condition for my sympathy was proximity. Unheard trees that fell made no sound to my ears, and hoards of the starving in India made no demand, at least not on me. Yet even those people near to me I cared for in some way that was more immediate than the sentiment politics required. If I'd been a king, I would have been more likely to have cared for the sick by touching them than by building a hospital.

I was neither as warm as people thought nor as cold as I feared. After an exhausting day of smiling and asking interested questions of everyone, I'd be kept awake by feelings not of hate but of unreality.

I discovered that every day I looked forward to seeing Maria. She was more curious about me than was Ivan or Paul. With them I was typecast as the precocious kid. I suppose they felt sorry for me too; people who knew me then tell me that I was terribly nervous, always fidgeting and biting my nails. I had a tic, a constant bobbing of my head, that was so bad I hated to have anyone sit behind me in a movie or, worse, a play. Although I thought of myself as a sinister young man, now I realize that most people back then felt sorry for me.

Not Maria. She liked my mind. She was like one of those characters in a Chekhov story, a doctor or army officer, who fills a silence by asking, "What do you think people will be doing a hundred years from now?" Now, a hundred years later, I distrust ideas and have few enough. Almost any assertion suggests its opposite to me, and a wide if careless reading has taught me that every enthusiasm, if genuinely embraced, turns into folly or fanaticism. But back then, developing an idea was as neat as doing crosswords. And with Maria our intellectual conversations were as romantic as Puccini duets.

One day, a Sunday after church, I went walking with Maria and Sam, her lover, a bearded Assyrian king of a man who, when he shaved later that spring, appeared weak-chinned and plump-cheeked. He raked his beard with his fingers as he walked along. His lips looked delicately pink inside the crisp curling beard. He seemed to find it amusing that he had a beard. He was very sure of himself, which I deduced from his smooth walk, his smile, and his mild spoofing.

Maria never sank into playing the happy couple with Sam while I was around. She didn't turn me into a sidekick. Of course, I was used to being a sidekick. I spent a lot of time with the guys from Eton and their girlfriends, counseling them when they were quarreling, and cavorting to entertain them when they were happy. I was the blur of motley they glimpsed through dreaming eyes. I was their intermediary in that they sensed I was somehow intermediate. I wrote a story called "The Hermaphrodite," about a creature full of longing who bound his breasts and worked at lowering his voice.

Yes, I danced attendance on my couples, confidant to him, cavalier to her. But Maria and Sam treated with me separately. They didn't aspire to be a couple. They were friends. Maria called Sam, "My friend." I was also her friend. And Sam seemed to like me in his beard-stroking way.

Now I sometimes think I don't feel enough, perhaps because I know myself too well. I've grown tired of myself. But then I was still a stranger to myself. I was shocked by the turbulent waves of feeling coming out of me—a laugh, a harsh word, a simper, a fit of tears that would go on so long my Adam's apple would ache. Now when I hunch over my solitary lunch in a Paris café I'll overhear a group of American tourists. I'm sure the Parisians dismiss them without a second thought, these men in bold plaids and women in big, lime green homemade pants, but I stare for an instant at the well-behaved boy or glassy-eyed girl at their side. I suspect the boy (isn't that a perfect church-attendance pin in his lapel?) may become an ax murderer, or the girl the president. They're like cute novelty jugs, but containing potent liquor, possibly poisonous.

During spring vacation Maria wrote me a long letter in pencil. She used the simplified spellings the *Chicago Tribune* had introduced ("nite" for "night," "thru" for "through") and lots of abbreviations. Despite these eccentricities, her letter was as varied as her talk—observations on the Cold War alternating with praise of Jussi Björling as Des Grieux in *Manon Lescaut*, flattering concessions to my opinions ("Your dislike of Faulkner is making me reread him") alternating with equally flattering rejections of my ideas ("You talk too much about happiness and not enough about fairness in your discussions of Communism. In fact your airy disregard of what's fair I find shocking. It's almost as though you are lacking a whole critical faculty").

Without transition she wrote, "I'm considering breaking off with Sam. I don't think he'll even notice, he hasn't called me or written in two weeks. I think I'm a much better friend than lover, anyway, at least I show more of my feelings to you than to him."

That was when I fell in love with Maria. I'm a nominalist; I believe only in what's named. Until then Sam had seemed so superior to me as to belong to another species. He had the lazy smile of someone many women had loved.

If Maria had been less elegantly reserved, I might have hashed out with her all my feelings of inadequacy and ended by losing her. But Maria didn't want to get to the bottom of anything but ideas. Her feelings were all impulsive and uncritical. I once told her I thought love was a hoax and I repeated something I'd read, that love hadn't existed in the ancient world and had only come in with the troubadours. She found this notion so absurd she'd often mention it to other people as a hilarious example of my gullibility. For her love was the one simple, painful or blissful fact in a world of shifting speculations. For her, love was as simple as Des Grieux's cry to Manon: "In your deep eye I read my destiny."

The wonder is that when she laughed at my theory of love no one ever defended me, since my theory is certainly arguable. But no one wanted to contradict Maria. She made her ideas—no, her very being—appear so likable no one wanted to be unlike her.

Because she'd been to the University of Chicago and had been converted to its Aristotelianism, she stripped every argument down to its starkest tenets and frequently asked, "What's your point? Can you put that in a nutshell?" That habit made her unpopular later among New York intellectuals, who seldom feel comfortable in a shell and prefer expanding to contracting their arguments. All those intellectuals who rely on their own prestige or invoke the authority of others filled her with contempt. Name-dropping, except by social climbers, struck her as silly; she forgave the social climbers, since she found them touching, almost novelistic in their pursuit of frivolously minor gods. But those people who thought eloquence could replace logic and considered the essay a transition toward the novel drove her wild with impatience; she'd brush her face with her hand as though rubbing away a cobweb. Not that she disliked make-believe; she read novels night after night, propped up in her single bed, the lamp beating back the darkness, her free hand blindly reaching for the glass of red wine.

My own habit of looking for a personal reason someone might have for holding a particular view ("Her idealism, of course, reflects her Christian childhood") seemed to Maria a sneaky way of stealing a march. She said my approach was as shoddy and as insidious as gossip and she ascribed it to my early and continued immersion in psychotherapy. Freud she despised as a thorough charlatan and she insisted that none of his views—that there is an unconscious, that sex is a key to motivation, that childhood shapes the adult personality—had ever been proved, nor were they susceptible to verification. She said these bizarre notions had merely been repeated so often that the cowed public had ended by accepting them. But she forgave me most of my follies, stroked my hair, and told me what a genius-dumpling I was with my chewed-away nails, bobbing head, and surprising bits of knowledge.

Maria read constantly but remembered little. At least she wasn't very handy at serving things up. When I read I squirreled away tidbits I hoped I'd be able to repeat. I read more and more just to entertain her.

She thought I was brilliant, but my only brilliance was my ability to appreciate her. Not as a woman perhaps, for I dimly sensed there was a passionate woman hidden in this slim body, housing an appetite capable of rapture and even violence. I felt awed by this force, but I didn't know how to make use of it. The rest of her I understood perfectly, with the best kind of devotion, the wide-awake kind. Nothing in Maria was wasted on me—that was the sole extent of my brilliance.

That spring Maria and I went on long walks together through the grounds of the school, past a pool stocked with fat ornamental carp, up to the Edwardian mansion of the Founders (maintained in sealed-wax splendor), down a hill toward the artificial lake on which the girls' school was floated. Then up along a wild tumbling brook to the Greek theater where plays were given in the summer. Now it was deserted. Behind the small amphitheater lay an atrium built around a rectangular pool, and there she told me shocking things—that she thought Jackson Pollock was a fraud, that she imagined we'd all be killed by the proletariat, that she considered the life of one African mine worker worth more than the Sistine Chapel.

. . .

I didn't know whether I liked Maria or I loved her. One day in her studio we sat around talking about our futures. The window was open a crack, and just outside a branch of bright yellow forsythia was preening. Maria was wearing an old, tan canvas hunting jacket that had belonged to her grandfather; she wore it over a beige turtleneck sweater. An empty Hills Brothers coffee can nestled sideways in another one which was upright on the ledge under the window. From where I sat I could look into the upper can. Its grooved interior seemed a distillery for changing watery light into sparkling *eau de vie.* Her black pants were bright with daubs of white paint and had fainter comet tails where her hand had smudged them. She'd penciled her plucked eyebrows in very black today, as black as the dots of her small nostrils.

"I can't believe you actually want to be famous," she said. "Famous as what? A writer?"

"I suppose," I said, "or an actor, or a general, or—"

"General!" She unnested the coffee cans and used the top one as an ashtray. "So you'd do anything, anything at all to be famous." She looked me in the eye suddenly, as though to surprise the answer there. "But why?"

"Freud says the writer writes for fame, money, and the love of beautiful women."

"Or men," Maria added. My heart stopped. Was she enlarging the definition to include the goals of women writers or was she suggesting I wanted beautiful men?

"Or men," I conceded, "though Freud, I'm afraid, didn't encourage women to be very ambitious."

"Who does? Certainly no one at this school. My *theology* professor at the University of Chicago was more interested in his women students than the painting instructors here are. I guess they believe the female spirit is earthbound and only the male is creative."

"Maybe they think the girls will all get married."

"Not me," she said.

I asked her why. She threw out one reason after another but none seemed to justify her indignation. When I teased her, as I'd heard other men do a hundred times, and told her she would surrender to the right man, tears of anger sprang to her eyes. Anger, I guess, or maybe she was hurt that I understood her so little. I took her hand and stroked it. I was sick I'd vexed her. "Good," I said, "because I'm never going to marry either."

"Really?" she asked, smiling as she slowly pushed the tears away with the back of her other hand. "Will you be famous all alone?"

"No, with you. You'll have to be famous to encourage the next generation of women painters and socialists and to keep me company."

She said she preferred reading all night and drinking bad wine. "Honestly, can you think of anything more inviting than fresh sheets and an open book turned face down on the night table? But if I can be famous and lonely with you, I'll give it a whirl."

Because I admired Maria, I wanted to be like her—or like the image of me she cherished. She said that I liked everyone so much and entered into everything so readily that life became more exciting around me. "How dull my life seems when you're away," she'd complain. But what she considered my enthusiasm for everything was really nothing but my love for her. To woo her I would inject color and motion into accounts of insipid events and sluggish thoughts. Since she was so intellectual, I too led the life of the mind— but with conviction only when I was with her.

Alone, back in my dormitory room, I'd become distracted by the small changes percolating through my body (an itch crystallizing on my knee, a cough scrabbling to get out of my chest, advancing and retreating armies of impatience and lassitude) and I'd toss aside Bergson's *Metaphysics* or Santayana's *The Sense of Beauty*, neither of which seemed likely to become an after-dinner story or a how-to book. My sense of guilt was too pressing to leave me the calm needed to contemplate the sense of beauty. With Maria I could take up such a question, perhaps, because my urge to keep her entertained led me to juggle with whatever I was handed by circumstance. The glamour of intellectual effort was on me. I pictured a dim study in a German town and could almost smell the hard, shaved face and touch the manicured, spatulate fingers of the great thinker as he sat in the glow penetrating the green glass shade of his desk lamp . . . But the second I was alone, this phantasm faded, the great thinker scratched his leg, longed to be somewhere he'd feel less tense, less empty. I liked to think I was a Buddhist disillusioned with the world, but I was caught in Maya's strong silk cords. I never doubted the world could make me happy, if only it would give in.

To make it relent, I was refining all the seducer's skills— his ready sympathy, his tight focus on the prey, his anxiety to entertain, his ulterior mission to lead every conversation toward surrender and conquest. The seducer grows ardent only in pursuit. Left to his own devices he feels shabby, the half-mask cast aside and worthless at dawn, even though last night it had flattered the face it had concealed. In conversation I took my cue from every smile or flicker of exasperation I read in Maria's face; alone, trying to reconstruct my warmth on the page, I'd turn stupid, lumpish.

Maria laughed at herself, teased me, and liked it when I made jokes at my own expense. The sudden shift of perspective that the long shot of humor required became habitual to me, something I've kept, though with less satisfaction than the practice is supposed to bring.

That summer, Maria went to Solitaire, an artists' colony in the Michigan woods, and in August my father let me join her for a week.

All of June and July I'd worked as a stockboy for my father's haberdasher—boxing and mailing garments, waiting on customers when things got busy, making deliveries, and endlessly repolishing showcases and restacking shirts and stockings. Now riding a train by myself through the hot, flat countryside seemed a rare freedom. I was free to eat, read, and doze when I wanted, to watch the afternoon light burn on silver grain elevators, to swoop past airless fields of luxuriant green and gaunt farmhouses or dilapidated barns painted long ago with now-faded Bull Durham chewing tobacco signs. The train hurtled through towns where cars waited at the crossing and a collie peered down its long nose at an alley cat and the sun found over there a single small window to dazzle—just as I imagined God, if He existed, might find in a whole crowd only one soul turned at the right angle to reflect His glory. And there, bordering that two-lane highway, was planted a row of signs that, word by word, asked a question, gave the joking answer, and ended with the name of a shaving soap, Burma Shave.

Those were the years, in the late 1950s, when serious literature was teaching the few serious readers that communication between any two individuals is impossible, that we are all isolated and that this isolation is no accident but due to the "human condition" itself. And yet I, who had been isolated, now found such perfect communion with Maria that I couldn't detect a single gap between us, and I exalted in our closeness. Of course, there were many differences and omissions, but now during the hot windless evening they were forgotten.

We went wandering through the woods, great forests of shabby birches unspooling themselves, until we reached the dunes, climbed them, and looked out at the late afternoon sun reflected by Lake Michigan. We took off our shoes and sat on the beach, digging our feet down into a layer of cold, root-thick marl so much blacker than the hot surface sand. We stared into the sun and talked, our words overlapping, our laughter ringing out across the still, orange water. A loon flew overhead, then dove for a fish. We held hands. I was wearing my suit for the train (for in those days Americans still dressed up for travel), but Maria had on white shorts, a T-shirt, and sneakers, nothing more, so for once I felt the older, graver one. I was pale from my shopkeeper's summer, she as tan as she ever became.

When she talked, she squinted as though sighting an idea in the distance. Her squint would even flutter slightly. A small colorless wen was attached to her lower left eyelid and, like a speck in her eye, this slight deformity added—oh, but it's hopeless for me to work up an inventory of this woman I've known now for three decades and whose looks and way of moving have become the argot of my feelings.

That night the summer heat did not lift and I lay naked under a wet sheet in a little cabin I'd been assigned on the edge of the woods. I listened to crickets. The sweat poured freely from my body. I was wide awake. The crickets throbbed louder and louder, as though they were rattles on the ankles of approaching dancers. When I closed my eyes, I still could feel the lurching and speeding of the train. The train would delve into a tunnel, then emerge and flirt with a fellow-traveling river that refused to stick to the party line.

I was so happy. Since the cabin had no closet, my clothes were hung on hangers along the wall or draped from hooks at different heights, and in the moonlight these shirts and jacket and pants looked like a flight ascending the white wall. I pulled on a pair of shorts and walked barefoot through the dew-squeaky grass down to the shack Maria had called the lithography studio. No one anywhere was awake, not a bird or dog or person. The cabins had no electricity, and even their kerosene lamps had been extinguished.

The moon was nearly full and almost directly overhead, like the hole in the Pantheon. But not an absence, rather a presence I'd call human except that it was nobler, at once tender and aloof—not a speaking presence but an intelligence I could address. Two big wooden lawn chairs, painted green, but looking almost blue-black in this light, conversed with one another sporadically like old people. The water scarcely moved but once in a great while lapped, as a sleeping dog will wake and hugely lick its lips before dozing off again.

Until now, looking at the night sky had usually made me long to be elsewhere, to escape, and had reminded me that I was alone, but here the night had changed and become friendlier. The moon was not the retreating face of a traveler seen through a veil of smoke but a concentrated attention bearing down on these cabins, these sleeping minds. I could picture the moon's rays as a protractor slowly turning to encompass us all in a perfect circle.

The next morning I had breakfast with Maria at the inn. Solitaire was made up of the paying guests, mostly older Sunday painters who came for a week or two and stayed with their husbands in the inn, and the kids who lived in the cabins for the whole summer and did odd jobs. Maria had befriended two of the older women; we stopped at their table on the way in. I was introduced to the artistic wives and their husbands, obese, amiable. Lots of loud polite talk—the skinny boy at the next table smirked with a thin Voltairian sneer. Maria was teaching a life-drawing class and she promised Marge, one of the two ladies, some extra time this afternoon.

The rest of the morning we spent on the porch in front of Maria's cabin. She was wearing a floppy straw hat and a halter top. She was painting a still life—wine bottle, apple,

Cinzano ashtray—and she laughed and said, "This is hard. Abstract Expressionism eliminated all this tiresome observation."

Although she was a Communist, Maria liked the songs of Noel Coward, Mabel Mercer, and Marlene Dietrich, and she played their records for me in the underfurnished rec room at the inn. She was the first to see the irony in this inconsistency, but her merely personal taste scarcely counted, she thought, when the question was one of a "scientific theory of history." I quickly came to love the tumbling wit of the Coward lyrics and the quixotic charms of Mercer and Dietrich, two stylists without voices and with a range of about five notes. Coward's rolled *r*'s and theatrical diction, joined to the gossip that he was "gay," interested me. "Yes," Maria said casually, "all slander, no doubt."

Closer to hand were Betts and Buddy, an ancient lesbian couple who lived in the most remote cabin at Solitaire. Just once I saw Buddy, who had been elected the local sheriff. I mistook her for a man, a short wide man, with grizzled, close-cropped hair and a swaggering walk. She was wearing her uniform and talking to the colony director, a much younger woman. I never saw Betts, but Maria often did, and loved describing her. "They're terribly poor, but Betts must have been a debutante fifty years ago because she has such fussy, elegant manners. She never leaves the cabin and is always wearing silk lounging pajamas and angora high-heeled slippers. She draws and redraws her makeup. She smokes with a cigarette holder and languishes. We're led to believe she's ill, but of what no one is crude enough to ask. Buddy stops at the bar in town for a drink every evening to shoot the shit with the guys, but then hurries home to her better half. Isn't it bizarre we find their marriage charming but we can't endure the heterosexual original they're aping?"

As I listened to Maria, I absorbed each small wrenching

of convention without a blink. The teasingly affectionate portrait of two such eccentrics stunned me, though I never let on. I knew I might be as diseased as they were—in fact, I had no doubt of it—but I'd never aired my neurosis as these women did, and if it were found out, I'd expect to be run to ground, not gently chided. But as the records spun, as Noel Coward talked about life coming to Mrs. Wentworth Brewster at the Bar on the Piccola Marina, when Marlene confessed that men clustered round her like moths to a flame and if they burned their wings she was not to blame, I felt plunged into a piquant world where sins were winked at, where in fact a juicy peccadillo was the price of admission. We sat in shabby rattan chairs under a naked light bulb inadequately screened by a lantern-shaped basket whose weave was too wide and let our eyes stray over the Ping-Pong table, the game of Chinese checkers, and the dart board, while just outside more and more moths, drawn by the light, or Dietrich, beat against the screens. Maria walked about restlessly as though she only half-believed her own daring words.

We drove into town in her station wagon. It felt strange to be chauffeured by Maria, and I registered this new awkwardness, which certainly I had not known last winter. But then I'd still been her little Dumpling, whereas now I was, well, what I imagined the other colonists took me to be: bourgeois visitor, friend, possibly suitor. Yes, complete with bourgeois male anxiety about who drives the car.

Maria led me in the slow dance at the bar, a noisy friendly hangout illuminated by the endless Niagara of the Miller's High Life sign and by the bubbling jukebox. I was too young to be in a bar legally, but no one noticed and we drank beer after beer and danced to polkas or slow hillbilly songs. Maria said she loved the hillbilly songs because they were about grown-ups, adultery, divorce, heartache. With her, even loss sounded as glamorous as gain.

TWO

■ ■ ■ ■ ■ ■ ■

My last year in boarding school during Christmas vacation in Chicago, I met a small Texan with bad eyes, bad skin, and the smell of Luckies on his breath. Tex ran a book and record store next to an art house showing movies near the Loop. "Art movies" were still new then. The label might mean Gina Lollobrigida jiggling provocatively up and down hills on a donkey or it might mean Gérard Philipe meeting an early death as the crazed painter Modigliani. Despite the range, art meant Europe, and something European shed its glow on Tex. I'd get on the elevated train in Evanston and ride an hour each way late in the afternoon just to escape my mother and sister and spend thirty minutes with him.

He loved books. I remember running with him down the street one gray winter afternoon when the sun, discouraged by a cold reception, had withdrawn. Tex had nothing on but a tweed jacket and a ratty scarf steeped in smoke, itself the color of smoke. He was racing like a kid to the post office to carry back to the store two boxes of books, all copies of *The Outsider* by Colin Wilson. I carried one box. Tex had ripped open the other and was juggling with it as he read random pages to me. "Listen to this, will you," Tex shouted with a sudden reemergence of his warm Southern accent. Generally he tried to sound contained, as though he'd just sucked a lemon, but now his mouth was filling up with hot sweet potato pie.

In another instant we were back in Tex's cozy store, which had been temporarily confided to the care of his pouty assistant, Morris. We settled into a heap on the pink velvet loveseat by the window to read *The Outsider* to each other in excited snatches. That was the way Tex read, as though a new book were a telegram addressed to him personally. This one was about a whole fortune that a spiritual uncle somewhere off in England had willed him, since the book told us about existentialism and its roots and suggested that, over there at least, to be an outsider was not a cause for shame but a condition that could be capitalized on, even capitalized. Tex talked to me about the Human Condition. Because he didn't introduce his ideas and he threw away the ends of sentences, he seemed to be letting me in on a conversation I'd be gauche to interrupt and question. The bitter coffee we drank, the sound of the discreetly murmuring announcer on the classical music radio station, and the sight of reflected spotlights tilting off varnished new books and records still in their cellophane wrappers—all of these things came together to excite me, especially since I knew Tex was gay.

Morris, the assistant, even used that word when there was no one else in the shop. He'd pulled up one trousers leg and caressed his calf and said, "I'm feeling so gay tonight." Then he shook his head as though he had curls instead of a close crop. He wasn't smiling; he was completely serious. I didn't know exactly what he meant but I knew he meant something quite precise.

"Shut up, Morris," Tex snapped in a cruelly direct voice

and jerked his head to indicate me. I turned just in time to catch it. "And Morris," he added, "lay off the fuckin' eyeshadow for chrissake. I'm running a respectable operation here. One more warning you're out on your little depilated tush."

I looked more closely at Morris. I couldn't see any trace of makeup. Why would he wear it? I wondered. Do queers like that? Is that how they can tell who's who?

The joy of reading *The Outsider* had turned ugly. Snow whirled in a sudden updraft, then fell through the streetlights.

Day after day the snow fell and the streets rang with the sound of shovels. People in fur hats and many layers of clothing tiptoed awkwardly over gutters piled high with the snow that street plows had turned back.

At home I felt a constant tingling excitement just knowing that yesterday afternoon I'd seen Tex and again today I would snatch a few minutes with him. In Evanston, I stood in the bay window and looked out at Lake Michigan beating itself up. Ticking steadily inside me was the thought, half-thrill half-fear, that within my grasp, or almost, lay this other world. This "gay world," you might say, with its mood swings turning slowly, then slamming you to one side like a roller coaster on a sharp turn. This world with its childlike enthusiasms and vicious attacks. I associated it with Morris's silent pouting and the way he'd stroked his leg, licked his lips, and said, "I'm feeling so gay tonight." Although I knew something would have to come out of my visits if I continued paying them, I feared what I hoped, and what I hoped I didn't want to know.

Tick, tick, tick. The excitement was in my pulse. I couldn't think of anything else nor did I want to. I'd look at the mashed potatoes exhaling steam and I'd hear the ticking in my ears. In my bed at night as I peeked through the curtains at the old man across the way reading his paper and luxuriantly picking his nose, I'd hear the tick taking me nearer to my next encounter with Tex.

The next afternoon Tex and I were alone in the shop. Morris was home with what Tex sourly referred to as a "sick headache" and Tex kept complaining about Morris's inept bookkeeping. He was looking through the accounts and a long gray silence installed itself in the room. For once the radio wasn't on and no well-bred announcer was reading to us from Pound's *Cantos* or playing us alternative interpretations of *"Nessun dorma."* People stopped and looked at the books in the window but hurried on.

Tex slammed the glass counter and moaned, "Honey-chile, your mother's in a bad way." For an instant I imagined my real mother had phoned in an emergency, but then I understood he meant himself. I was flattered that he was about to confide in me. My mother often told me her secrets, and I was an experienced listener. I could look sympathetic and I gave only welcome advice.

"Your momma's done hocked her jewels for her man and now I's too hard up to buy needles and thread for my notions shop. Oh sweetheart, tell me, who will feed Baby?"

Instantly I grasped that this funny, imaginative way of talking was a form of politeness, a way of conveying his distress in general terms without treating me to the unpleasant details. "Are you completely broke?" I asked, though I wanted to ask, "Who is this man?"

"All my money is here," he said, pointing to his glossy books and records. "If she can't sling this hash, Mom will have to close the diner." Every time Morris had started to substitute female for male pronouns, Tex had shut him up out of deference to my supposed innocence. Now Tex himself was inverting genders—was it a sign of embarrassment?

"Who's your man?" I asked.

He slid off the stool behind the cash register and came

over to me on the pink loveseat. His shoulders dropped. He was really very homely, with clammy skin, small boneless hands, a meager sparrow's torso. When he took off his glasses, his eyes looked huge and wet.

"You see, my lovers always turn out to be straight." I must have looked confused, despite my efforts to appear all-comprehending, for he added, "Heterosexual, normal. My current beau is a cop, Bob, and I just paid three hundred bucks for his wife's abortion."

"Does she know about you and Bob—what you are?" I asked, not quite sure what they were. How could a bona fide heterosexual like a queer?

Tex lit a cigarette. He was strangely likable, despite his melancholy air—likable because he carried his whole story with him wherever he went, like the housekeeper who worked for my father and stepmother, scattering her ash in her tenth cup of coffee, chatting away about the men in her life, still wearing her bathrobe at three in the afternoon, her sympathy universal even when her understanding was partial.

As for Tex, he was so intimate that he erased the distance between adolescent and adult. I had heard my mother and her friends discussing the "man problem"; now Tex was doing the same, and I was listening as a provisional equal.

"I think she suspects her husband's fooled around with me, but it suits her to look the other way. She knows they can count on me for loans, like for this abortion. They already have three kids. I like her and she knows it. We all go bowling together in Rogers Park when she's not wore out."

"Then what's the problem?" I asked briskly to cover my confusion. His novel way of looking at things was so human and unconventional. You could say he wore down the spikes of moral imperatives by holding things—dangerous explosive things—in his soft hands and turning them this way and that. At least right now, sitting beside me, he spoke of his cop, the wife, the abortion, the loans, the bowling evenings, with such domestic sighing familiarity that I took them all in the same way, his way, touched them all over in a friendly way.

"The problem, my Poor Little Rich Girl, is money, moolah—not that you'd understand," and he ruffled my hair and smiled with fond exasperation, his eyes supplicating heaven for patience. I didn't feel spoiled; I felt neglected. Nor did I choose to step into the role he was holding up for me. I took his hand and said, "But I do understand," and I did.

Then, out of a reflex of good manners, he cocked his head to one side speculatively. "But tell me, Baby Doll, what are you looking for in a man? What kind of sex? Start with that."

"Sex?"

"Do you like being screwed—we call that being browned, and the person is a brownie queen." When I looked embarrassed he politely turned philosophical. "That's more European, of course. It's your Continental gentlemen who like to brown each other. We Americans are better known for giving blow jobs. Are you a suck queen?"

The pink velvet felt as rough as wool under my legs. "Can I ask a dumb question? Do you actually blow?"

"You suck, silly." Tex turned away to hide his laughter, but his skinny back started quaking and then he was sobbing into his hands the way my Texas grandmother did, a big country woman who'd weep with merriment. I smiled in mild resentment at the wonderful joke I'd become.

"You suck, silly, but"—he wiped away his tears—"ooh-ee, I needed that!" Suddenly serious on a downbeat of breath: "But gently, not like a Hoover. The main thing is plenty of spit. The juicier you make it, the better they like it." He straightened his tie fractionally and flicked a glance at the street. "Will you listen to me, teaching you, and you just jailbait, how to service peter, and me not even a chickenhawk. That's what we call the young stuff—chicken. Honey, I'll have to give you a demonstration one of these days; I can't *believe* how *naive* you are." He sang out the rhyme and gave the impression he was as pleased by his own worldliness as by my innocence. "Me, I was never naive. Your mother was a born slut. That's the name of my fragrance." He dipped his wrist beneath my nose: "Born Slut. Like it?" Then he edged away from his extravagance. "Shouldn't corrupt you too soon. You know the expression, 'Today's trade is tomorrow's competition'?"

It took quite a bit of explaining for me to grasp the thinking behind that one. *Trade* turned out to mean a heterosexual man willing to let a homosexual blow him. But the idea was that a "piece of trade" didn't remain straight (that is, desirable) for long and soon was corrupted and turned into one more useless "nelly."

"But can't two nellies go to bed with each other?" I asked.

"Miss Thing," Tex hissed, indignant. "And do what? Bump pussies?"

I shrank back from this image—then laughed, feeling suddenly too big for my clothes, compromised. Did Tex think I was trade, attractive for an instant, like highly perishable fruit that's edible only for a day before going off? It seemed a tragic situation, because whoever succumbed to homosexual desire became immediately undesirable.

"But I really don't think about sex too much," I said. "I'll do whatever the . . . other person wants to do." I often said "other person" to avoid mentioning that person's sex.

"Yeah, but what kind of other person?" Tex asked.

"Someone older," I said dreamily, ashamed of having a fantasy, though entranced by it. "Someone rich and handsome who'll take care of me, pay for my boarding school, free me from my parents."

"Be real—the rich ones only go for each other. If you were rich and handsome, wouldn't you look for another one just like you?"

Until now, I'd considered wealth a latent capacity realized only in giving itself away, but now I saw that it was a closed club. I recognized Tex was right, since I could find plenty of evidence for his view among my father's friends. Hadn't my father said to me only last summer, as I started attending my first debutante parties, "I'm not saying you should marry for money. Just make sure the girls you go out with are all rich."

Two days after this talk with Tex, on a Friday evening, I told my mother I was going to a sock hop at the Y, but I headed right for Tex's shop. The elevated train lurched past squalid apartments, and I could look right into a room where an old woman sat hunched under blankets trying to keep warm, beak sunk into feather ruff. Down there, kids played in a garbage-littered backyard, and through another window I saw a man in a torn undershirt eating directly out of a refrigerator, his silhouetted hand lifting the milk bottle to his lips. I looked at every man, on the train or in these lit cubicles, and asked myself if I could marry him. Could I live with him forever?

Now I know myself. Now I know "forever" is a word that excites me, that just the word *marry* (not marriage itself) is a stimulant and I'm afraid of wounding others or trapping myself. But then? Then, in the winter I'd see a couple, man and woman, out walking in the snow, both of them hooded, torn plumes of vapor streaming from their mouths, or in summer, in the blue electric flash struck by the El, I'd snap a mental photo of those two people on the fire escape, beers in hand, he bare-chested, she in shorts, both pale as moths, and my spirit would hover over them, restless, half jealous, trying him on for size, now her, not finding a good fit.

That evening there was no hint of disaster at the bookshop. Morris, his lashes suitably brown, not black, was seated behind the cash register, ringing up sale after sale. Despite his shyness, Tex was circulating among the customers in a dim parody of a Southern belle. The polite young male announcer on the FM station was reading long sentences with a venom in their bite and a rattle in their tail. Then he announced he'd just finished the first part of tonight's story, "The Beast in the Jungle." Tex silenced him and put on a record of Callas's mad scenes. I myself preferred the radio and the idea that other listeners liked Henry James.

At one point, Tex whispered to me that the man in the corner owned several quality bookshops in New York and, though he was married, might make a nice date for me.

"But if he's married . . . ?"

Tex said, "My pet, he's a New Yorker. They're all bisexual, at least a man of his class. He's here alone without his wife, you're here, not an uncomely ephebe. If you're subtle about it, he might let you demonstrate the difference between sucking and blowing." A crazy Texas laugh, so at odds with his modulated tone, wildcatted up out of him till he capped it over by slapping himself and saying in mild admonishment, "Miss Me." And he slid toward a potential customer and said professorially, "The Kierkegaard boom seems to be continuing, doesn't it? Sartre's influence, no doubt."

I had an image of a vast city in which people ate breakfast when it was still dark out, drove to work in patient files under raw red skies, peeled off boots in fluorescent-lit offices, at home after work practiced the Hammond organ or dozed, joked about their "spare tire" and patted it fondly—a whole gray world in which I was biding my time, stupid with

longing and fear. But here, in Tex's shop, something dangerous was glowing as bright as the waste gas flaring day and
night off exhaust stacks above the factories in Gary, Indiana.
I felt exhilarated by the presence of so many sophisticated
adults: the woman in a black turtleneck examining *Either/Or*;
Morris playing efficient behind the cash register and conspicuously effacing himself like a glamourpuss actress in a
nun film; Tex tapping his cigarette in a Ricard ashtray, his
fear of bankruptcy temporarily pushed aside; and this suc-
cessful New York heterosexual who might tolerate me in his
bed.

Tex introduced us. The man's first name was Lester
and the last something Russian that ended in "iak." He wore
horn-rims that he kept taking off as he spoke or examined
a book, as though they served no function other than rhe-
torical. He wore a shaggy coat as a metonym for the hair I
felt certain must cover his entire body. He had the bulging
forehead, shaggy brows, and strong jaw of Beethoven in the
hand-size, chalky busts that my childhood piano teacher,
Herr Pogner, doled out to students as prizes.

And now Tex had proposed this New York Beethoven
as a prize for me, someone I'd be allowed to service later as he
reclined on the anonymous hotel bed, his thoughts winging
back to the East Coast a full day before his heavier body.
Surely this man had no need of me. Surely Beethoven was
entirely self-reliant.

At that time I had a horrible brush cut my father had
chosen for me, neither long enough to comb nor short enough
to be marine-sexy, and I wore not ivy-league horn-rims but
thick black glasses that girls said made me look "intellectual,"
a dubious compliment in the 1950s. Although Tex had assured
me only the other day that New Yorkers prized intelligence,
I wasn't sure mine could be counted on. It didn't feel like a
thing in our very thinglike world, a world where identity

began with the choice of massive automobile (my mother was a "gay divorcee" as could be seen from her powder-blue Buick convertible with its upholstery outlined in red piping; my father was "no-comment" rich in his midnight-blue Cadillac).

I asked the man what he thought of the Kierkegaard boom. He mouthed the word *boom* and picked up another book. I was left standing there.

But then, despite or maybe because of the rebuff, it became more and more important to me that he be aware of me, realize that I was "feeling gay tonight." I kept standing next to him, like a horse whose bridle has been dropped. I picked up a book and turned the pages without seeing them. I inched closer to him and let my shoulder brush his. He stood there taking it, until suddenly he looked up, frowned, put the book back, and moved away.

For the next hour I kept inching close to Lester while maintaining a space between our shoulders or stationing myself in the next aisle face-to-face with him over bookshelves. If he caught my glittering eye he'd smile the pained smile reserved for possibly crazy people. I guess Lester must have been waiting for Tex to close shop.

When I desired someone, especially a stranger, I poured myself into him ("Don't stare," my mother would tell me). Not that I found Lester so handsome; it was just that he was a chance, some sort of chance.

My face burned and my hands were cold. I was terrified the other people, the normal people, in the bookstore would detect my desire, that it was steaming off me like a bad smell. Worse, Tex stole up behind me and rested his hand on my shoulder. I blushed. We were two men touching! Real men (athletes, soldiers, workers) could touch each other with impunity. They even flaunted those pats on the ass and playful punches. But the rest of us must keep our voices subdued, hands soldered to our sides lest a gleam of desire or a shriek or lisp or limp wrist betray us. That staring of mine, the complete absorption in another man, would incriminate me yet, I felt certain.

Finally Tex closed the store at midnight, and he and Lester and I walked down windy Rush Street. When we came to the corner of Rush and Clark, Lester said to me, off-handedly, "Do you want to come up to my room for a moment? I'm staying here in the Ambassador East."

"No, thank you," I said. We shook hands and he and Tex made plans to have lunch the next day. Then he was gone.

"What got into you, chile?" Tex asked gently. "Lose your nerve?"

"Oh, Tex," I said, "I don't know him. He doesn't really want me. He likes girls. Can't I go home with you, Tex?"

"Hon, I'm bushed," he said, but he smiled with weary kindness at me.

"Just for a few minutes," I said.

We went up to his modest hotel room, devoid of personal touches aside from a half-empty bottle of bourbon and, pinned to the lampshade, a photo of the cop, a beefy guy with ears that stuck out.

Tex's body, pale and hairless, looked much younger than his face, which was large and endowed with too much humor and mobility to go with such a featureless torso. I worried about what he was going to spring on me, but he kissed me and massaged my shoulders and back with surprisingly strong hands, then he explained step-by-step what we were about to do. Always the good student, I responded competently, never guessing I was meant to feel any pleasure.

The minute I came, a wave of sickening guilt rushed over me. The hotel room looked depressing. I noticed the stain on Tex's underpants and the hole in his stocking. Down the hall someone was coughing. Tex's obsession with the policeman had reduced him to this. Compared to my father's solid if cheerless fortune, Tex's poverty was too great an expense of spirit.

I pecked him on the cheek, barely able to conceal my shame and disapproval. He yawned. I hurried down the cold street, my mouth sour from Tex's cigarettes, my cock and ass glowing, my heart sinking, sunk. I swore to myself I'd never, never sleep with another man. Defiance against my mother, no doubt, had propelled me into Tex's bed. It was her fault that I was "acting out" on my homosexual impulses (my psychiatrist, Dr. O'Reilly, had explained it all to me).

As the elevated train clattered back to Evanston and rewound the film I'd seen coming down, glimpses into slum apartments, these pitiful cuttings from the domestic life I'd been taught to admire but could never like, flickered past, educational and tragic.

THREE

■　■　■　■　■　■　■

Soon after I entered the University of Michigan, I joined my father's fraternity, Alpha Tau, simply to please him. Friends of mine who complained about the "lack of communication" with their fathers always amazed me, since it never occurred to me to hope for or even want from mine an exchange of confidences. He lectured me about the impersonal things that interested him—stocks and bonds, insurance policies, politics, civil engineering principles—and I provided him with a simulacrum of the son he wanted: I joined his club; in the summers I escorted debutantes to balls as he wanted me to; and I wore the clothes he chose.

I couldn't, of course, be the athletic or heterosexual man he wanted. He knew I was homosexual, although we never discussed it. I'd told him in a letter in order to get the money I needed to see the shrink, Dr. O'Reilly.

The next summer I spent with Dad at his Michigan cottage. My stepmother and sister and the maid weren't allowed to join us until the end of the season. Until then I was alone with my father. He put me on a strict regime of yardwork, mainly raking the pine needles that formed a thick carpet from top to bottom of the slope on which the house was built. When I asked him what possible reason there could be for removing the needles, he turned red, his already thin lips grew thinner, and he said, "Goddamn it, you'll do what the hell I goddam well tell you to do."

When my stepmother finally arrived, she revealed that my father thought he would drive the queerness out of me through manual labor. For weeks we had circled each other wordlessly, my father up on a ladder, me with my eternal rake and wheelbarrow, his anger between us, mysterious as the stone the Muslims worship. Since he knew how to cook nothing but steaks, every night we'd sit wordlessly over plates overflowing with fat and blood. He'd read the newspaper. I couldn't guess why he hated me so much. In the past I'd always welcomed his indifference, since that was what I felt for him, though I took care to hide it, but his program of hatred frightened me. My stepmother told me my mother had accused my father over the phone of having brought about my "sickness" through his absence; my father was countering the charge by administering to me his grim discipline. Although I'd finally done something to grab his attention, that same thing repelled him. My stepmother said, "Your poor dad, this thing is killing him, he stays awake all night worrying; he was so angry at first I was afraid he'd kill you."

At college I was finally free. I'd smoldered against other people's rules for so long that now I felt freedom as a form of loneliness, a disturbing withdrawal of love. Certainly I was lonely and I wanted friends. I wanted to be popular, not just with indulgent bohemian grown-ups, but even with attractive people my own age, for here, being intelligent was, if not quite a social asset, at least not a liability.

English class was taught by Winthrop Shelley, a pale-

skinned black man whose blue eyes seemed to be a constant
source of pain, as though their blueness were a form of en-
croaching blindness. He was always taking off his wire-
rimmed glasses, which were so pliable that they had to be
handled gingerly, and massaging his closed eyes and particularly the delicate bridge of his nose, the place where he
located his objections to a student's remarks. What Mr.
Shelley said was always precise, quizzical. His queer air of
listening to himself, the way he had of responding to his own
idea in a complex sequence of feelings by a wavering, then
pinched smile and a line of doubt drawn on his forehead—
such scrupulosity vaguely irritated me. Didn't Mr. Shelley
see that most of the class couldn't parse the syntax of so much
refinement? And what kind of Negro was he, anyway, with
his tweed jacket and the gold pocket watch he ceremoniously
placed on his desk to indicate class was beginning? With his
Oxbridge accent, his soundless chuckle, and his dumbshow
of glee (titter behind an exquisitely manicured hand) when
someone said something stupid?

Not that he was taken in by stylish but empty chatter.
He'd run his lacquered, dusky pink index finger over his
tweezed mustache and say, "Mr. Larkin, I'm not sure I follow
your point. Are you suggesting we should turn against a
friend who's an enemy of the state? Or do you agree with
Cicero that loyalty to a friend must outweigh up to a certain
point even patriotism?"

Like any agile debater, I could defend either side of
the question, but I was too immoral to wonder which side
was right. I didn't care and I couldn't imagine anyone else
did either. When it was revealed at this time that a young
intellectual had cheated on a TV quiz show, I was amazed
that other people were so scandalized. I looked around for
winks of complicity and sly grins but found none. My own
immorality didn't trouble me, since I knew I responded to

other people and I mistook this ready sympathy for goodness. Besides, I wanted only to survive; other people, the ones with power—their acts might count.

Kant's idea that one must act as a universal legislator setting a precedent for everyone seemed the purest nonsense to me—in fact, so pure I admired it.

I discovered the toilets in the student union. One afternoon after class, I burst through the door in a rush to piss and hurry home. Shoes scraped, bones cracked, I turned a corner and saw a student huddled over a urinal, face blood-red and turned down, his white shirttail sticking out in back. Just two urinals away from him in a line of eight was a beefy businessman, obvious toupee, out of breath. In the stalls a scurrying and the clank of belt buckle against metal partition. I chose my urinal, the farthest one away, and I too looked down.

The silence was intense, intensified by the timed flush of water. Then silence again, the throb of my pulse in my neck, the businessman's impatient, audible exhalation, the scratch of a match in a stall and soon the rich scent of burning tobacco creeping out over the ammonia smell of disinfectant. The concentration was strong and focused, every heart pounding, every sense open. When it became obvious that I, too, was waiting and no longer pissing, the businessman shot his shiny black mohair cuff and consulted his massive gold wristwatch. Face burning, fingers going cold on my cock, I turned to look at the businessman. He regarded me expressionlessly, leaned his head back hoping to glimpse into my urinal, took a step away from the wall to expose his short, engorged, nearly purple penis. I stepped back to show mine, though I knew he didn't want me, just as a sign that I was a friendly player in the game. In a flash he was squatting, the student turned to feed the businessman's mouth, the smoker in the stall dropped his cigarette in the water, quick hiss, and he and his neighbor in the next stall were on their knees, hands reaching under the partition between them and grabbing each other, as I could see by stooping over. No one cared about me one way or the other. I was one of them.

I looked at the student being sucked. His soft white belly with its explosion of black hair and wet cock shiny as glass were flashed on the screen of my mind as was that rush of male hands under the partition. I listened to the quick clink-clink of a belt buckle on the tiles.

Then the muffled sound of an approaching step, followed by someone pushing open the door, released the echoing chatter in the corridor. Instantly the couple in the stalls regained their seats; the businessman and his client broke off their deal; and I revolved to face my urinal. The intruder, a big, pigeon-toed athlete, splashed, dribbled, left, but not before he'd made us feel like Sleeping Beauty's courtiers the moment before the prince melts the rime of sleep. . . . If I use that implausible image I do so to cool my burning face, since the athlete, after buttoning up, flicked his hair out of his eyes and voiced a simple grunt of disgust.

Home to Chicago for Thanksgiving weekend, I managed to slip away for a wild evening with Morris, the clerk in Tex's store. Tex had disappeared but had left a note promising to come back with money. Morris opened the store only when it suited him. He hadn't been paid in months, and besides, there were no new books to sell.

Tonight he was wearing pocketless black trousers molded to his full buttocks. "Not bad, hunh?" he said, standing on tiptoe, sticking out his ass, hand on hip, and looking back over one shoulder like a wartime pinup.

We piled into a car with some friends of his, all a few years older than I, and as we passed a policeman directing traffic, the driver lowered his window and shouted, "Love your hat, Tilly!"

"Hush, you're a caution," someone in the back seat said, "don't upset Lily Law, she be *bad*, that girl."

In my middle-class way, I tried to show interest in my neighbor by asking him where he lived, what he did, but he peered right into my face and licked his lips slowly like a silent movie vamp. "Hey, it's cute, this one, it's real cute," he announced to Morris in the front seat, pointing at me.

"Like it?" Morris asked, bored. "You like anything in trousers, shameless hussy," he added, stifling a tiny meow of a yawn with a fluttering palm. Morris's hands, I noticed, were huge and ropey with veins, strangely ill-suited to the frivolous gestures he liked to sketch in.

"Look, bitch," my neighbor growled at Morris, "don't get me started, or your mother will claw your little red eyes out—I'm on the rag tonight."

"Certainly," Morris said, smartly turning around and deliberately staring at the other man's crotch, "you've certainly been ragging something; I never saw a white woman pack such a big box, I don't mind if you tuck in the odd hanky coyly stuffed just to provide a little front interest, don't you know, but Mary you've pushed a double bed sheet up that cooze of yours—not that you feel anything down there anyway, stretched out as it! must! *be*!" he said, ending his aria on an upbeat. He snapped his fingers and turned away.

"I'll read you if you wreck my nerves, girl," my neighbor said. Then he added a loud wailing "Oo-eeh!" just as Mahalia Jackson might have done after an all-out gospel hymn.

We were all smiling. I was mute and ponderous beside my new companions. I assumed each bit of repartee had been coined on the spot. Only later did I recognize that the routines made up a repertory, a sort of folk wisdom common to "queens," for hadn't Morris recklessly announced, "Grab your tiaras, girls, we're all royalty tonight, why I haven't seen so many crowned heads since Westminster Abbey—"

"I know you *give* head, Abbie, but the only crowns you've seen are on those few molars you've got left." The speaker turned to me, nudged me in the ribs, indicated Morris, and said, "Can you fathom a slut pulling her teeth just to give a smoother hum job?" and then pulled his lips back over his own teeth to demonstrate. "She covers the waterfront, poor dentureless crone, looking for seafood trade."

We stopped at a gay coffee shop. As the youngest and quietest, I was pushed to the aisle, just beside the next table of straights, two couples on dates, slumming, I guess. I prayed for the guys in my group to calm down. But the presence of hostile, if mesmerized, heterosexual spectators made them hysterical. Morris leaned across the table and asked a "sister" huskily, "Like my lashes? Ronnie dyed them, said it'd give me definition."

"Honey, the only definition that fits you starts with Q and rhymes with—waitress, *beer*, please," he shouted at an old tattooed man in white shirt-sleeves who worked the lobster shift. He looked at the waiter more closely. "Oh, you're a waiter, not a waitress. Sorry, Dearie, I thought you were a Fish for a moment, there's such a strong smell of Fish in here tonight, wouldn't you say?" He was staring aggressively at the two girls beside me. "Can't bear Fish or Fisheaters, smell like cans of old tuna."

The girls had stopped chewing their gum and were noisily sucking the ice melt in their Coke glasses. I smiled conspiratorially at them, as if to say, Aren't these guys weird, but I noticed that they were looking back at me with open disgust. One of their dates said, "Some people are sick, real sick," which touched off a volley of birdcalls at our table ("Are you sick? Who's sick? You don't look sick") and a whole dumbshow of fever tests (palm on forehead) and tongue checks ("Say ah"). For the first time I'd crossed the line. I was no longer a visitor to the zoo, but one of the animals.

My mother had just moved to downtown Chicago, to a brand-new high-rise along Lake Michigan, a place where the floors were raw concrete and had to be covered by wall-to-wall carpeting. Hers was gold, as were the sheer curtains woven with metallic thread, and the upholstered armchairs and sectional sofa. The windows were sealed shut; cooled or warmed air seeped in through vents.

From the twenty-fourth floor I looked down on the older buildings and across to the newer ones. Their windows reflected the light or sank into shadow or glowed from within as the heavens turned, as a construction crane turned atop a rising tower or stood, dozing, inert against the night sky. Twenty-four stories below, over and over again a traffic signal gave its crude demonstration of spectrum analysis: red, yellow, green, and back again, a primary lesson sometimes imparted to the glossy hood of a car, sometimes wasted on the rain-slick pavement.

Out of another window the winter lake at night, unheard behind glass, flickered with foam like the black-and-white television I kept on, sound off, for the wan company it provided, Sid Caesar doing a pratfall, Imogene Coca mugging.

When my mother was out for the evening I'd take off my clothes and dance naked, barefoot, through the dim apartment on the shaggy carpets. The glittering spires outside surrounded me like astounded adults. Snow fell, swirled, slalomed past our windows. A cloud got caught between our building and the next. The second Sibelius symphony provided me with exalted feelings to interpret. What a relief to feel longing in my arms, passion in my legs, craving after beauty in my hands rather than in my head for once.

When I returned to school I started cruising all the time, all the time. Every free moment between classes I was in the student union or the third-floor toilet in Main Hall. I'd sit for hours in a stall, dropping cigarettes into the bowl, studying a book on Chinese social structure or Buddhist art, awaiting an interesting customer, like one of those gypsy fortune-tellers who prospect clients in storefronts where they also live. Their mixture of homely paraphernalia and mystical apparatus (TV beside crystal ball) might serve as an analogy to my blend of scholarship and sex.

I was obsessed. Hour after hour I'd sit there, inhaling the smells other people made, listening to their sounds, studying the graffiti scribbled all over the thick marble partitions in Main Hall or the metal ones in the union.

Someone comes in, heavy brown cordovans before the urinal, worn-down heels and scuff marks on the leather—neglects himself, can't be gay. I can hear his urine splatter but I can't see its flow. I wait for it to stop—the crucial moment, for if he stays on, then I'll stand in my stall, peek through the crack, soundlessly unbolt my door as an invitation. Now, in this indeterminate second, I can put one head after another on his unseen shoulders, invent for him one scenario after another. I get hard in anticipation, stiff before the void of my own imagination.

Nothing. His calves flex slightly as he buttons up (heavy weight to lift) and then he's gone. One of the toilets two stalls down drips and I picture the mad anesthesiologist mixing poison, drop by drop, into the sedative.

Time and again I'd focus on this stranger on the other side of the door, will him into wanting me, impart to him perverse demands, blond hair, full lips, only to see him through the crack in the door: the middle-aged janitor with hairy ears. But then, just as I was ready to cash in my chips, someone sat beside me, dropped his pants to the floor in a puddle, revealing strong tan calves above crisp white ribbed athletic socks. A silence like a storm cloud gathered over the room, blocking out the hall noises. He tapped his foot slightly; I tapped mine. Then two taps, matched by two of mine. Three and three.

And without further prelude, he sank to his knees shoving his brown thighs and white groin under the partition, and I also knelt to feast on his erection, inhaling the clean smell of soap, my hands exploring the lichee-size testicles, then traveling up smooth skin. I'd dreamed about this moment so long that now I wanted to freeze the frame.

In my anthropology class I was learning that although man had started off as an animal subject to natural selection, he had soon begun to evolve in a direction determined purely by culture. Human beings stood upright to free their hands, they needed their hands to hold tools, the tool-and-weapon-wielding parts of their brains developed to accommodate their newly prehensile grasp, language was enabled by tool-wielding—but now, if culture were yanked out from under us, we'd be destroyed, like one of those cartoon cats who scamper off a branch and tread thin air until sudden awareness makes them plummet.

Here, under my gaze, was this creature half-natural but half-invented by himself. The tan line suggested poolside swimsuit, frosted glass, sunglasses—everything as symbolic as the life pictured by advertisements. But the hickory-hard straining of this cock upward spelled animal—a straight line of ascent inflating slightly as the balls rose and tightened for blast-off, a thrust that propelled life upward. The cleanness, however, the feathery lightness of the blond hairs, the neatness of the circumcision were all preppy, while the heavy hamstrings (and now the jets of semen filling my mouth) were primate.

For an instant I stayed attached to him, though here

I was on a dirty tile floor on hands and knees before a stranger I'd seen only from the waist down but whom I remember to this day because he'd presented himself so fearlessly, because his body, at least the half of it I knew, seemed ideal, and because his desire was so strong it was as expressive as words or deeds, the things that normally define individuals.

Then he was gone. His exit was so hasty I couldn't see him, just a flash of blond hair and white shirt collar through the narrow vertical slit of my sentry box. I waited patiently for someone else.

I was alone with my sexuality, since none of these men spoke to me, nor did I even know their faces, much less their names. Their most intimate tender parts were thrust under the stone partitions, like meals for prisoners, but if I poked my head under the partition and glanced up at them, they'd hide their faces with their hands as a movie star wards off a flash. I'd rush from one toilet to another between classes. Sometimes all four stalls in Main Hall or all eight in the union would be occupied, full house. I'd wait for someone to emerge, but if no one did I would realize I was spoiling their fun and leave. Perhaps my presence was interrupting an orgy that would resume the second I left and even now eight doors concealed eight erect penises.

Someone with a convict's patience had drilled a dime-size hole in one of the marble slabs in Main Hall. I'd sit on the toilet, suddenly remember the hole was here, between this stall and the next, look up and see a black pupil glossy, quivering. If the eye persisted in its liquid restlessness, at once thoroughly anonymous and shockingly vulnerable, I'd look back toward this live camera, this unseen seer. I stood up to expose my erection. I posed a bit self-consciously, turning halfway toward my audience while still keeping my feet forward in the usual position so as not to arouse suspicion in anyone outside glancing at the floor.

His lashes squeezed shut for a second as he blinked. The effect through the judas was of a carnivorous plant swallowing a black, trembling life. The soul and intelligence usually attributed to the eyes had been annulled by this extreme close-up: nothing left but motility. "The quick," I thought, as in the phrase, "The quick and the dead."

Then I exploded, he flushed and shot out of his booth, the door to the hall sighed shut behind him, and I was alone with the faintly blue light filtering down through overhead frosted glass onto white porcelain and with the sound of the leaking toilet and a paw full of come, which I licked clean and swallowed like a savage or a cat. If I'd had the courage, I would have advised my anthropology class that primitive man believes in the conservation of energy through the recycling of bodily fluids.

I was a Buddhist, or would have been if I could have given up this hankering after a penis attached to two furry legs below and one Cyclopean eye above, as black and wobbly as black-currant jelly. Because of my Buddhist longing for peace, I'd decided to study Chinese. Wherever I went— fraternity house, dorm room, student union, dinner party, toilet—I had my handmade flashcards with me. Chinese character on one side, on the other its pronunciation and correct tone above the definition, or rather dated definitions, since meanings shifted over the centuries.

We were just a handful of students clustering three nights a week around our conversation teacher in the one lit classroom in an otherwise dark building. The stairs creaked. Our teacher, an ageless Chinese woman in a dark blue lusterless silk dress, asked me in Mandarin to run out and see if it was a strange "nose person" (*bi ren*)—and in that instant we kids, all Caucasian, learned that's what the Chinese called us because of our big noses. Our teacher clapped a hand over her mouth under her own suitably snub nose and blushed.

We called her the "straight lady," because she could have been drawn entirely in straight lines, her pageboy and bangs, her eye slits and thin wrists, her breastless body. She was quite proud of her up-to-date attitudes (she was both a Methodist and a lifetime member of the YWCA), but she retained odd scraps of folk wisdom (and the Chinese inability in English to distinguish between *he* and *she*). She said to me, "You look tired" (pronounced "tod"), "very, very tod. Me too, I always tod. One day I look at my dog and say, 'Why he never tod? She never tod.' Then I realize he never tod 'cause she sleep all the time. Now I sleep all the time too. When I have moment between class or food cook, I sleep. I sleep all the time. I never tod."

Through her and a Chinese social club I met a large group of students from Taiwan and Singapore. Two girls, Betty and Kay, invited me and other friends to an enormous dinner served Chinese-style with no tea ("Tea is for every time of the day except mealtime," they explained) and dozens of tiny plates flying through the air, and, in the center of the table, big bowls of soup and steamed rice.

Somehow I'd imagined Chinese women would be—well, Japanese, that is, modest, self-effacing, tittering. But, in fact, Kay, who wore her black hair held back by a wide pink band, was strong enough to defy her family's insistence that she study medicine or law. All her Chinese friends had an artistic bent, but she alone had the courage to pursue a music degree (she played Chopin études for us on her overly live upright). And she and all her friends loved to tease, not titter, and

even played rough practical jokes on one another. Her roommate Betty, women's tennis champ of Hong Kong, was
minuscule and looked no older than fifteen, though she was
finishing a doctorate in chemistry. She was wound too tight
and kept gaining time; obsessively efficient, she was able all
at once to run up a dress, jot down a stream of formulae,
practice her backhand, bicycle to the lab, and plan an elaborate evening of amateur theatricals to spoof several friends.

At the dinner, Kay decided to test how gullible and distracted a friend of hers, a Chinese grad student in physics,
actually was. As we listened, she phoned him at his apartment,
where she knew he'd be lost in calculations. She told him she
was the operator calling to test his "unit" and, despite her
heavy Chinese accent, he believed her. "I want you to walk
across the room and put your unit in the top drawer of your
walnut dresser, close the drawer, return to your present
position, and say, 'Wong, wong.' " The physicist's compliance,
coupled with the fact that dogs in China say wong-wong
instead of bow-wow, made us sick with laughter. Soon Kay
had him whistling, hooting, and grunting at his unit.

Betty was at the same time quickly loading the table
with dishes. We were drinking beers, and the cold imperious
Kay had turned bright red from drink: "Autumn Moon"
became her new name.

Then it was Betty's turn to be teased. She'd made the
mistake of complaining that she felt fat, though she carried
no more excess weight than a cricket. Kay told us how
she'd recently called an exercycle company in Detroit and,
in Betty's name, asked for a free demonstration. One afternoon while Betty was deep in her chemistry book, a big
blonde in black high heels clomped-clomped up the wooden
fire escape, rising into Betty's view like a sea monster. "Are
you Betty Wong?" she demanded.

"Yes."

"One minute please while I assemble the horse."

Before Betty could say *ee, erh, san,* which is one, two, three in Chinese, she'd been strapped, all eighty-five pounds of her, onto the weight-reducing demon.

"That night," Kay was saying, "when she asked me in tears how they'd come up with her name, I told her they go through the infirmary files and approach anyone who's overweight."

The two other male guests were Chinese in white shirts, sober ties, and gray suits, smiling and nodding, knees together, hands to either side flat against the chair seat as though ready to spring up at any moment. Before long I'd grasped the underlying idea. The girls were supposed to have all the personality, but everyone, men included, was meant to be a "character"—Betty a cheerful but driven maniac; Kay the severe kidder, until she became "Autumn Moon"; the men polite and neat, but each harboring his secret though innocuous foible: gluttony for cherries, passion for Elvis. This jokey, satirical style was far more pointed than the mirthless Midwestern joshing I was used to, the flaccid wordplay, and the tiresome envisioning of dull improbabilities ("Wouldn't it be really neat if the moon really was made of green cheese?")

For white Americans of that time and class and place, the only alternative to public joshing was intimate confession; we gave too little of ourselves or too much. But the Chinese students I met were guardedly friendly when alone and gleefully satirical in groups—but satirical of minor vices, none too close to the bone. We white Americans were grim psychoanalytic theorists, sure that sex (greedy sex, guilty sex) was our sole motivation, whereas the Chinese were capricious, artistic. Kay told me, "You always wear blue because you like blue eyes," and it was perfectly true that the boys who attracted me—the boys I fell in love with, not the brunettes

I lusted after—were blue-eyed blonds. Or she'd say, "You eat as fast as possible, like a badger," or, "You always drawl out your *yes* when you really mean no," or, "You rub your nose with the back of your hand like a cat." Knowing I was being scrutinized flattered and alarmed me.

Into the party burst a thin Chinese woman in her fifties, salt-and-pepper hair drawn back, black pants, black sunglasses, fingernails and lips unpainted. Everyone grew silent and uncomfortable. The newcomer spoke rapidly in a maddening whine; I couldn't pick out a word in her dialect. After half an hour she stood and left, nodding at Kay and one of the men and ignoring the rest of us.

"She's a sort of princess. That's Fukienese she's speaking," Kay said. Our party, discouraged, broke up. One of the men walked me partway home and said, "That woman doesn't like Americans and she hates speaking English. She teaches Old High German—"

"What!"

"Yes, at Cornell, and she takes a bus all day and night just to come here to speak Fukienese to Kay for four hours. Then she turns around and goes back. She writes Kay and me. I'll show you her letters. They're very beautiful and literary. She'll be watching college boys racing around the track and in three words she'll make an allusion to a Han *fu* about swans skimming the old palace pond. . . . She lives in a mental China still. She arrives without warning."

"Was she upset to see me at the party?"

"Maybe." He smiled. "What a dialect! We say she speaks five languages, all with a Fukienese accent."

For the next few days I couldn't stop thinking about the contrast between my happy Chinese friends, the plentiful table, the laughter and harvest-moon faces—and then the perfect stillness of everyone's eyes lowered under the bright ceiling lamp while the visitor nattered on and on, half her royal face concealed behind sunglasses, hand cutting the air. Her rank or distress had intimidated everyone except Kay, who seemed proud to be singled out. Maybe I was studying Chinese in order to have precisely these fleeting contacts with even a remnant of a society so different from my fragmented and compartmentalized life.

My university had twenty thousand students, which makes a big school but a small town. Despite the smallness, I was able to keep several different lives separate from one another—I hid the Chinese from my fraternity brothers, the brothers from the bohemians I was mingling with in the middle room of the student-union cafeteria, and all three from those hairy legs and hard penises I was meeting under cold thick marble partitions or thin metal ones. When Kay or Betty would flirt with me I'd blush, and that became a new joke with them: I was nicknamed "Your Holiness" and teased for being a puritan. "We've heard about the American puritans," Kay said unsmilingly. "Thoreau," she said, pronouncing the name as though she meant the Hebrew holy book, the Torah.

Since I'd read so many books about heterosexual sex and was specially well informed about the mysteries of the clitoris, my frat brothers thought I was a secret cocksman. Their stories were all about getting so drunk they were sick on their dates; girls were seen as good sports who held their heads over toilets and murmured, "It'll be okay, honey."

The fraternity house was an Edwardian mansion. The outside was crosshatched by dingy timber on cream stucco like an old tic-tac-toe game. The fraternity was famous in the South for drinking, football, and racism; here in the North, we'd retained the drinking. Two or three of our members were jocks, but no one paid them much attention. As for the racism, we'd start quaking with laughter whenever we had to put on hoods with Halloween eyeslits for our secret ceremonies and pledge to protect white womanhood. There were at least three Negro star football players the brothers would have pledged if the bylaws had permitted them to do so, but this whoring after gladiators seemed to me only another form of racism. Our swords, the flowery Masonic language, and the Klannish sentiments would make our president scratch his head. He was a hawk-nosed man who liked to sleep and drink, always seemed to be genially confused, and appeared to be freshly hatched or peeled, certainly minus a vital protective layer. "Come on, guys," he'd say, sheepishly holding his sword aloft, "show some respect."

"Let's skip it and have some brews," the vice-president would suggest, and soon we'd all be sitting around the chapel-size dining room in our fancy dress, drinking beers in the middle of a Tuesday afternoon. We never even succeeded in making a float for Homecoming, though we bought the chicken wire and crepe paper.

A hard core of juniors on warning and suspended seniors would play cards and drink all night, sleep all day, and stagger down to roast-beef dinner in their bathrobes, never leaving the house, sending out pledges for brews and smokes. I could hear them all night downstairs, shouting and laughing, someone roaring with triumph, someone else laughing like a hyena. The fad of the moment was to say the opposite of what was meant. "You *are* a wit," was addressed to an idiot, "He *is* a face man," of someone brutally ugly.

In ranking pledges during rush, the brothers would say someone was a legacy (as I was, since my father had been a member down South), a jock, a brain ("He'll pull up the house average"), or a face man. Until now, all the heterosexual men I'd known had pretended they were unable to tell whether another male was attractive or not, but the reputation of the house required the brothers to measure even such an elusive factor and they did so, protected by this strangely objective term they'd invented, "face man."

The frowsy, boozy camaraderie of the fraternity amounted to permissiveness. The brothers frequently said to one another, "You're *not* a pervert," but they were referring to yet another lapful of beerbarf or a vaunted preference for cunnilingus ("oyster diving" or "beaver heaven"). Of course they didn't even whisper about a real perversion such as mine.

They could be seen strolling with sorority girls through autumn leaves or dashing out distraught into the garden during a dance ("Hey, Sal, I'm sorry, I *am* just couth"), but when they replayed the weekend for the guys on Monday morning, their reports contained no mention of feelings beyond nausea and highly localized lust ("I'm such a beaver man, just put a shaving brush to my lips when I'm asleep and I'll start munching"). Whereas I was the real pervert, worshipping men I knew only from the knees to the waist, but at least I loved them all—especially if I thought behind the partition they were straight, blond, athletic, indifferent.

Of course there were the john fairies, the "tearoom nellies" like me, and them I despised. One man would establish shoe contact and then slip under the partition a questionnaire written on toilet paper: "Inches? Cut or uncut? Body hair? If so, where? Underarms? Chest? Stomach? Crotch? Legs? Heavy growth?" I'd simply pass it back unanswered, which would provoke a peeved "Tsk," a storm of flushing, and a hasty exit. Something about that guy's fetishism offended me, not because it was abnormal, but because it was unromantic. I sat on my toilet shuffling Chinese flashcards and aching—not to be loved but to be permitted to love.

I was still seeing Dr. O'Reilly, the psychiatrist I'd first consulted in prep school, desperately trying to go straight. He'd told me I couldn't attend Harvard but must remain at the local university to be near him. "I'm the only one who can save you, old boy," he'd said, "because I love you and you know it." I borrowed a friend's car and drove the fifty miles each way twice a week to see him. Dr. O'Reilly swallowed amphetamines by the handful in the morning to get going and started calming himself in the evening by sipping bourbon. His waiting room was full of angry birds, the gift of a patient, and Japanese prints.

He introduced me to Annie Schroeder, another patient. "Those stuffy Freudians would split a gut," he said, or rather mumbled, since the pills and alcohol slurred his speech. "But Annie's a good gal, though she's got a psycho for an old man, right out of Dostoevsky, and a mother who wants to be Annie's daughter." He clapped me on the shoulder with too much force. "A fine gal, Annie, but don't think I'm jealous. I'm not the avenging father."

If I started from the premise I was sick (and what could be sicker than my compulsive cruising?), then I had to question everything I thought and did. My opinions didn't count, since my judgment was obviously skewed. If I found something beautiful, perhaps it was merely decorative; if I regarded a couple as happy, admirable, I was sure to have chosen the wrong example, the people most likely to confirm my neurosis and lead me deviously back to my illness. If I argued a point, I was being over-intellectual (a sin I'd already become aware of from the painters and which Dr. O'Reilly considered the most serious impediment to my mental health). The mind as its own enemy. The mind desperate to outwit itself. The mind claiming virtue but intent on preserving its own viciousness. The mind a boat at sea rebuilding itself while under sail. The mind a rotting meat under expensive spices. The mind a pure spirit (the unsuspecting wife) under the sway of a murderous will (Bluebeard). Perhaps that's why Buddhism appealed to me. It denied the existence of the soul, the will, and even the self and sought to show that only illusion lends a spurious unity and dynamism to so many separate, detachable sentiments. For me, Buddhism was the welcome prediction of cosmic collapse, spiritual entropy.

What I desired most was a man; desiring men was sick; therefore, to become well I must kill desire itself. "Or kill men!" O'Reilly shouted, triumphant, half rising from his chair behind the analytic couch where he usually dozed out of sight or bit his broad white mustache and fiddled with his drink. "You want to murder men! You see, old boy, you think I'm sleeping, that I'm counter-transferent, but even when I'm dozing I'm listening, putting the pieces together in the preconscious, creative part of my brain. You want to murder men by sleeping with them. The stiff cock is the torero's sword. There's a lot of bullfighting imagery here."

Any reference to my own penis embarrassed me; moreover, I was reluctant to explain that my penis played little or no part under the partition. I had no desire (no *vulgar* desire I might have said) to obtain sexual release. In my eyes, my preference for service to others over personal pleasure mitigated my corrupt desires.

Annie Schroeder was also a student at my school. I gave her a ride the fifty miles back to our campus. She told me she planned to be a model. I wondered out loud if she'd photograph differently than she looked.

"Do you think I'm *fat*?" She poured scorn into the word.

"On the contrary."

"I suppose O'Reilly's instructed you to say that. Don't play dumb. I know he thinks I have an eating disorder. But if so, I'm not like all those little Jewish girls at school fretting over their waistlines. I have a real reason to obsess over food."

"Oh?" I had the sensation I was giving a lift to a fire. And yes, her hair was red, twisted around her head in a beehive too old for her thin young face, the face of a soldier wearing a bloody bandage.

"Didn't O'Reilly tell you?" She looked at me searchingly. I took my eyes off the slippery road to look into hers, outlined in kohl, her lips painted almost black, her face a long slice of Persian melon.

"Tell me what?" I asked guiltily. My general moral discomfort was so swollen it could be lanced at any moment by anyone. The rain lashing the four-lane highway was turning to sleet. Big trucks buffeted our little Volkswagen, bison rushing past our ladybug.

"I'm sure he told you about my father."

"Just that he was a character out of Dostoevsky."

"Literature has nothing comparable," she said grimly.

"Tell me about him, won't you?"

Annie told me of her father, a drunk madman who would be sober and sane a month at a time. Then he'd snap. Annie and her little brother would come home from school to their remote country house, and there Dad would be, grinning knowingly, pistol in hand. "Okay, wise guys, I found out what you've been cooking up. I'm going to give you one last chance to make it up to me." And for the next three days he'd force them to work at gunpoint as he kept pulling at his bottle of scotch. In the snow, in the mud, they'd haul bricks, sniveling, pleading for forgiveness, but he'd keep them at it, laughing, sometimes brushing off voices and wings he alone perceived.

Annie stopped talking. Then she said, "Someday I'll show you the barn my brother and I built with our own hands." She seemed very close to tears again. I wanted to say something right, to make it all up to her, not because I felt such sympathy (I feared her too much to pity her), but because I wanted that sort of power over her—the sort

O'Reilly wielded. Maybe I envied the horror of her child-hood; she had a legitimate reason to be messed up now.

"The worst of it was when he would come out of it. Then he'd be so repentant he'd crawl across the floor, kiss our feet, and cry. He'd force us to hold the gun to his head and beg us to pull the trigger. We'd kiss him and comfort him and forgive him. Though he'd hurt *us*, though it was *our* nails that were torn, *our* faces covered with dirt—we'd forgive him so quickly."

Now she was crying, and the huge semis hurtling past, creating a momentary vacuum that sucked us into their wake, seemed for a second like the passions that grown-ups wreaked on their children. In this little car every revolution of the wheels, every segment in the pavement, was registered as a shock; we worked for every mile we gained. But perched high above us, comfortable in their crow's nests of nude pinups, dangling foam dice, family snapshots, a dashboard twinkling with lights, the truckdrivers were smoothly guiding their liners through the night, politely saluting each other with doffed brights.

FOUR

■ ■ ■ ■ ■ ■ ■

Maria and I never stopped ex-
changing letters. She was back at the University of Chicago
completing a graduate degree. Or she was in Iowa for the
summer working for a socialist candidate for the state legisla-
ture. "It has nothing to do with being pro-Russian!" she
bitterly replied to my note of muted caution (the McCarthy
era had just ended). "The Midwest has its own tradition of
populism, which you'd know if you ever read some political
history instead of all that crepuscular fiction. Or at least
some honest Midwestern novelist like Sherwood Anderson or
Dreiser rather than your putrescent Barbey d'Aurevilly!"
And I could just hear her laughing with her beautiful musical
laugh at her own fulminations.

At Christmas I saw her in Chicago. My mother invited
her to dinner. The only other guest was my mother's new
secretary, a suburban simpleton in penny loafers, knee socks,
a tartan skirt closed by a giant safety pin. Maria (chic black
dress and stiletto heels, brilliants in her upswept hair) helped
Beth wash my mother's dishes, as guests often did out of
neighborliness in those days in the Plains states. I overheard

Beth say to Maria, "Don't you just love that song 'When you walk through a storm, keep your chin up high'? Isn't it inspiring? Doesn't it make you want to cry?"

"I think it's sickening rubbish," Maria said evenly.

And yet Maria doted on my mother, admired her for her courage and resourcefulness as a woman on her own. Indeed, through Maria's eyes I began to see my mother as a character of some interest, although what most redeemed her was simply the distance that allowed her to be seen at all. As a boy, I'd loved and loathed my mother with the same relentless energy I'd devoted to myself. Or perhaps I should say I studied my mother instead of myself as though she'd been a mirror to my failings. Now I was a student and, as Maria claimed, an "intellectual." This identity by way of an honorific allowed me to look at my mother as someone brave "for her time": condescension permitted admiration.

After the Christmas Day dinner, which began at three in the afternoon but continued until seven-thirty, Maria and I escaped. Once again we were driving through loose wet snow that melted on contact. After living in a college town with its noisy dorms and hushed libraries, its meteor crater of a stadium, its dark streets lined with illuminated fraternity houses, its sketchy downtown of textbook stores and hamburger joints, coming back to a real city made my pulse race. Here were all these adult men and women with money to burn—burn in the form of *crêpes flambées*, of smoldering cigars, of burning whisky, of steamy sex, fires flaring up against the cold night.

I was still too young to go to a bar, so Maria and I sat in the Italian coffee shop next to Tex's bookstore. Before entering the coffee shop, we looked in through Tex's windows. Gone were those glossy new novels and records, the plush carpet, the spotlights. Now nothing but concrete floors, dangling wires, and on the door a bankruptcy notice. Where was

Tex now? Morris? Who was fleshing out the cop's domestic expenses? Tex, like a torch singer, had ruined himself for love. He'd hocked his jewels to win one more smile from the policeman with the jug ears. Once Tex had said to me, very sister-to-sister, "Aren't we mad, we gay boys, starving ourselves to sylphlike fragility, all so we can attract a straight cop with a beer belly?"

As Maria and I sat in the coffee-shop window and drank hot cider, I told her about my friendship with Tex. Something about the passionate opera music stirred me; this scene was scored for confession. Just as the betrayed Des Grieux sang, "Be silent, you're breaking my heart," I spoke up. "I don't know what you'd think if I told you, uh, that guy next door? Tex? was a little weird?"

Des Grieux was singing *"Nell'occhio tuo profondo io leggo il mio destin"* as I looked into Maria's eyes for my destiny, her scorn or disgust.

"Are you trying to say your friend Tex is homosexual?"

"Yes."

"These are my kisses," the lovers sang, "this is my love," as I added, "So am I."

"So am I, Dumpling," Maria replied with a puzzled smile. "I thought that was the whole idea. I thought we were both gay."

"But what about Sam?" I asked, naming her bearded ex-lover.

"Oh, I have a *faiblesse* for men," she confessed. "I even prefer making love with men, but I only fall in love with women." Her thoughts went on silently until a sigh replaced her jaunty smile and she said, "Alas. Women are no damn good."

Maria sketched in her gay past. "Women are so impossible, always hurtling about in station wagons and Pendleton shirts and swearing drunken vengeance on Cuddles or

Babs. And then this fatal attraction to the *country*—you can't get the farm out of the girl. And no fashion sense. Nothing wrong with a dyke that couldn't be cured by six months in finishing school." She went on talking in the lightest, most frivolous terms, concocting a heady mix of diesel dykes and sulfurous *femmes damnées* ("Damn women, as Baudelaire said"). Although her lesbianism relieved my anxiety, the ease with which she apparently went from men to women dismayed me, as did the glamour of her milieu. There was nothing glamorous about my time in the toilets, that long sentence I was serving.

Although I was appalled by the hair fetishist who slipped his questionnaire under the partition, at least his tastes were specific enough to be fulfillable, whereas mine were raging but shifting, leaving me no peace. I couldn't find the answer because I couldn't phrase the question. After I ejaculated I felt full of self-hatred every time, and every time I swore I'd never return to the toilets.

Every time I had a free moment during the day when I could roost in the poultry house, I felt the excitement of anticipation creep over me. My hands went cold, a blotch of blush would float cloud-slow up my chest and neck, cover my face. If a girl stopped me to chat in the hall, I'd be torn by anxiety. What if he got away, the one big fish to cruise our pond today?

I'd never said one word to all but one of the other campus homosexuals who were john queens. But I knew them all: the beetle-browed man whose outsize glasses touched his hairline above and his beard below and who, in his stall, would lower his ponderous haunches just far enough for my hand to touch his canine penis; the tall law student bearing a heavy tome of torts and investing his stall like a city under siege—no cough, no tapping foot, no lightest emery board of a sigh; the businessman in monogrammed shirt and glossy sharkskin I'd seen give a blow job that first day; and Jeremy, the only one I spoke to, a fat boy with a huge mouth and pomaded hair who waddled out of his booth with a diva's disdain, gathering his reversible windbreaker around him as though it were a sable. None of us wanted each other but contempt had bred familiarity and we'd raise a weary eyebrow or stifle a yawn as we passed each other on our rounds as though to say, "Still at it?" or, "Slim pickings tonight."

The thrill came when one bagged not another old fruit but a hot young college kid, for although I myself was at least young and in college, I already saw myself as vampire-cold, turned prematurely old as a punishment for vice, and not nearly enviable enough to be that exciting thing, a "college kid." I'd learned to feel nostalgia for my own youth while I was living it.

I started dating Annie Schroeder, although I sometimes felt I was carting an aunt about. Her makeup was too elaborate and her clothes too stylish for the Beatniks I was meeting, among whom the women wore little other than black wool sweaters and skirts and black tights and paisley babushkas. For variety, they might tote a green bookbag or paint on badger eyes or let their bushy, waist-length hair bounce over their shoulders.

Sorority girls, unlike Annie, had lots of "personality" of the sort I still see at airports ("You guys! I can't believe it! This is too incredible!"), a pantomime that can go nowhere beyond being repeated for someone else's benefit ("Come over here, you won't believe it, look who's here, Holly is here, I can't believe it, Holly in Paris!"). Some were sweet and big-sisterly, good shoulders to cry on; others eternal cheerleaders, all freckles and bobby sox; still others were serious campus leaders with their blond hair in a severe twist.

My Annie, although she'd pledged a rather dim sorority

that seemed to have nothing but sluts and Home-Ec majors as members, was too moody and far too shy to have much personality. She looked on with confusion, even fear, as other girls kept digging their spurs into their own flanks, neighing louder and louder, pawing the air. She wore that scared smile that the partially deaf produce or that foreigners evince at boisterous parties of people speaking in another language. She didn't get it.

The Beats didn't make much sense of her either. After all, she wanted to be a "top New York model," as she said. The Beats were proud to feel they were outsiders against a majority that included nearly everyone else. She was histrionic, but not in the Bronx Ophelia manner of Beat women, who went about scattering black flower petals.

Nearly simultaneously, we discovered William Everett Hunton, a first-year law student. I hadn't slept with Annie. I was (I am) afraid of all women, but especially one so bony, painted, and breakable. Annie pretended to be hurt by my lack of ardor, but only to gain an advantage over me. I suspect she was actually relieved. William was as gay as I but far more eager to try sex with women. I'd conveniently adopted O'Reilly's theory that homosexuality was only a symptom—a theory, to be sure, that made my urge to love men no more acceptable than Annie's urge to vomit her supper, but at least the theory didn't rush me into trying anything so flighty as tinkering with the symptom by literally sleeping with women. I could look forward to years of speculation about Mommy-Daddy; once all my mudpies were neatly stacked, in principle I'd wake one day finding my penis pointing due south, no longer north.

"What do you think of him?" Annie asked me. We were walking diagonally across campus. The snow lay in dirty piles all around us as though it represented all the soiled linen we'd ever slept on. "Isn't he exciting?"

"And just a bit phony," I said.

"Does he excite you?"

I swallowed. "Yes." I'd never discussed these things with her before, although O'Reilly had told her of my diagnosis.

"He excites me," Annie declared. "I love his big blue eyes. They look like they're going to pop out. And the cute way his teeth are gapped. He's a real little dynamo. And that baby skin—I'll bet he's smooth all over. Well, I may be finding out tonight."

"Aren't you going too fast? I think you've got sex on the brain," I muttered.

"And you don't?"

I pinched my mouth sourly and said, "Chinese is not exactly an easy major, Annie." We fell into silence as we squeaked our way through the black sludge. The wind blew a shelf of snow off a low eave.

"Are you jealous?" she asked. I glanced over and I could see from her reined-in smile and nearly crossed eyes that she wanted me to say yes. I ducked out by taking a higher philosophical line: "I'm not sure what jealousy is." Then, bearing down on her as O'Reilly might: "Why are you so eager to wound me? Have I become a substitute father for you, someone who tortures you (in my case by not sleeping with you) and whom you must punish because you could never punish your real father?"

And we were off. She and I ascribed the most appalling motives to each other out of some seemingly scientific zeal, but unlike a real scientific proposition, which can be verified or at least negated, ours submitted to no proof, since the very things being discussed were unconscious, hence unknowable. I say "things" because I hesitate to speak of them as feelings. An "unconscious feeling" strikes me as an impossibility; the one thing we know for sure is what we are feeling. At least now I believe that no one else can correct our feelings; they are pure, incorrigible.

Always, at the onset of such a conversation, I had the half-thrilling, half-dreadful sensation of being cranked up to the first, highest hill of a roller coaster. We were scaring each other ("You want to castrate me," or, "Have you looked at your incestuous feelings toward me?"), but the mutual attention was flattering, as when a lovely palm reader holds your hand, looks into your eyes, and predicts tragic eventualities.

There was also a Talmudic fascination about the exercise. If the real horror of living is its failure to mean, to accumulate, then our constant decoding was a comfort, for it found design everywhere—still better, a design of one's own making. It was easier for us to accept that we were sick than to acknowledge that we were powerless and life vapid.

Of course, we would have been insulted if someone had accused us of cheating on an exam or confounding *lie* and *lay*, but we smiled charmingly when charged with wanting to murder our father—smiled and shrugged our shoulders. The attribution of Sophoclean passions to ditherers could only be heartening.

William Everett Hunton was one of the first handsome homosexuals I'd ever met, a small, neatly made little guy who would flounce and languish around me but turn gravely masculine around the other law students. Even though he was hoping to reform himself and was quite optimistic about a cure, at least for a while he had been gay, and could still be considered at least a transitional case. Annie and I would sit around his room in the law quad and listen to his adventures, presented as evidence of his depravity but with a suggestion that *his* scarlet sins, at least, had been mink-lined.

We were alone, he and I, for a moment. He was shaving and dressing and I watched him as a child might, as though I myself didn't perform these same rites every morning (or in the case of shaving, every third morning). When I told him in which Midwestern city I'd been born, he laughed and said, "But that's where my patron lives, the real Everett Hunton."

"Come again?"

William widened his blue eyes, smiled, and came over and sat on my lap. "Oh, look, I've gotten foam on your neck," and he brushed it away. He swiveled in my lap, linked his hands behind my neck, and leaned back to look at me. With one more wiggle of his bottom he whispered, "I was wondering if I could get a rise out of you." He stood and pretended to be a matron slowly raising a lorgnette to her eye to inspect the degree and angle of the damage she'd done. "I can't tell if you pack a big basket or not."

"What do you mean exactly?"

"You're not that naive." He went back to his sink and mirror. "God, but do I feel like a tarnished angel around you." He turned and held up a warning finger. "Equal emphasis on tarnished *and* angel."

"You are angelic, William, a naughty angel," I said, surprising myself with my low tone, which was the vocal counterpart to a lazy pat on a chorus girl's fanny. William instantly responded with a shiver. "You think so? Oh, I was telling you about my 'patron.' He'd die if he heard me using that word; he tells everyone we're cousins, though that's just as dangerous—with these really old families the cousins are all present and accounted for." He clapped his hand over his mouth. "No, I must change the subject. So, tell me, Ducky, are you hung or not?" He slapped himself, looked at his reflection, and hissed, "You slut, I didn't say that."

"Do I have a big penis? Oh, I suppose it's just average."

"*Suppose?* Darling, a real man might get away with vagueness about that one vital statistic, but it's not as though you haven't done major comparison shopping." He laughed as an actress might, tossing his head back to emphasize his long neck.

His things were all severely, unexceptionably masculine and patrician—his cologne from Panhelicon, his shoes from Church's, his suits, shirts, and ties from Brooks, his black lisle stockings knee-high and held up by garters, his hat from Lock's in London: exactly the wardrobe lots of money and no confidence would have selected in London or New York, but here in homey old Michigan, where mothers ran up their kids' clothes on the sewing machine, or ordered them in bulk from J. C. Penney's, such garments looked exaggerated, certainly conspicuous. He even had a monogrammed silver hairbrush set, an old Vuitton trunk, a cut-glass sherry bottle. "Such a hoot!" he shrieked when I teased him. "Mad for High WASP camp! Only a retired English officer makes me get really hard."

Suddenly he turned sad, sat on his bed, and hugged his knees, again as an actress might, this time for a meditative head shot staring into the setting sun beside a lake. His speech rhythms were unpredictable and snagged deep into my mind. "You see, we were dirt poor, real white trash. River rats— that's what they call people who live so far down the hill they're washed out every time it floods. We were river rats. William . . . Everett . . . Hunton, what a hoot . . ." He buried his face between his knees for a second. "Some day when we're sisters I'll tell you my real name, but if you snitch on me I'll pull your braids and dip them in the inkwell."

He was up and laughing again. "Champagne, I feel in the mood for champagne." He twirled the two bottles ready and waiting in an ice bucket. "Where is that girl? Isn't she fabulous! *So* glamorous! I can't believe she likes me. I suppose you think it's all frightfully lesbian, you horrid cynic!" And again he was back at my side, this time kissing me. His mouth was wet and sweet from the full red mouthwash he was always swigging. I felt a floral rapture springing up inside me, as though a huge sunflower were about to poke out of my mouth, my entrails about to turn into soft ropes of wisteria, my cock into a red-hot poker. Everything in me rose up to greet him, and Willy grabbed my pants and shook my erection as if it were a hand: "Average, as you say." He bit my ear. "Sorry, doll, I don't go for pencil meat. I'm a hopeless size queen."

He seemed delighted to have demonstrated his power over me. Buffeted by his own witticisms and sexual splashiness, he was smiling a really huge smile. I saw in him the wide-eyed boy I sometimes impersonated, which made me concede the field to him. He was so much better at it, so much more appealing. I could still feel in my palms the girth of his tight, muscled, turned waist as he'd wriggled out of my arms a minute ago, exactly as though he'd been a small but powerful fish, a rosy trout breaking through the ice with the thrust of his tail.

Then Annie came in and she and William flattered each other about their appearance and kissed, standing, for a long time as I sat and looked on—crotch-height, child-height. They were certainly aware of me and were posing for me.

I left the young lovers after they'd assured me how much they adored me. They had even laughingly asked me to be the best man. Outside, it was dark already although only four o'clock, and fresh snow was falling in the quadrangle. I could hear typewriters clattering and see genies of steam lifting off the heated shower windows in the dorms. I passed the chemistry building and looked down at a lecturer in a basement laboratory. So much activity, I thought, and none of it immediately productive. I considered only farmers and steelworkers to be truly productive. The notion of intellectual labor struck me as purest sophistry.

I turned back and headed for the student union. I'd

heard tonight was nude swimming for men only in the union pool. The showers were full, two facing rows of cubicles without curtains. I stationed myself in one and looked and looked across the aisle while trying not to stare. There was the man with the enormous black glasses now squinting glassless, and there, tucked in a protected pocket under his gut, was his penis. Two down was a swimmer with high, molded buttocks. As he turned, his ass seemed to be shaped by invisible hands, like the rubber balls boxers knead to strengthen their grip. I wondered how William Everett Hunton would evaluate the size of each penis—and suddenly a panic seized me, for I realized that I truly was limited by what God had given me, that I wasn't a cloud of uncertainty but an animal with certain attributes and not others.

Perhaps because I hated my sexuality and believed it could be redirected, I'd come to see every aspect of my being as vague and shifting, and in that very cloudiness had lain my definition: I was the boy who hadn't started living yet. But now I felt stigmatized by my actuality, by the mole between my shoulder blades, by the botched job of my circumcision, so that a dewlap hung down on one side but not the other. A Psych major had told me just yesterday that the army could spot queers by showing them slides of nude men. In spite of themselves, the queers' eyes dilated a fraction—and that "in spite of" enraged me and scared me, for my pride, yes, my pride insisted I could be whatever I chose. Every morning the *tabula* was *rasa*. Maybe that was why the Buddhist doctrine of the non-soul, the *anattā*, attracted me so much, because it suggested I was potentially everything and actually nothing. I could wake up one morning gay or straight—or as nothing, since Buddhism seemed to annihilate such essences. I was afraid to make a choice of any kind.

From the showers and toilets my cruising moved out into the world. Although my school reputedly had a large percentage of gay male students, no one was open about it and street cruising was too blatant. The real screamers, as I learned years later, drove hours and hours to a bar in Toledo, a lively spot with drag queens, hustlers, bull dykes, and couples dressed identically and sporting matching wedding rings, the site of nightly brawls and weekly police raids. Nevertheless, in our college town some married men cruised in their cars and a few students discreetly hung around late at night outside the union.

I became the most persistent street cruiser in town. For someone who till now had had a rather irritable, short-fused fussiness about wasting time, I was suddenly willing to turn whole acres of time over to pasture. Like a hunting lion, indifferent to the beauties of nature and the night but excruciatingly alive to even the smallest twitch or chirr, I paid no attention to the buildings around me and after staring at them hundreds of hours could not have told you if they had Ionic or Corinthian capitals or even columns; yet the moment someone male lingered for even a second, slowed his pace a fraction, or looked back with a frown, conspicuously snapping his fingers in the air to mime remembering something (transparent alibi), I had taken his photo, cured it, and glued it into a special identity kit just for him. I learned I couldn't go home unsatisfied. At the beginning of the evening I'd rush haughtily past Fatty or Gramps, but four hours later I'd be on my knees in an alleyway doing him.

And I learned once is never enough. Nor is twice.

I felt a blind hatred for (and shame before) anyone who interrupted my cruising—a strolling family or a boy and girl on a date who sat on a bench to neck, if that bench was my territory.

The boredom I underwent was intense, painful, hard work, since all disciplined thoughts had been crowded out and soon in the toilets I'd even traded in my Chinese flashcards for unadulterated stupor. I learned that everyone else in the world was less interested in sex than I. The others reached a point where they'd had enough. They stood, buttoned up, and hurried off, irked they'd wasted so much time on nothing. But I had no shred of dignity left to button. The other fairies could be spooked by a slowly passing cop car, or they would withdraw when the prey became too scarce. Not me. I was still there, blue with the cold, beating my gloved hands for warmth.

I'd had the same feeling when I was a child. I was the one who wanted to play late into the cold and the dark and to roughhouse (you be the rough, I'll be the house). Just to feel that contact with other boys' bodies, their knees burning into my biceps, their weight resting on my chest, or a strong forearm choking my neck from behind (I leaned closer into my tormentor)—to feel this contact, I was willing to defy the other boys, refuse to say *uncle*, or say it and recant.

Now I spent so much time on this harsh exchange, where I was selling myself for free but still could never find enough takers, where the buyers I despised despised the merchandise I'd become, that all other human reciprocities (between friends, teacher and student, parent and child) appeared excessively kind, extraordinarily considerate. And yet I couldn't help thinking that other people were nursing illusions of which I'd been disabused. Other people were somehow naive. My mother prayed every day of her life that my father would come back to her—or, failing him, some mystical Herb, Abe, or Will—and she listed her own attractions, her professional standing, her fine character, her accomplishments as hostess and conversationalist, her cultural background; but I knew she was fooling herself, that men were quantitative not qualitative, that they only knew how to count years, inches, wrinkles, dollars. Just as my chest was too narrow, my glasses too thick, my penis too small, she was too fat, old, poor.

When Annie would tell me she was sure William Everett Hunton would come to love her because she had an inquisitive mind and a true heart capable of devotion, I thought, "Cut it, lady, just show me the figures."

To that primitive skepticism I now added cynicism—not a mustache-twirling glee but a cynicism I took and ate with barnyard docility. People were bodies, I thought; the only valuable people have beautiful bodies; since my body isn't beautiful, I'm worthless. That was the humble feed I pecked at night and day.

Every time I returned to the Main Hall toilets I thought to myself, "Well, here we are again." Unlike those babied straight people, I was incapable of self-deception. Paradoxically (and this thought was as real as it was slippery), the toilets—their very degradation, my enslavement to them— struck me as the "big time." Something so debased must be real, I thought. Like a whore who returns to the strip, I said, "Okay, here I am again, back in the Life."

O'Reilly at my next session said, as he picked a red spot on his nose that had become infected, "For chrissake, what the hell have you done to our Annie, fixing her up with that sicko?"

"I didn't fix them up," I said.

"She's in a hell of a mess. I had to work with her all night. She's sleeping peacefully now. I have to get this off my chest with you. I'm not one of those goddam Freudian tin gods claiming I have no feelings."

"But what happened?" I resented O'Reilly's meddling, feared his rejection. I needed him. My addiction to homosexuality must end, must end soon, and he had said only he could save me. I was being shaped and stunted by my desires—sex with men had even entered my dreams. The army test would pick up a dilation of my pupils, and William Everett Hunton had sworn I was getting a "cocksucker's mouth—like mine!" he'd added brightly. "Big pouty lips. And our skin is smoother, like a girl's, and our hips fleshier, maybe just a millimeter, and our nipples are more sensitive; one of mine even gave a drop of milk once. You can tell who's gay—the little mincy steps, the loose wrists, the overly mobile features, lips always pouting in a *moue*" (which he pronounced "mooay," on the theory that sounded more French), "the cadaverous chest and skinny waist, the estrogen-shiny hair, and of course the *voice!*" He shrieked to demonstrate, ran to the window, and called out, attracted the attention of grinning law students passing by: "Yoo-hoo, young boys!" He was being the giddy matron with the warbling operatic voice. "Young boys, cuckoo, cuckoo! Up here, Duckies, come up here to your very own Gertrude and Alice." Sotto voce: "That's you, Gertrude—suits you, today's mannish woman on the go, the avant-garde scribbler."

"What do you mean 'sicko'?" I asked O'Reilly. "What did William do?"

"You'll have to ask Annie, if she'll be good enough to ride with you."

"William's rejected me," Annie told me with a faint grin and excessive blinking, as though she'd just removed the bandages. "The awful thing is that he won't let me go entirely. He likes the *idea* of me, he wants to be normal sexually, but he feels horribly claustrophobic when I'm around. I try to hug myself into vanishing, take up as little space as possible, but it's no good; he's frantic—the law school takes twice as many freshmen as it keeps on, really vicious system, the poor guy's a genius, but not at all disciplined, and does he really want to be a lawyer I keep wondering or is it just the High WASP camp of the Brooks sack suit and the monogrammed briefcase from Mark Cross, but one thing's sure he sure can sting, speaking of wasp, he says he loves me but all my girlie things drive him nuts, can't bear my slip and garter belt and makeup, though he's better than I am at making up and he's really a tyrant about my appearance; O'Reilly thinks he's a sicko out to murder his mother but could O'Reilly be just the weeniest bit jealous 'cause I think William is oddly *curative* for me in that he's more obsessive about appearance than I am and he makes me feel tired out by narcissism, speaking of negative psychology and he's"—deep breath, the recollection of a smile—"*wonderful*. He really is, you know."

Like a baby who's panicked crawling through a tunnel but emerges smiling, Annie had pushed away her fears and was now quietly discussing "our future," by which she meant hers with William. "He really does want to marry me, at least we've spent hours lingering in front of jewelry windows and he even sashayed into one and demanded to see the *costliest* diamonds." I could hear an echo of William in the way she said "costliest." "And now we both know everything about minks, how to let them out and match skins."

At my fraternity we celebrated founder's night, a "bachelor evening" when we all dressed in black tie, ate shrimp cocktail and well-done steaks, then went to the party room in the cellar and drank ourselves into a blackout. The style of the house was hang-dog: seasoned, weary, alcoholic. Our president, the one who looked freshly peeled, would wake up at six in the evening, climb out of his hooded sweatsuit and two pairs of athletic socks, his costume for sleeping in the un-heated "fresh air" dorm, spend an hour shaving and showering and emerge, flushed, in impeccable black tie and diamond studs, his debauches betrayed only by his red nose. He mixed potent cocktails, but he refused to serve them unless every detail was perfect—correct glass correctly frosted, the right kind of garnish, the right monogrammed paper napkin.

The camaraderie of founder's night seemed doubly warm

because we were all decorous and idle in a new way. At dances everyone was naturally devoted to his date, and at the weekday dinners a third of the members were missing and another third critically hung over. The rest read magazines, staged lackluster burping or farting contests, or threw bread. The house had been built by the first dean of music, and the dining room, with its minstrel gallery, had been the university's original concert hall—Caruso had stood up there, right there, and sung, "Oh Ginnie whisky late burn air." The shiny, very dark, and turbulently ornate woodwork made one think of hobbyists who do sculptural things with their own body wastes and keep their successes in jars.

After the white wine and the red, we sang our way downstairs, underground, arm in arm. I suppose for the others there was something sad about such a gala evening without women, and obviously men alone don't work up that glitter on their canines or press with the same suave, competitive leaning into the circle—alone they don't even have the right excuse for joshing with each other.

But for me, the tuxedos (which depersonalize waiters and lend distinction to friends), the banquet, and the toasts all permitted me for two minutes at a stretch to imagine we were a club of lovers—not the freaks at the toilets or those zombies endlessly laundering their genitals under the showers, but regular guys at ease in their skin, carelessly reaching a meaty hand back in a giant arc to scratch a shoulder blade, big panda eyes taking in the world, voices too loud for indoors. If I elaborated this fantasy it fell apart, since I knew a man stopped being desirable the moment he desired another.

By three in the morning the President's Punch had been delivered as the coup de grace to the few survivors. On every buttoned leather couch, unconscious men sprawled, as "totaled" as the cars they liked to wreck. Some of the brothers sat bolt upright, mouths open, ties and shoelaces undone.

Their snoring bleated and gasped antiphonally from room to room. The lights on all four floors were blazing. I was the only one awake.

No. There was one other person, another pledge, Mick, a guy who grinned too much and who talked about weapons and physical fitness with a creepy enthusiasm, as though everyone must agree that hacking through the ice to swim in Lake Michigan was a self-evident pleasure as was the prospect of parachuting out of a plane into enemy-occupied territory. Like certain religious fanatics who supply their own chorus of assent ("That's right, by golly, Lord knows"), he murmured to himself all the affirmation he needed.

Mick was from the South. Everything about him was glossy. Each hair on his head looked as though it had been individually dipped and twirled in hot mink oil. His prominent temples, his bony jaw, the machine-tooled grooves of his ears, his sealskin eyebrows all threw off highlights, and his big black eyes looked like the reservoirs of that lubrication, just as his shiny black nipples looked like the controls. He wasn't "masculine" with the full pachydermal weight that word carried back then. He was more like a ferret—quick, intent.

And a loner. He was always alone, backing out of rooms with a grin and that nearly subvocal chorus of yea-saying ("Yessiree, better get crackin' if I'm going to make ROTC"). He'd hang on the witticisms of the older guys with that huge grin. It was hard to look at it since there was no scrim over it, and only if someone teased him ("Stop eatin' shit, Mick") did he become conscious of his smile. Then he used it defensively; he'd dial it bigger and brighter, rotate and beam it into every corner. The brothers didn't think he was a "face man" only because he wasn't given to an eye-batting awareness of his own beauty. But he did have the sort of good regular looks that go with a parade uniform. One could picture his features under a helmet, deep-set eyes sunk into the shadow cast by the brim.

He had a girlfriend whom he never stopped touching when he was with her—fingering her sash, stroking her hair, massaging her neck, guiding her through the door by patting her shoulder. They were always the first to hit the dimmed make-out room at a dance and the last to leave in complete dishevelment. She wasn't a "Greek." In fact, she had no distinction in our eyes except as Mick's girl. Mick seemed much less complicated than everyone else about sex; he didn't talk about cunnilingus for hours and didn't vomit on his date. He seemed curious in the same uncomplicated way about men. When he was on wake-up duty, he'd tap me (I slept on an upper bunk) and then he'd just stare at my early morning erection in my jockey shorts. He didn't smile unless I caught his eye; then he'd sort of come out of his trance and give a grin. He was what the other fellows would have called a horny bastard, except he never posed as one. Maybe he wasn't very intelligent.

Now he and I were the only people awake in the whole glittering after-party house, surrounded by wheezing and gibbering penguins. I was sitting stunned by drink on a broken-down couch on a landing at the head of the grand staircase. Someone had passed out beside me. "Do you mind if I join you?" Mick asked. It was almost as though we'd had an appointment. Several times during dinner he'd caught my eye with his usual curiosity. His black hair had just been cut very short and I had the strongest urge to run my hand through it and before I'd thought twice I'd done it and suddenly his mouth was pressed to mine and we were rolling in each other's arms and our hands were blindly tearing at shirts to open them and to feel that skin. Mick's mouth tasted of crème de menthe. His hand had wormed its way down my trousers and was on my cock and I was thinking, We'll become lovers we'll live together forever I love him why were there no signs. He looked and acted like a ferret and now his hand became one; *my* hand stroked his stomach, so taut from all his sit-ups a dropped dime would have bounced on it and I thought, Does he love me too much, will he become a nuisance always underfoot in the fraternity house, this is probably a mistake.

And then we'd half undressed each other, my cummerbund was cast on the floor, my studs had popped, and shifting streams of red and yellow light and heat flowed up from my legs through my chest and blazed across my closed eyes. "We're crazy," I whispered in his ear, "the other guys . . ." He pulled back and looked at me quizzically and then his tongue, muscular as a snail's foot, was washing my face, the tip probing my nostril, now licking inside the arch above my eyelids and a second later back on my tongue and I was grateful for the ferocity of his desire because I felt borne up by it, just as though I were flying on the back of a stork—yes, one of those babies the stork wings down to its parents.

His hand, calloused from all his commando workouts, closed over mine and led me into the room he shared with three other guys. Not a tender squeeze, just the practical pressure of horniness. His roommates were asleep, snoring or groaning only a few feet away from us. We finished undressing in a flash. Mick was standing naked beside me, smooth torso, furry legs, as though he were still wearing hip-length black stockings but had peeled off the matching tops. Then he slid in bed beside me and took liberties, we took and took liberties touching each other all over in all those secret places our eyes had glanced at obliquely in the fraternity shower room.

Now my fingertips found that long muscle that ran from the anus up to the base of the penis—this second submerged penis, the father penis, sheathed by the body itself. And his fingers were digging into my buttocks as though he hoped to push me into him, blend two willing but separate entities, less separate now that his mouth was on my ear, thundering breath into me. Certainly my thoughts were inflating and floating upward. Now he was straddling my chest and his cock was sliding over my lips. A second later he'd swung around and we were sucking each other, lying on our sides, Romulus and Remus before the wolf arrived to nurse them. In the hall light that came in through the open door I could see the red veins in his translucent scrotum, autumn leaf, and I looked up the crack of his ass. My mind reeled in a drunk waltz back and forth between my cock and his, between getting and spending.

Then he said, "Why don't you stick it in me."

I said, "Okay . . . ," with a trace of hesitation.

"I've never done this before," he said.

"Neither have I," I lied. "But maybe it's done like this," and I folded his strong legs back, plowing into them as a lineman digs into his opponent's shoulder. His calves hooked over my shoulders. His legs, long and firm in their black stockings of fur, felt cool. He was like a trick bottle that must be turned at a queer angle for it to pour, but then it pours freely. Since he had been built to stand perfectly still at attention under a general's glance, he knew how to take orders, even silent ones. For once he wasn't keeping up his stream of self-encouraging comments. Nor was he smiling.

When I started to enter him, he said "Jesus Christ" out loud and grimaced with pain. The closest roommate stirred. I pulled out and he dashed for the toilet. I followed him. He sat on the toilet, door open, and said in a loud voice, "You're really a pain in the ass," and smiled that big unveiled smile. I stood there while he winced and talked and looked down into the toilet to see if anything had come out. His body had been tanned so often it retained a permanent swimsuit line.

We didn't go back to bed, neither then nor ever, but the next semester I had a room of my own in a boardinghouse and Mick would borrow it every Tuesday and Thursday afternoon when I was in class. He used it as a place where he could sleep with his girlfriend. Once I found a single drop of blood on my sheets. Often I could smell the scent of his clean but athletic and unperfumed body. By that time he'd been teased so much for his smile—and had even had a caricature drawn in which he was all teeth—that he'd lost his naturalness. The next year he dropped out of school and joined the paratroopers.

Two days after the bachelor dinner, William Everett Hunton called me at three in the afternoon and begged me to hurry over to the law quad. When I arrived, there was Annie slumped outside his door, barefoot, wearing a pretty rose silk slip and nothing else, her beehive collapsed. She looked up at me with huge muddy eyes, but the clinch of recognition quickly relaxed and she glanced away, hopeless.

"For God's sake, Annie, get up!" I shouted, as concerned about the scandal she was making as the pain she was suffering.

The minute I spoke, the door flew open and framed William. "Thank heavens you've come." He looked with fear and loathing at Annie. "I see you've met my little doggie. Don't pet her. We're leaving her out here to punish her. She barked all night. You can call her Sam."

He yanked me into the room, after I caught a glimpse of a mad grin on Annie's face at the name Sam. She even mouthed it silently. And then her mouth turned from comic to tragic, and her eyes filled with tears.

As soon as he'd closed the door he leaned up against it, as though to keep Sam out. "Oh, my dear, you'd never guess the cheap paperback I've made of my life, pure *roman de gare*—why wasn't I content to stay a thoughtless queen in quest of big dicks? This GF (by which I mean 'genital female' to distinguish her from us, darling, who are women by choice, not by necessity, though in your case I do see the iron hand of fate)—this GF has been turning my life into hell. I haven't been to class for a week and, listen!"

We stood stock still.

"Do you hear the typewriters? They keep that up night and day, typing up class notes, they never stop. Or do you think it's just a tape of typing on a loop to torment me? I may be *smart*, but more in the sense of isn't-that-a-smart-hat, anyway, there's no way to fake an exam on the tort, which I persist in seeing as a soggy onion quiche—or as what you are, a cheap Southern tart who's plumb wore out."

"But what about Annie? We can't leave her in the hall like that."

"Why not, Miss Priss? Are you afraid she'll tattle to Sheila?" That was William's name for Dr. O'Reilly. "Too late. You're already in the bitch house with Sheila, who incidentally is on her way up here now (if she doesn't nod off first) to rescue Sam—so careless of you to hire a shrinker who's a juicehead and goofball artist; I *mean*, my dear, I talked to the old fright on the blower and she was as incoherent as I get with ten inches up my bum, only she wasn't happy about it. She got more foam on the receiver than you get on your skirt when you see a film starring Montgomery Clift, who's not even worth soppy panties since Monty's just a tired old fruit herself."

"O'Reilly's coming here? My God!" and I felt the most terrible guilt. The day was brilliantly cold and sunny. William had thrown a window open, which let in the cold above the sizzling steam heater.

Annie came in. Her eyes were huge, enlarged by the smudges she'd made of her mascara. Her body looked all the more emaciated in her slip, and when she started to sob I could see her poor flat belly shaking under the flimsy fabric.

William and I sat on the edge of his bed and looked at her as she bent over the sink. She studied her face in a small mirror. Then she splashed cold water all over herself, which at first seemed ordinary except that she didn't stop. She bent her head farther and farther down and her hands continued to scoop up water and fling it over her shoulders, splashing her back and the varnished floor behind her.

"For chrissake, Ophelia, give us a break. Medical help is on the way in the form of bourbon and amphetamines and Big Sheila, so just hold tight. Or get tight. Here's a bottle."

I couldn't bear either her suffering or his vitriol. Until now I hadn't realized how much I'd wanted them to make each other happy and how sickened I was by the mess they'd—wow, maybe *I'd* made. I put an arm around Annie's shoulder, dried her off, and seated her on a chair. She was surprisingly docile, but the instant I turned to find her blouse she'd risen and was pacing the room, touching everything as though she were a miser counting her possessions.

"I can't bear this," William said. "I thought I was getting a girlfriend, but I've come up with one of Sheila's botches, just scrambled eggs for brains." He threw a tweed jacket on over his striped button-down shirt and headed for the door, but Annie sank to the floor and wrapped her arms around his legs.

"Don't go," she said in a normal hostessy voice, "I promise to be more amusing," and she actually managed a beguilingly sociable smile, but then a high moan, an Algerian widow's moan, started in the back of her throat and grew louder.

William went white. He said, "You've spoiled everything," kicked free of her, and headed out. Then we were all three out in the brilliant blue-and-white day, a day so surgically clean and sharp that even the clouds looked like cotton soaked in alcohol. It was the ten-minute break between classes. The walkways, bordered with snow-laden bushes, were jaunty with red scarves flowing into the wind like blood the instant it's drawn up the pipette. William was walking briskly ahead, his baggy khakis luffing around his legs. He was talking to himself, chatting up the wind. I was embarrassed, wishing my cigarette smoke would condense and turn into new friends or at least conceal me from the ones I already had. I looked back, as did William, and there was Annie, still in her slip, but on her knees in the snow, her mouth an oblong of grief, her hands raised and hyperflexed. She was crawling on her knees in the snow.

I had to take charge. She should be hospitalized, but it wasn't my place to do that; yet I could get her indoors, warm her up, dress her, try to calm her. Suddenly I saw her as my sister, not the hard tyrannical sister I actually had, but another waif.

William had vanished. He'd left his door open and Annie and I returned to his room. Hours later, long after sunset, O'Reilly arrived, his nose inflamed from the way he kept clawing at the infected spot with his mini-nails, for he'd chewed them down nearly to the quick. His white hair was flying. He was wearing sandals in the snow. Nevertheless, he had an expensive silk-lined cashmere overcoat on, the sort a broker wears, but underneath he wore his embroidered cossack shirt, and a rope for a belt. He embraced Annie, whom I'd wrapped in William's plaid bathrobe. He crushed her against his chest. The two of them stood there rocking back and forth for a long time.

I didn't know which way to look. My only feeling was embarrassment and relief, relief that I was no longer responsible. But O'Reilly said to me, "Okay, you can come over for your share too," and he raised an arm and beckoned me to his side. I didn't want to go. I didn't want love of this kind, love from a man who didn't really like me though he professed he did, a humiliating love to promote "regression," for O'Reilly subscribed to the theory that his patients must revert to infancy and grow up all over again under his benign tutelage. I preferred loneliness and pain. The wolf in me trotted away from the campfire, threw back a finely modeled head, and howled—but the sheep went to O'Reilly, because I didn't know how to say no. Taken out of his office and spirited here, O'Reilly looked crazy and ill—puffy, disordered, breathing laboriously, reeking of bourbon. I was ashamed of him.

Over the next few weeks, Annie stopped eating. She'd got it into her head that William had found her repulsively fat, and she'd spit with scorn at the reflection in the mirror of her meager breasts and nearly fleshless hips. She longed for the purity of a boy's body (a boy before puberty).

She'd found another girl at school with the same obsessions. They slept all day, prided themselves on their luminous paleness, grew their hair very long. They wrote poetry and began to go to cocktail parties with professors; they were invited by a teaching fellow in art history whom they'd befriended. At midnight they'd get together in Annie's dorm room, light candles, and take several hours to eat two cucumbers. The rest of the time they lived on vodka, cigarettes, and black tea. O'Reilly hospitalized Annie for not eating, but she tore the intravenous tubes out of her arms and trotted frantically up and down the stairs to work off the disfiguring calories.

I took her home to my father's for Christmas. My stepmother gave us a tour of the house, as Midwesterners will do. We looked at cedar closets, the linen cupboard with enough sheets to outfit an infirmary, the whole cooked turkey and cold ham waiting in the fridge for our midnight snacks. We inspected the basement, saw the furnace, the bar locked tight against pilfering maids, the Ping-Pong table. "If you kids feel in the mood for a game," Dad said, "even in the middle of the night, go right ahead since it's soundproof down here."

"Anyway, *you'll* be up," my stepmother said to my father sourly. She launched into a recital of his annoying nocturnal habits. "He doesn't get up till late afternoon, and at six in the evening he sits down to a breakfast of a pound of bacon. I've had to go my own way. Otherwise I'd never have had a life."

Which was my father's cue to brag about his wife's social successes as chief Friend to the Symphony, as docent at the art museum, and as the star of Mr. Feltrinelli's painting class. She said, "I did a portrait of your dad as a sad clown and then a sort of Michigan landscape that got out of hand so I made it abstract but it's kinda cute anyway." She was also going to play Scrooge in a Christmas production for the Home for the Incurables ("If only I can get my lines down. Will you help, Annie? I've got a wonderful costume and beard and bah-humbug all worked out"). In her busy life, slide shows of trips to Mexico alternated with four-hand piano renditions of "Mister" Haydn's symphony ("Thank heavens he wrote so many; we girls just adore him, he's easy to count to and the bass part is good for beginners").

My father distrusted men and felt uncomfortable around them, but he came to life near a pretty girl. Annie counted as a pretty girl in spite of her skinniness and her professionally applied makeup, so in contrast with the faintest pink our local debutantes touched to their lips and then mumbled away on Kleenex. Although she could scream "Shit!" at nurses who force-fed her, she also knew how to ape the manner of the debs—or almost. Actually, Annie simpered and languished, whereas the debs were thrillingly alert to everything. I noticed the difference and I'm sure my stepmother did, but my father was sufficiently seduced to change his habits. He who usually stayed up all night and flooded the house till dawn with Brahms symphonies, who never spoke except to lecture ("You may have been wondering about the comparative advantages of long- versus short-term bonds"), now sat down at nine to eat a proper sociable meal with candlelight and conversation and even a bottle of vinegary wine he'd dusted off. "Just the tiniest thimbleful for me," Annie said, overplaying it, I thought, since she lived on vodka.

"I'll stick with coffee," my stepmother said reproachfully.

My father called Annie "Young lady" and laughed at what she said. When he laughed, he cocked his head to one side and held his cigar away from his mouth. It gave me goosebumps to see his teeth—I suppose partly because they were so yellowed from tobacco, but mainly because his smile looked so fake.

I knew geniality was a strain for him. He preferred solitude, and if he was forced to socialize he wanted to do it with employees. If he had to entertain equals, his idea of a party was a once-every-two-years blow-out for which the house would be repainted, bricks pointed, gutters cleaned, lawn rolled. Every room on every floor would be thrown open for white-glove inspection. Not a speck of dust lurked behind a single figurine, not a vase went without a bouquet, not a single blown-glass, kidney-shaped ashtray that wasn't spotless beside its gaping "silent butler," not a single lamp unlit, not a bathroom rack without its full rigging of guest towels. Outside, drinks were served and a band played and couples danced in a tent. For days in advance my stepmother would ask, "Do you think people will want a banana daiquiri? What if someone orders a Rob Roy?"

"Let's get all that," my dad would say. "We don't want to be caught short." Just as Mormons stockpile their basements with canned goods and weapons in anticipation of Armageddon, my father's approach to any festivity was apocalyptic. The appalling moment when Betsy McAllister, past president of the United Fund, might ask for a B&B and be told there was no Benedictine must be staved off at all costs, as must the equally shocking moment when a guest would inflict a wound on himself and not find in each of the six bathrooms a fully stocked medicine cabinet. But if high, unforgiving standards were ascribed to real or potential guests, the hosts were as eager to judge their friends. A man who dropped in would be laughed at for wearing cologne or even the chastest ring or for showing his calf when he crossed his leg or for turning the creases in his trousers when he sat down as poor men do, and his wife would invariably have too loud a voice and too much jewelry and she'd smoke and drink too much, availing herself, in other words, of those very bottles we'd laid in and those silver felt-bottomed lighters we'd posed on side tables with such anxiety to make them appear casual. It was a milieu where even the most passing acknowledgment of the body was considered "off color." Now that I'd lived away from home for several years at boarding school and college, I found myself breaking the delicate membrane that sealed off decent talk from the world's grossness.

That night, my stepmother escorted Annie to her room, far from mine, since in those days there was no question of putting an unmarried man and woman even in adjoining rooms. My father lit another cigar and said, "Damn nice young woman. And seems to have a good head on her shoulders. She asked good solid questions about group versus individual life insurance." I doubt whether my father thought Annie was either solid or nice, but she *was* a woman—a step in the right direction.

My stepmother discovered in the morning that the entire ham and turkey had vanished from the refrigerator overnight. That evening, when my father arose, he found that his sink had stopped up. The blocked drain was located exactly one floor below in Annie's bathroom. When he put on his special, comical plumber's cap and overalls and roguishly opened the pipe leading down from her sink, his face fell, his mouth turned down in disgust, and he pulled out stinking, half-chewed gobs of turkey and ham with his bare hands.

"I just don't understand," my stepmother whispered. "Why couldn't your friend get sick in the toilet instead of the sink? And it seems such a waste of good food—I was planning a cold supper."

Annie had tried to prevent my father from opening the drain, but once he did she calmed down and packed her bag. My stepmother drove her to the station and waited as I put her on the train. On the platform Annie said, "Are you furious?"

"No, it serves them right," I said smiling. "I wish I had your guts—they need to be shocked."

"I wasn't trying to shock them. But no matter. I don't see how you came out of this family. You're so much better than they are—sweeter, more open."

I tasted her praise but suspiciously, as though the candy might be poisoned.

Like my sister, who scorned our real mother's habit of praising herself, I felt I was being honest only when I said the worst things about myself. Now, all these years later, I realize one self-evaluation is as true as another and that my mother's relentless Pollyannism was a less melancholy and more efficient way of muddling through than my gloom or my sister's saturnine honesty. Nor did my sister's honesty keep her from talking herself into marrying a man she didn't love and becoming the suburban mom she had a drive but no talent to impersonate. My sister was ashamed of my mother and me for being so weird. She locked herself into an iron-maiden normality that gave her no room to breathe. She was stifling as she mixed the frozen orange juice on wintry mornings, attended PTA meetings, baked brownies, suffered the attentions of a dull, doting husband. Her upper lip would swell every time he wanted to make love to her. She sipped from bottles of liquor she'd secreted all over the house (mouthwash bottles, perfume bottles, Coke empties under the sink, a Lysol bottle in the spare bathroom).

After Christmas vacation back at school I was invited by William Everett Hunton to a gay dance. "Spit-polish your Mary Janes," he said, "and pray a man will see reflected in them up your skirt that you don't have any panties on, you naughty thing."

Someone had a studio apartment just above a used-textbook store on a corner of an otherwise nonresidential block. There at ten on a Saturday night in January, I found myself armed with a cigarette and beer (one of the four cans William had had to buy for me with my money, since I was still below drinking age). We sat on top of stacks of books, sipped and watched the twenty men squeezed into the small room. I didn't know any of the other fellows. I'd never seen any of them at the toilets. I suspected that handsome gay men all knew each other and avoided public cruising. For the first time William seemed shy, but he said he was simply trying to butch it up. "Look, doll," he whispered, "people think a queen's a hoot, but the life of the party goes home alone while everyone makes a last-ditch play for the idiot hood who's been standing in the corner all night by himself. My dear, who did the lighting here? I should get my own light man written into my contracts just like Marlene. Nothing like a baby-pink follow spot to take years off a gal." At twenty-two William was terrified of aging. "I'm going to kill myself when I turn thirty. Thirty is gay menopause. I've always liked that saying, 'Live hard, die young, and leave a beautiful corpse.' 'O Rose, thou art sick.' Maybe that would make a good drag name for you: Rose. *Sick* you certainly are." And William laughed with his special blend of mischief, compounded of humor, spite, and sadness in a ratio even he wasn't sure of but that he mixed by feel.

I saw a big blond man in a blue crewneck sweater and tan slacks and suddenly I had the impression we were all here to please him but no one could. Pagans would have known how to worship him as the temporary perch of a winged demon; poor monotheists blind to all gods but the invisible one must ascribe their attraction to love rather than fear. And yet actually everyone in the room was afraid of Harry, the huge biology major from Canton, Ohio.

Not me. I'd always had good luck with gods if I could make myself believe in their disguise as a shepherd, messenger, or biology major. I asked Harry questions which he answered politely but from a great distance, as though the neural impulse had to be translated into several intermediary codes before reaching me as speech. There were two things going on, completely incongruous: his response to my questions about trilobites, dialogue for an *Encyclopaedia Britannica* science film; and the damage done to the air every time he moved or smiled. If his laugh was a hollow boom, his gestures studied, the timing of his great smile off just a second, that was because his demon wasn't yet quite comfortable in this incarnation—or perhaps he was receiving instructions from another star, which accounted for the fractional delays. I was relieved that his eyes, wild as beasts, were securely caged by long lashes.

I asked him to dance. He looked startled by the impiety. Maybe he wasn't a god but just a handsome guy from Canton (though a misfit in high school) who now at last wanted to dance with someone else cute, not a troll like me (William called the tearoom regulars "trolls" or sometimes "dragons"). Or maybe Harry, like me, had never danced with another man before. Who would lead?

"Sure, why not," he boomed. And a second later I'd glided into his arms, his hands rested on my shoulders, my arms reached around his waist, we closed our eyes and the blind led the blind. Brenda Lee was singing, "Break it to me gently," but I ignored the words. I rested my cheek on his chest and thought, All I've ever wanted is to rest here, the word really was *rest*. (For me desire is always static.) I thought dimly that I have to go round the world impersonating a grown-up and a man and a heterosexual, whereas I'm none of the above. But I had no desire to think things out precisely. It was just a relief to be here hugging this big man. He was wearing a cashmere sweater and we were both sweating. The best explanation of masochism, the appeal of masochism, is that it accepts shame; the sickening shame one must swallow and hide is at last accepted, employed, even loved— the shame about a mutilation, hairiness, too much or not enough fat, the shame about wanting to serve, to be a dog, son, wife, slave, horse, prisoner. If so, my feelings then were masochistic, since for years I'd felt ashamed of my longing to dance with the swimming captain, to be worthy of him. Ever since, shame and gratitude have been for me the caste marks of passion.

And yet there was no cause for shame here, not even when I looked up for a kiss and got one. He didn't desire me (what god would?), but he would let me stay in his arms until the end of this song or the next and that was more than I'd ever expected. Of course I felt foolish, a grown man wanting to be sheltered by another. Even the tenderest wedding between two men is always hooted at by their own overly active sense of the ludicrous. The freedom to dance with a man (I don't say "another man" since he was the only person here who counted as a man) seemed remarkable enough to be a one-time-only privilege, but maybe parties like this one went on all the time. Was there a secret fraternity that

linked homosexuals across the states, countries, centuries?
Was I being rushed?

Shame and gratitude, I said a moment ago, but surely
gratitude was normal enough. Anyone who ever let me in his
body or arms I still feel grateful to. That's why so many of
my friends are old lovers, I suppose. And that includes, these
days, dying and dead friends as well, to whom the flesh, my
flesh, still connects me.

The smells of sweat and English Leather or Canoe after-
shave and cigarettes and beer and, now, cooking popcorn in
the kitchen all floated around me. "You gave him a hard-on,"
William hissed in my ear. "I could see it in his pants. Not as
big as it should be considering his height but acceptable;
family size," and he nodded sagely as though he were a grandfather whispering, "An acceptable dowry."

William was obsessed with size, and because I spent so
much time with him I started checking out men's crotches too.
We'd be walking down the street and he'd say, "Catch this
one. It's not as huge as he'd like us to think. That's all balls,
the man has a beach ball for a scrotum. Now *this* one's big—
darling, don't look in the zipper area for the bulge. The
really big ones can't wear jockey shorts, too binding, just
like your mother's love. No, they wear boxers and let it hang
down their leg. Be on the lookout for baggy pants. Believe
it or not, the really humongous dicks are embarrassed, they
try to hide it in loose folds. Now Negroes are good bets, but
not invariably. Italians are reliable, if you don't mind fur-
balls in your mouth, they're so hairy, and if you go for
pecorino."

"What's that?"

"Italian goat cheese. They're all uncircumcised and on
a hot summer day It—Can—Get—Pret—ty—Smel—ly—in
there." He shook his head and growled: "*Love* it." A glance
at my shock and he coolly added, "An acquired taste."

He had other guides to cock size—big hands, big feet, big nose, fleshy ears, early balding ("Due to an excess of male hormones"), big thumb-to-palm ratio. He favored tropical people over those from temperate climes, though he'd discovered that as one approached the poles, cocks become larger again ("Nothing like a big Swede"). Short thick ones ("But *beercan* thick") he preferred to very thin long ones. "But *you*, I don't think you'd know what to do with a truly big dick except throw it over your shoulder, burp it, and weep. Are you Irish?"

"Yes."

"I *knew* it, you Irish boys all have small mouths and small dicks, the worst of both worlds. *Why*," and he rolled his bulging eyes up to heaven, "do I always keep running into Irish boys? Punishment for being a Lit—tle—Bit—Pig—gy in my last life, you think?"

When the new semester started I had my own room in a boardinghouse and I was free from all supervision for the first time in my life. I'd moved out of the fraternity house, although I continued to take my meals there. Indeed, I continued to juggle all these elements—fraternity brothers, Beats, Chinese, and my anonymous, half-seen lovers. I painted everything in my room white except the old desk I'd bought at a junk store, which had a tiny escritoire that folded out and a small oval mirror placed high above my head on a ladder-back of carved black pegs that inscribed the wall with an abacus of shadows. There I did my homework; everything else in my life was so chaotic that I needed to receive good grades. I covered the bed with a white blanket bordered in whitest, widest ribbon and I'd lie on it and watch the sunlight singing to itself out of that small Irish mouth of a mirror.

I met a pretty Korean ("Forget Koreans," William

hissed angrily, "it's clit size") who lived next door. Whenever the mechanical world frustrated him—if his bike jammed
or the laundry machine swallowed his coins, or his key
snapped off in a lock—he'd ring my bell, trudge in, take off
his clothes, fold them neatly on my white wooden chair, and
lie face down on my white bed. He'd take it like a man, bite
the pillow if I hurt him, and nothing had ever felt quite so
good as those small taut muscles under that chamois-soft skin,
the color of cinnamon when it's sprinkled on cappuccino.
That's my way of saying that a low fire, a pilot light, burned
under that glove-smooth skin, and that he smelled excitingly
of that foul fermented cabbage the Koreans like to snack on.
The minute it was over he'd dress and leave, his eyebrows
raised in painful doubt as though he didn't quite understand
what had just happened. He had the whitest teeth.

And then, after I closed and locked the door, I was alone.
I had a record player and twelve records, which I played over
and over again, especially the Bartók violin concerto, its
harmonies edgy enough to make me feel modern but its sweep
romantic enough to hurl me back on the bed in a flood of
ardor. Until then I'd always wanted to write, but when I did,
I wrote down nothing but the time and key signatures of my
feelings or the chords. Most of the melody, as it were, remained in my head, and all the orchestration. Endless scenes
of he said–she said poured forth from my pen, the automatic
transcription of what I was currently living through, but my
characters remained voices in the dark. I never described
them or said what I was feeling. I took a creative writing
course from a published novelist, who told me during a
private conference, "You should arrange the nouns in each
paragraph like the heads in a painting by Uccello."

"Utrillo?" I said brightly.

He turned away in disgust.

But now I read a collection of short stories by new

writers, and I saw they did something I can only call "braiding," the interlacing of phrases, details, snatches of dialogue. Until now I'd written mindless confession in a desperate effort to keep my head above the rising waters of despair and confusion, which could also be called the flood of circumstantiality. Nothing had ever seemed more important to me than who said what first, what she said back, and where it happened, but now I was toying with the idea, gleaned from my recent reading, that a design of sorts, not a stencil but a weave, could be teased out of all these balls of yarn.

I'd drag men back to my room, one after another, guiding them up the fire escape into my window; they didn't want to be seen by the other boarders any more than I wanted them seen. Afterward they'd smile awkwardly, dress, stand on tiptoe to comb their hair in my pointlessly high desk mirror, say, "Well, see you 'round," and duck out the window and back down the rusting metal steps that boomed faintly with each step. Once the man was gone, I'd return to my story. I'd switch on my record of Puccini's *Manon Lescaut* or Bartók's violin concerto and pour myself a shot of Drambuie, a liqueur I didn't realize was meant to be a sort of liquid dessert, not a steady drink. In a moment I'd weigh anchor, the white room would drift into a fast current, and I'd be alone with my characters. No mother to say, "Lights out," no dormitory master patrolling the corridors, no fraternity brothers interrupting me, just four walls of my own, rent paid, and five months to go until summer vacation would spoil my sport. My lights burned their way into the dawn.

At first I'd feel lonely, afraid, itchy, very afraid to go on with my story, afraid it wasn't any good, afraid it was terrific and I was about to spoil it, afraid it was better than I understood and I would never know how to equal it again, afraid it was cold, repellent, inhuman, and my friends would see through me and realize I wasn't such a nice guy after all.

I'd jump up, pace the room, get halfway down the fire escape in search of the third sexual partner of the night— and then this partial retreat would calm me sufficiently so that I could pick up the signal my page was faintly beeping. What if I were to give my character, Sally, a version of Annie's poor beehive?

I sat around the middle room of the union and talked about art and poetry and fiction for hours with other Beatniks, for I thought of myself as a Beatnik even though I didn't have the courage to wear a black turtleneck or sandals, or carry a green bookbag. All that serious talk, as enthusiastic as it was imprecise, between companionable sleepwalkers, each cut off by his dreams but convinced that he was in air-tight accord with the others.

Some afternoons, after twenty uninterrupted hours of writing, reading, drinking Drambuie, playing my twelve records, and hectoring and praising myself, I'd stagger into the union and there find a woman sculptor who had the un-settling habit of nodding before I'd said ten words while murmuring, "Yep. I can see it." At some minor point in my account of my artistic struggles she'd blurt out, "That's it! brother, is that ever it," and I'd smile foolishly, not sure whether I should go on or correct her misunderstanding or coast on it and just give in to the wash of good feeling, mis-placed as it might be. I usually gave in and said, "God, I'm glad *you* understand." And she did seem to understand the most important thing about my work, which is that I'd lived through something, as though I'd saved a child from drowning.

That room was a debriefing room. It was also the room where a potter from New York, as small-shouldered and full-bottomed as her own vases, told me, "I was a math major six years ago, until the day I saw some Japanese porcelains and decided to pot. I was a complete klutz. I threw pots for three years, night and day, before I could get one even to stand up.

Any kid at arts-and-crafts camp was better than me. I'd cry
and hit myself out of anger."

"And now?" I asked, eager for the sequel.

She shrugged and, opening her hands as though to show
four aces, radiated all the uncomplicated happiness of a self-
made genius. I envied her in a knotted way it took me a
moment to untie. Yes, envied her clear picture of what she
wanted to make and her strength in submitting to a discipline
she'd invented. I wasn't like her. Everybody said I was
intelligent, but I feared I wasn't artistic. Unlike the potter,
I had lots of facility but no goal and very little taste. My
mother had convinced me I was or would be "brilliant," and
her belief in me kept me writing. But I didn't trust my own
instincts. I didn't know what I ought to feel.

Just as school was ending, Maria drove up in her old
station wagon to stay with me for a few days. She brought
a bottle of Armagnac, a carton of cigarettes, and Nietzsche's
Thus Spake Zarathustra, which she finally hurled across the
room in exasperation. "I like poems to be poetic and prose
to be prosaic, religion to be prophetic and philosophy to be
crystal clear. Give me Bertrand Russell any day."

The days were hot and the nights warm. Fraternity boys
were staging panty raids on sorority houses, but there was
nothing unconscious about such bacchanalias; everyone referred wearily to Bacchus. I'd never confessed to Maria that
I'd joined a fraternity at all (although I liked the brothers
and went to the house nearly every day). Now we stuck close
to the Beat poets and chicks I'd collected—the lanky painter
next door who copied Larry Rivers and strode the halls nude;
his hearty "old lady" who'd thought he was complimenting
her when he called her the Venus of Willendorf, until she saw
a photo of the prehistoric fertility goddess; the New York
poetess who proudly claimed she'd been conceived in Greenwich Village and whose father had fought in the Lincoln

Brigade but now provided janitorial supplies to factories by day and attended Trotskyite meetings by night; the bearded sculptor with the eternal smile who roared with laughter when he fucked his girlfriend, another sculptor, up in the freezing tower of our boardinghouse. I feared Maria would find me dull. I kept making luncheon and dinner dates for us with my friends until she burst into tears and begged to spend one evening alone with me.

We could sit for hours talking art, love, politics. Other women offered me as a man one kind of deference (my opinions prevailed) and expected another kind (their wishes were to be obeyed). Maria neither gave nor wanted such courtesies. She'd light my cigarettes and tell me I was a fool. She teased me when she overheard me agreeing coquettishly with every absurdity uttered by a handsome athlete.

In her ponderous old station wagon we drove to Flint to spend the weekend with a college dance teacher, Anita, who'd been Maria's first love. Around Anita I was demoted back to being a kid, and Maria would literally pinch my cheeks and roll her eyes as though to remind us that kids will say the darnedest things. Anita was not only on the school staff but also toured with a company versed in the Graham technique, all to earn money to send her sister to graduate school and to support a widowed mother. Her family responsibilities somehow neutralized her lurid status as a lesbian. Although I pretended to be sophisticated and could listen to tales of erotic mayhem without blinking, privately I still considered us all damned. This disparity between my surface smile and inner anguish condemned me to savoring my guilt in silence, a guilt I couldn't expiate since it was thoroughly secular.

Back in my white room after the weekend, Maria stopped playing the big sister. Now that we'd lived together for five days, we'd pressed beyond a border into companionable silence. Much as we might protest our devotion to each other, until now our bodies, tense, edgy animals, had stayed on guard. On this fifth day, they sighed and lay down to sleep side by side like two cats who've finally stopped prowling and hissing their rival claims to the sewing basket and squabbling over precedence at the water bowl.

Now we sprawled on the bed, smoking and reading and listening to Bartók. One afternoon we started kissing. In a second we'd undressed. Maria thrashed with shocking passion in my arms and in my ear her smoky mouth breathed with short, voiced gasps. She was so fragile, so supple in contrast to all the big clumsy men I'd known. I'd thought a heterosexual man must weary of always having to instigate things, but there was no question of aggression and passivity, we were both swept like lovers into a tempest that raged around us, and, yes, *for* us. We were its victims.

Maria stayed two more days. When we'd go to the student union, I'd cast hungry looks at the boys and yearn to escape Maria and reenter this anarchic fraternity which had, instead of secret handshakes, matched taps on the toilet floor, and instead of one hell night, endless nights of perverse pleasure and excruciating remorse.

Once we were alone again I'd forget these distractions, and Maria and I would lie on white sheets fading to blue in the long, late May evening light. I asked her if she'd marry me, and she laughed, rubbed my cheek with the back of her cool hand, and whispered, "My child groom . . ."

She sketched me as I wrote. In the warm summer rain we walked through the night. We sat for hours in a booth at the back of a Chinese restaurant. I told her how I was convinced the Buddhists were right, that the self is an illusion, and yet as a writer and even as a person (in that order) I responded to the individuality of everyone I met. How could I reconcile my religious convictions with this artistic response?

"I've got it!" she said, silencing me with her raised hand as she pursued a thought. At last she sipped cold tea and said, "But that's just the way American life is anyway, because we all move around so much and keep losing touch. We have these smoldering encounters in which we tell everything to each other and pledge eternal love, and then a month or a year later we've drifted apart, we're making new pledges and new confessions and—you see? American life is both Buddhist and intensely personal. It's nothing but these searing, intimate huddles and then great drifting mists of evanescence that drown everything in obscurity. Write about America and you'll reconcile these opposites."

I heard the doubt and reproach in the midst of her disquisition and wondered how I could assure her I'd never drift away or stop loving her. I knew we hadn't yet quite found the form our love would take, doubtlessly because of the conventionality of my social imagination. I didn't have the insider's advantage of refashioning public forms to suit my private needs. Yet I did have an ecstatic apprehension of her, of what she meant to me. I'd never let her go.

After school that spring I went to my father's for three weeks before going on to Chicago for the long summer holiday. I was allowed to drive one of my father's Cadillacs and accompany a debutante to a ball. My stepmother had found for me a sweet girl from a *nouveau pauvre* family. She was too poor to give a proper ball so she held a square dance in her grandmother's barn with a genuine country caller and fiddler.

At the bachelors' cotillion, a catered event for two thousand guests, I shook hands with Everett Hunton, the *real* Everett Hunton from whom William had stolen his name— William's "cousin" or "patron," I couldn't remember which. I mentioned William's name and Everett, a thin, balding blond whose bony nose moved and even went white as a knuckle when he spoke, quickly cast his eyes up to beseech the cupid-heavy cupola for my complicitous silence.

I drifted away, but half an hour later Everett was at my elbow, guiding me through a back door into a service elevator and, on a tower floor high above the city, into a room he'd rented for the night. There we undressed efficiently, word-lessly, and he screwed me without a flicker of affection cross-ing his intelligent, indifferent face.

We washed and dressed again, all very quickly. As we were going out I referred to William as his "cousin."

"But he's just a tramp I picked up and sent to school out of my—well, no one ever said my heart was *big*, but out of my small heart. I felt sorry for him, but he's nuts. He took my family name, which really isn't cricket, and he stole things, good leather and crystal things, gold blazer buttons, a hunt cup, my grandfather's signet ring. Then he met some appalling starved girl who wasn't even from a social family but a sort of mannequin or tart. Then he flunked out and just vanished. He called me once drunk from a phone booth in Dayton, but I wouldn't let him reverse the charges."

As we were going out, he patted my back and said, "The girl, that mannequin—she's in a mental hospital somewhere, I heard. Oh, American life, it's past belief." Thin smile. "He did give a good blow job though, didn't he?"

FIVE

▪ ▪ ▪ ▪ ▪ ▪ ▪

That summer, Maria flew home to Iowa and my mother went to Europe for two months. She left me twenty-five dollars a week to live on and the key to her apartment. She'd estimated that the allowance was large enough to feed me and small enough to force me into getting a summer job. I did work for a while loading trucks all night. To get the job I had to tell the boss I'd be staying on in the autumn. I'd dropped out of school, I said, and wasn't seeking just summer employment. But once I started working, the other men drew me aside, one by one, to tell me that I must go back to school. "Don't get stuck here," they said. "It's shit. It's a dead end."

In the sweaty Chicago night we'd squat bare-chested inside the holds of semis, stacking cartons. Our sweating hands and arms would leave phantom brown prints on the tan cardboard boxes. My partner, a beer-bellied man whose five-o'clock shadow had deepened to midnight by dawn, never spoke to me; I could imagine marrying him, living in a trailer with him, and cooking him meatloaf. On the third night we worked together he finally opened up. He told me that when he was a teenager his father, a young doctor, had died suddenly of a heart attack. No insurance. My partner had been the oldest boy and had gone to work to support his mother and to send the three younger kids through college. "But I got stuck. Now they're all in professions with nice homes in the suburbs and they're ashamed of me, don't like me coming around. So I'm stuck in this shit job."

We talked about books. He liked Stefan Zweig and Nelson Algren. And he liked Beethoven, especially the symphonies. When he talked about books and music, his flat Midwestern voice (he pronounced *milk* as "melk" and *wash* as "warsh") warmed up, almost as though through the smoked window of his face I could see a young man approach, smile, then go away.

Two nights later he stopped talking, and when he had to say something he mumbled. Once again every noun was double-decked by "fuckin' " or "mother-fuckin'."

I'd return to my mother's skyscraper apartment, my face fierce in its warpaint of dirt, my T-shirt clinging to my wet body. The city at last was cool and the streets had run dry of traffic. I'd bow my head under the shower for twenty minutes, scarcely moving, then stand nude in the window and watch the city below slowly constructing itself like coral under incoming tides of light.

My father had told me his father had become a professor so he wouldn't have to work the fields of his parents' Texas farm. Now I understood my grandfather perfectly. I felt pride in my strength and shame over my position just as the other men did. No one respected them for their labor in a country where the idea of honorable poverty had vanished. And yet we had done something, we'd loaded transcontinental trucks. More than most fuckin' men did in a night.

But mostly I just ached. The pain of work, real labor,

had driven splinters into my muscles, into the crouching muscles, the climbing muscles, the bending-over muscles, the lifting muscles, the just-standing-there muscles. My upper body had rusted shut in its basin of pelvic bones and couldn't turn anymore. I was a tired animal, and I tied a feedbag of milk and cereal over my nose.

I couldn't tell if I was big or small. In some ways I felt big, because the men said I was strong and could get stronger, but the boy in me was skinny and losing weight fast in that sweatbox. I couldn't figure out my size, because in my mind I kept modeling a wax effigy of myself, now puny, now a big bear of a worker, now a supple girl without breasts or vagina although responsively female: treat me as a woman and you can rule me. The wax was soft and getting softer, nearly fluid, and as it melted its color became milkier. It would flow out of the chubby cool forms of a child, his sturdy legs, big head, lips lucent as fruit jellies, into lanky adolescence. A moment later it had set into a thick neck, barrel chest, thickening biceps, and even my penis, a moment ago nothing but a tiny urine spout, would thicken and grow, the river god's sex in a bed of ropey moss.

On my day off I went to the Oak Street beach. Luxury apartment buildings lined the lakefront and the six-lane Outer Drive. On one side of the drive strolled businessmen in coats and ties and women in dresses and big summer hats. On the other was a wide, white-sand beach and bathers in swimsuits surveyed by lifeguards. Between these two worlds, one formal, the other nearly nude, the traffic streamed ceaselessly.

I felt my grip on this, the "nice" part of town, was slipping. I had no confidence I'd ever land a decent job after school. Would I be condemned to loading trucks? My shoulders thickened brutishly.

On the beach I saw a group of older gay guys, and I

spread my towel beside them. They quieted down as I stripped to my swimsuit, and one of them even put on his glasses. I couldn't tell what the verdict was.

But Midwesterners are friendly people who chat and joke easily with strangers, and soon enough I was talking with one of my neighbors, a rosy-cheeked countertenor with a haze of silky hair unexpectedly covering his back and shoulders. His nose and the bald top of his head were painfully red. He put on a shirt and baseball cap.

Next to him lay a man who was introduced to me as Lou and who gave me a warm, brown, limp hand, which he presented at an odd angle as though I were meant to kiss it or touch it to my forehead. He was in blue jeans he'd sawed down to the briefest shorts I'd ever seen, which were held up by a thick bicycle chain and safety lock for belt and buckle. He was thin, which my mind stupidly attributed to the long, beautiful scar that traced the entire inner lining of his ribcage—up from the chain belt across the solar plexus and down the other side. His hair had been cut fuzzy-wuzzy short with clippers. When he smiled, his teeth looked like expensive replacements. Although he was clean-shaven, black Benday dots traced the narrow pathway of his thin mustache and the stippled edge of his jaw. His jawbone and nose looked out of joint, as if they'd been broken by the same event that had smashed his teeth and inscribed the scar. Even the index finger of his right hand didn't quite lie down smoothly. It looked as if it had been snapped, rotated slightly, then rewired.

And yet nothing gruesome or shocking was suggested by these alterations. Rather, they counted as painful but elegant tribal decorations cicatrized into the flesh, a sort of allover circumcision. This tribal idea was emphasized by his hairless torso, his long, smooth, slightly bowed legs, and his small-pored, high-cheekboned face, which fit as tightly to his skull as a swimming cap. He was half American Indian, the countertenor told me later that night.

I took the countertenor home with me. He held me against his capacious chest and sang in his piercing high voice. Later I stood over him in bed, which led the singer, who was serious and sentimental and full of imported beer, to smile and blow me kisses.

"Do you live here all by yourself?" he asked me, looking around my mother's gilded cage.

"Yes," I said.

"Are you in school or do you work?"

"No, I don't do anything," I said. "I know that sounds terribly un-American, but I haven't decided yet what to do with my life."

The tenor nodded and hugged me.

The next morning, after several telephone calls, he arranged for us to eat with all the other men we'd met on the beach. It turned out Lou lived in the same building, in the identical apartment twelve stories down.

We all went to a coffee shop on Rush for breakfast. I ate so many syrup-soaked pancakes and drank so much bitter coffee that I got a stomachache. Maybe it was due to the excitement I felt looking at and talking to Lou. He was wearing a blue velour sweatshirt.

No one I've ever known before or since had his curious way of moving. When something excited him (usually something he was saying), he'd sit up straight in his seat, widen his eyes, and talk with hushed, oracular intensity. A second later, God, that bored puppeteer, would drop the strings and Lou would lie splayed all over the table, nearly comatose. On the street he'd stop in the middle of a stream of pedestrians to make a point, and as he did so he'd hold my hand between both of his, but lightly, lightly, almost as though he were a medium who needed only the merest touch to establish contact with the other world.

I found out that he was an advertising man who wrote poetry, but when I trotted out my newly acquired urbane ironies for him ("The Muses Bow to Mammon," I think I actually said), he flushed with anger.

"I can't bear middle-class ruefulness," he said. He was sitting straight up, fully inflated. "I love advertising. It's an art in no way inferior to poetry and not much different from it. Lofty disdain toward making money strikes me as . . ." He adjusted his head to an odd angle. "Yes!" Now he was in full cry. "Yes! all that well-bred ruefulness. That's exactly what I despise about *The New Yorker*. A cartoon shows a middle-aged man in front of his typewriter typing, 'This is the story of my life'—and *that's* supposed to be a *joke*!" His features froze in horror as he looked through me. Then a rich baritone laugh, so at odds with his light speaking voice, poured maniacally out of him. "A *joke*!" he shrieked in agonies of disbelief. His laugh, soundtrack for a horror film, rang out through the restaurant.

He turned on a dime into a low, father-explaining-to-son voice as he took my hand across the table and said earnestly, "Don't you see, Bunny, middle-class rue is a way of condescending to our noblest feelings out of middle-class embarrassment."

Suddenly, the divine fire passed out of the oracle and he slumped to the table, almost inert.

"Lou," the countertenor said, trying to defend me, "you're just creating a federal case, probably because you're embarrassed about making so much money."

I didn't want to be on any side other than Lou's. "No, no, I see your point and I'm sorry I took such a cheap shot."

"Don't go overboard," the singer said to me. All the

previous night he and I had exchanged classy book titles and well-bred quips and shared information about discography, but now he could see I wanted to push all that aside for this, what Lou represented, which was something new.

The countertenor went back to Bloomington, where he was studying voice. Lou said nothing when I shook his strangely cocked hand. I said, "Well, we do live in the same building. I'd love to have dinner with you some night." Lou lowered his eyes like a beautiful woman used to hearing compliments, and when he raised his eyes, like a beautiful woman's they looked right through me.

A week later I found him on the same beach. He was reading Alexander Trocchi's *Cain's Book*. "It's really one of the best books I've read in a long time. It's about an artistic junky in New York." He looked at me for a reaction. "Does it sound very ladies' club to have opinions about books?" His horror-movie laugh seized him and he rolled on his towel and laughed. I imagined he was someone without a sense of humor in any ordinary sense. My body ached from my night job. In another hour I was due to go in, though we were paid in cash every morning by the foreman and no one cared if we didn't show. It was a drifter's and drunk's job; men often went on a week-long bender if they earned a little overtime.

Suddenly he'd stopped laughing and had taken my hand in his, as heavy and nonhuman as a dog's padded paw. "The truth is," and he was looking me right in the eye and putting his soft tenor voice across like a lyric jazz trumpet player who for once plays the tune straight, mute in, "I don't have the right to talk about books. I never went to college. I never studied English."

"Neither did I," I said triumphantly, and I told him about my classes in Chinese with the Straight Lady. But Lou ignored my explanation, which didn't fit in with the point he was making.

"You've studied the classics," he said with rapture. "You have a solid foundation in the literature of the world. You can read Ezra Pound with understanding. Pound must be one of your favorites. He has the most perfect ear in English since Herbert. Never a bad line." He placed his hand, as limp and expressive as the dead Christ's in a marble *pietà*, on my ass.

"Can we have dinner tonight?" I asked him, though I wanted to say, "Can I sleep with you?" The *pietà*, yes, with Lou's thinness, mortified flesh, wounded hand, the excruciated angles he assumed. But also, I thought, an Indian chief: thick nose; tawny skin; and eyebrows that grew together. Pontiac. That Ottawa chief who led an Indian federation against the English. Lou had an Indian's lithe, strong legs, and I wanted them wrapped around me, but now his eyes were swooning shut, sleep came over him as suddenly as in a fairy tale, and I was left alone with my erection in a swimsuit and this handsomely ugly man in full glorious sunlight. He wore a big silver ID bracelet, the sort I'd worn in high school, and he slept with his exquisite damaged hand across my back, the metal links burning cold into my skin.

That night we ate dinner at the Cape Cod Room of the Drake and I spent twenty of the twenty-five dollars my mother had allotted for the entire week. A chubby bald man named Charlie joined us, and I learned he was a concert pianist, or had been, but now he couldn't play in public anymore for some reason.

He liked me, I saw, and we argued about Tchaikovsky. That was during the full confident flush of the Baroque Revival, and I'd been quick to learn that the Romantics should be dismissed as gushy and empty-headed. "But what about Tchaikovsky's own counterpoint?" Charlie asked. "If that's what you admire so much in Bach and Handel, then you have to admire Tchaikovsky's inner melodies, so fresh—and always powered by that breathless, passionate syncopation!"

All I could admire was us, the three of us in our white shirts and dark ties and still darker jackets and tan faces. All my life I'd sat with my mother and sister in restaurants and studied the handsome young men at the corner table. Not that many men ate together in those days, but when they did, I poured myself into the wine they drank, I threaded myself into the napkins they fingered.

Now I was one of them. It was a civil summer night and it was raining. We were here, drinking too much, joking with the waiters, who were men too, after all, and our hands looked very brown next to the silver of white shirtcuff. The curse of being the little creep my sister said smelled bad, of being the town queer as I scuttled from one toilet stall to a choicer one just vacated—this shame seemed to be lifted by the flaky turbot, the pale green Pouilly Fumé, the slivered green beans and toasted almonds.

Lou and I left Charlie at the corner. He hopped into a big cab. And then we were in our own cab heading in the opposite direction along the curving Inner Drive, which Lou said made him think of New York and Riverside Drive. He held my hand, not with the consciousness of exploration but with invasive familiarity. He sprawled on the back seat and hooked a leg over mine. Although I was ten years younger than he, I was the one who felt stuffy and elderly. I could see the driver's angry, disapproving eyes in the rearview mirror, just that part of the face the black band cancels out in pornographic photos.

We stopped off at a bar. I don't remember much about it except the respect Lou felt for it. A large oval bar with two bartenders corralled inside it, a jukebox, smoke drifting through colored lights—I couldn't see why we were here instead of home in bed. He never stopped touching my knee or shoulder, sometimes tapping me, then abandoning his nerveless, unexpectedly heavy hand to my care. "Now look at little Jimmy here," he said with a curator's pride, "isn't he fabulous?"

A round-faced man of thirty trying to look twenty in skin-tight black jeans and white boots and an open white shirt tied high at the waist to show a hairless midriff came hopping up to us. He kissed Lou in a crisp stylization of a kiss and revolved into his arms as Lou reached down from the stool to embrace him.

"Hi, toots, who's the brainy chicken?" Jimmy jerked his head toward me, effortlessly lifted my horrible glasses off my face, and perched them on the tip of his adorable snub nose. "Don't let me wreck your nerves, doll," he whispered to me, very gal-to-gal, "I'm just the frisky type."

Lou lowered his eyes, charmed by such brassiness.

We drank beer after beer, darted across the street to another bar, so I could see that bartender's "perfect buns," then headed down Rush toward the Chicago River where a little gay dance spot was hidden behind a restaurant with checked tablecloths. We watched couples foxtrotting cheek-to-cheek to Timi Yuro singing "Make the World Go Away." A black man the color and shininess of eggplant was dancing with a white boy the shape and golden paleness of a pear. A thug with a porkpie hat and a cigar guarded the door.

At last we stumbled into a taxi. I got out a block away from home because I didn't want Gerald, the doorman, to see me with Lou. Gerald was very thick with my mother. But then at last I was in Lou's apartment; he bolted the door and we stood in his living room, not floating above the night city as in my mother's apartment but rather surrounded by it. Between two unlit glass-sheathed buildings I could see Lake Michigan and its trails of breaking foam on black water. We picked our way over the debris in the dark and drank one more beer on the low couch. Lou kept dozing off. At last we undressed, our clothes thrown on the floor. But when I held

Lou in my arms and kissed him all over, he whispered, "Let's wait till the morning. I'd like to sleep with my ass pressed against your hard-on," and he drifted off.

Several times at the bars he'd introduced me with a laugh as his new "college-boy trick," and now I could see myself as just that. It all fit, the brush cut, the glasses, the stuffy opinions, the ruefulness about advertising, even my rock-hard college-boy erection placed between the smooth muscular buttocks of an older man who was neither butch nor femme but as plushly ambiguous as the blue velour sweatshirt he had worn to breakfast at the coffee shop, or as the crewcut that went along with his broken nose to give him a boxer's toughness, except that now, as I ran my hands over the bristles, I could think only of a Persian cat's silky fur as it sensuously flexes against a hand. For Lou, though asleep, was snuggling richly against me, and I thought of him for a moment as a beautiful kept woman. He'd left the classical music station on, and the Brahms violin concerto, my father's favorite music, was at last accompanying a tender longing that had an object. When I had waited on my father's green-and-white-striped silk couch through the night, smelled his pipe, and listened to his calculating machine, I'd wrapped myself in empty regret, hugged my arms to my chest, and sorted through odds and ends of fantasies, none substantial enough to work into a quilt of desire. But here I was, suddenly awake, the room surging drunkenly around me every time I closed my eyes, with a lavishly asleep adult man in my arms, his body a degree warmer than mine, his clipped head full of intense opinions; when the violin shimmered like starlight that glints blue then green, signaling someone but not me, I felt at last I had been given the code for deciphering the message. I held still, I didn't want to trouble Lou's sleep, but I was warming myself against his body.

The next morning, lightly silvered in hangover sweat,

he finally let me plunge into that strong ass, but not before he'd greased me up with KY and produced his "trick towel." He wouldn't kiss or let me face him when I took him. But I could reach my hands around his waist and feel the shifting muscles of that long flat stomach working as he twisted and pushed back against me. It dawned on me the stomach scar was there from the time when the doctors must have inserted extra muscles, the long sexy kind—the interior ones gripping me now. I had to say the alphabet backward to keep myself from coming. The moment I looked at what I was doing to him, I could feel myself ready to explode. My come wanted to enter him in order to stake even the smallest claim on someone who seemed superior to me in every way. William Everett Hunton had talked as though the one who does the fucking is the "man," but with Lou that didn't make much sense. Obviously he was in control of everything we were doing. It didn't occur to me that this shockingly intense pleasure could be sought after. If you're someone mainly eager to please others, you don't think much about your own pleasure; taking pleasure is not a survival skill, while giving it most certainly is.

Lou and I saw each other every day. I stopped going to work, but it didn't matter, since Lou had lots and lots of loose money in his pockets and he picked up checks without seeming to notice; his carelessness made a mockery of all those hours I'd crouched inside trucks. With a red face I started to explain the lie I'd told the countertenor, but when I confessed the apartment was actually my mother's, Lou wasn't interested in either the truth or its distortion. He'd never stopped to wonder how a college kid had his own apartment on the Gold Coast or why it was full of matronly clothes.

He was only concerned with realizing his own myths and explaining them to me in order to convince himself. He found anything extreme to be "beautiful" or "moving," even "heart-breaking," and his favorite phrase was "shimmering with ambiguity." He divided all homosexuals into "boys," "men," and "vicious old queens." A man (laborer, truckdriver, even "high-powered exec") must lust after and love a boy, who would be "beautiful" or at least "cute" but given to sudden enthusiasms, usually reckless and foolish. A man was brawny, cruel, except to the boy, whom he cherished, although sometimes cruelly. The man could be forgiven if he beat someone up, the boy if he bleached his hair. The boy felt a natural affinity to girls, with whom he was always exchanging makeup tips. The man had once fucked girls but now had no further use for them.

When the man fucked the boy, the boy always had his rump up in the air, propped up on a pillow, and the man would lick his anus and tongue it and finger it before greasing it up with KY and fucking it, long and hard, while the boy squirmed in pain or pleasure. While being fucked, the boy ignored his own dick and even lost his hard-on, proof of how thoroughly his was concentrating on his ass. After the man shot his load, he'd stay in the boy, they'd roll over on their sides, and the boy would now be free to masturbate quickly while held tightly in his man's arms. Once in a while, the boy was permitted to fuck the man, as a loving concession to the boy's own masculinity, espaliered but still rawly alive, shimmeringly ambiguous. As soon as the boy came, they wiped off with the already stiff and greasy trick towel, and the boy sat on the toilet and shit out sperm. Lou reserved special scorn for boys who whispered to their lovers on the way to a midnight movie, "I've still got your babies inside me."

"Don't they know those *babies* are dead spunk festering up their filthy bungholes!"

A real boy, someone skinny and under twelve who walked around with his mouth open, sent Lou into raptures. One sweaty afternoon in Chicago we rode the elevated and sat behind a boy of eleven or so in shorts and T-shirt. The boy stared out the window and wagged his right leg against his stationary left leg, in a ceaseless, thoughtless way. A hard little erection could be seen pressed flat against his tummy in his white shorts. Unconsciously he kept batting at the erection with the back of his right hand, now to one side of it, now to the other, as though despite trial and error he had yet to find the exact spot. His skin had no pores, no bulges, and no sheen—it was as mat and consistent as face powder, except it looked cool, firm, and alive. It drank the light as soil drinks water. His shoulders and thin arms hung limply down with sublime inconsequence, though his shoulder blades looked too knotty under the cotton, as if they were about to hatch wings. The same fine, nearly invisible gold down that covered his cheeks, and had collected in a haze just below the line of his light brown hair, dusted his nape in a precise pattern, the shape of a cursive letter M, rising on either side and dipping in the center toward his spine. If the down had been molten it would have roared as it rose to descend that glistening chute. "Yes," Lou insisted, "*if* it made a sound." He sank into a silence then sighed: "*If* it were gold . . . just look at that nape." Lou spoke as loudly as if we were conversing in a language all our own.

I don't mean to suggest, by the way, that I was or am dismissive or even critical of anything Lou was saying. His vision of sex, of boys, and of poetry, even (as I was to discover) of drugs, was my first and strongest encounter with a pure theory of beauty. I'd always heard sensible down-to-earth values praised, but they were the only kind I'd ever observed, and the repeated endorsements seemed redundant. Now at last I'd met the man everyone had warned me against.

I realized he'd never love me. Not that there was anything so wrong with me, but we didn't form a couple he would have considered sexy. We were companionable, but I was too big and educated to be the boy, and too much younger to be the man. For a week or ten days, Lou tried to turn me into the man, but I was too affectionate in a puppy-dog way. "I'm afraid you just put your dick in me, Bunny, wriggle around and kiss my neck, and shoot like a twelve-year-old," Lou said, "which is sweet but ineffectual. You need to focus more on cock and ass, pull out farther and plunge deeper, balance your weight on your elbows and toes, that will give you better leverage, go slow. Do everything with deliberation."

I was terribly wounded. Until now I'd never had any anxiety about performance because I hadn't realized I was on stage. Just as William had made me self-conscious about cock size, Lou made me so nervous about fucking that I kept losing my erection. By default I became the "boy" and occasionally Lou fucked me.

Lou was fired from his advertising job, but he told me that happened every six months anyway in the biz. "Every time they lose a big account, they can the whole team. I want to write a book called *Love You, Love Your Work, Gonna Hafta Let You Go.*" Now that neither of us was working, we were free to go to the Oak Street beach every day or sometimes a mile or two farther north to some slabs of broken concrete, the Belmont Rocks, where the gay boys had staked a claim and which Lou called "Homo-lulu." Now I knew the whole adolescent world I'd missed out on, the world of idle summer days, of tinny portable radios and coconut oil, of towel hopping and shared Cokes, of desultory exclamations ("Ow! That bug really bit me") followed by wave-lulled silence and the indignant nursing of the glossy shoulder or silky thigh. Lou wrote a poem about cruising the Oak Street beach at night, but he felt the only good line was "the pollen-streaked lamplight."

Ezra Pound was his true Penelope, and even Pound's criminal politics and weird economics Lou was able to justify when it suited his mood. For Lou, Pound was strategic in any dismissal of Eliot's absurdly English posturing, and both men rose serenely above the local American battle between the Beats and Academics. Lou couldn't be an Academic. His fear and hatred of schools forbade that, as well as his contempt for sterile exercises. But the Beats, despite their appealing cult of drugs and Whitmanian sincerity, lacked the cool elegance Lou venerated. The values he really embraced were those of Negro jazz musicians who divided the world into what was square and what was cool. Things labeled cool were highly controlled if sometimes arbitrary and decorative, an expression of a narrow range of feelings: happy-guy exuberance, cerebral noodling, or a foggy but anxious melancholy.

Each of those few times Lou wanted to like someone over fifty, he repeated Pound's phrase about "old men with beautiful manners." Only twenty years later did I stumble across the line and realize Pound was mocking the statesmen who brought on World War I. Lou had no sense of irony or history and none of comedy save the grand guignol of his indignation. At about this time, a homosexual magazine, *One*, began to be published in California. Lou was appalled. "Why should a bunch of criminals be allowed to have a *magazine*, for chrissake. They might as well let thieves publish *The Safecracker's Quarterly*. *One*, indeed . . . "

If an apology for homophilia struck him as a bad joke (or was he afraid it might make gay life seem too square?), Lou was a respectful reader of the boy books that were emerging then, those magazines of black-and-white photos of teenagers with shaved chests, sucked-in if unexercised stomachs, and cloth posing-straps who stood on a dais silhouetted against a sunburst of seamless paper. They were pictured lifting a spear or throwing a discus so that the alibi of classical Greek homosexuality could be produced. Lou would roar with laughter over the short articles by a minister about Christian fellowship or by an athletic director about a sound mind and a sound body or by a "scholar" about Greek love, but he stared for hours at the boys, especially one, Bobby Phalen, whom he followed from one publication to another, month to month, and whose greatest shots he'd blown up and framed. "Look at that perfect ass, Bunny, the way it's almost too big, nigger big, but just misses by being not all high and hard but perfectly round, pneumatic with youth, just as though it'd been drawn by a compass, no flattening here, no sag, and then the *roundness*! of those hairless arms and legs, imagine what they'd look like in cross section, and the full, vulgar mouth redeemed by that truly classical nose, so severe and martial, the only truly Greek thing in this whole fuckin' cheap rag."

I said, "Mnm, yes, Lou, he is well-built."

Lou looked up at me startled, then a funhouse laugh rumbled up out of his depths, "Well! *Built*!" the laugh quickened in astonishment and sent him down the rapids. "Bunny," he said, gasping for air, "you look so pained. How dreadful for you to be with a moony old queen like me," and he rolled on his bed with fiendish glee.

The only dreadful thing was my realization that at nineteen I was already too old for Lou. I'd been waiting and waiting year after year to grow up so I could lead the gay life, and all the while I'd been wasting my most precious capital, my youth. Now my face was already disfigured with a beard I had to shave every second or third day, my legs were grotesquely hairy—at least there was some fuzz below the calves—and I had none of the baby fat left that Lou searched out with a magnifying glass on Bobby Phalen's thighs or just above his small waist ("Do you see the shimmering ambiguity of that impertinent randy young maleness and those packets of girlish softness, just like Donatello's *David*?").

Lou recognized, as everyone had to, that homosexuality

was sick; in fact, he insisted on the sickness. Although not spontaneously given to campiness, he'd catch my eye in the midst of his own lip-licking perusals of Bobby Phalen's thighs and touch his chest with his great broken hand and murmur, "I'm *not* a well woman . . . "

But through some curious alchemy he'd redeemed our illness by finding beauty in it. He loved Baudelaire, and like Baudelaire he searched out beauty in whatever was foul, artificial, damned, although those words, too Continental to be hip, would have embarrassed him. He liked everything deformed by the will toward beauty, whether it was a ballet dancer's mangled feet and duck walk, a nun's pallor and shaved skull, or a trumpet player's split pulpy lips. In those days S-and-M had not yet become popular. Lou was forced to admire things too tame for his radical taste (peroxided hair, drag), but those he admired fiercely.

Whereas William Everett Hunton wanted to go straight (or said he did), and spent a lot of time wanly imagining how warm and secure marriage must make men feel, Lou despised squares. He would proudly hold my hand as we walked down the street, and loved shocking the little old ladies in our apartment building with his sawed-off blue-jean shorts. If I got too folksy-chummy with the waitress or came out with an opinion worthy of our fathers, he'd blush and hang his head. He didn't go to museums or read highbrow books, at least not systematically; he wasn't interested in improving his mind or coming off as cultured. He did prize his taste, and that he imposed tyrannically on those few people he liked.

He and Maria were very different from one another, and I never introduced them. She read compulsively, but no poetry, not much fiction, lots of philosophy. Lou read the same books over and over, trying to coax from them their secrets, not of meaning but of lilt. He loved the poems of John Wieners and would quote again and again the stanza:

He's gone and taken
my morphine with him
Oh Johnny. Women in
     the night moan yr. name.

or he'd say, "Don't you love the way he uses proper names as in:

And I am lost beside the furs
and homburgs at Fifth and
Fifty-seventh where Black Starr
& Frost holds

Its annual sale of diamonds?

Could anything be more beautiful than 'Black Starr & Frost'
which really is the *definition* of a diamond?"

Lines from songs would move him just as much. "I'm
Travellin' Light," he'd murmur, or, "God Bless the Chile
That's Got His Own," or, "Good Morning, Heartache," which
he insisted was the only way to translate the title of Françoise
Sagan's new novel, *Bonjour Tristesse*. He didn't have much to
say about why these phrases were beautiful, but he'd obviously scrutinized his small hoard with a jeweler's loupe, and
he'd bring all his gems out often and place them one by one
against the plush of his admiration.

One day he came back from a drag contest and said that
a Mexican boy named Spinoza had won it (his drag name,
Gigi). "Bunny, there were all these other tired numbers with
their falsies and pancake and falls, but Spinoza just walked
out with his tough little mug unpainted and his duck's ass
haircut and his young boy's arms with the tattoo in the web
of skin between his thumb and index finger and his bare
wetback feet and just a dumb black dress on, zipper broken
down the back, and he looked like a teen killer someone had

forced into a frock at gunpoint and—Oh!" Lou let the intensity of his stare melt. He lowered his eyes, while a smile, a shy smile, dawned: "Oh, Gigi. Women in the night moan your name."

We lay in his disordered apartment on dirty sheets surrounded by coffee cups growing mold and piles of cast-off clothes. Since Lou had been fired, he never arose in time to get to the laundry before it closed; his only solution was to buy new shirts at Brooks Brothers on their late night, Wednesdays. He had expensive groceries delivered from Stop'n'-Shop, but he forgot to eat them or even refrigerate them. They rotted and had to be dumped down the incinerator. I had friends to see and things to do, but like a vampire, Lou hated the daylight and slipped into a coffin of sheets every dawn only to emerge that evening, impeccably groomed. I suppose he and I were like my father and stepmother in our staggered hours.

I loved his tawny skin and the medals of hair radiating out from each nipple as though he'd been decorated twice for the same act of heroism. I loved his own ambiguity, shimmering from male to female. He could nuzzle against me like a woman, back his ripe hips up against me and be certain he was exciting me. On television a popular idea for a big dance number was for a beautiful blonde to stride past a line of flabbergasted men and domino the whole line over with just a fingertip; Lou had that effect on me. I had a constant erection around him, and I forced myself to disagree with him now and then lest I bore him with the uniformity of my admiration. As for the man in Lou, I never stopped seeing in him Pontiac, the Indian. His sense of ritual about sex only heightened this impression, as though he retained a brave's respect for performing any physical ordeal. We still had sex from time to time, but I assumed Lou was doing it partly because he'd found no one else and because his poetics of life required nightly intercourse. Between us sex was never love, that sudden flux of affection that causes two people to break stride, pull apart, and stare smilingly at each other. Lou never broke stride. He delved into me with a force and regularity unbroken by words or kisses or gasps. He disliked a spasm of delight much as he disliked any sudden visitation of feeling that broke through a form. He was a sexual formalist.

Late, very late at night, he'd start raving. He'd try to convince me of some absurdity that appealed to him only because it was the opposite of what all right-minded people believed. He'd oppose divorce because it put asunder what God had joined. Yet I was sure his opposition was inspired by the beauty of the word *asunder*. He wanted the chance to say it, and to say it in the only proper way, with Old Testament fury. Or he'd fulminate against travel and insist that everyone should stay in his own country, nourished by his native soil. He decided that Soviet-style censorship was defensible, even commendable, since people had no need to know what was happening in other lands.

One hot summer night, so late all the neighboring apartment windows were dark, he decided we should go out in search of jazz. He showered and combed his wet black hair back, tore a new shirt out of its Brooks package, and put on a perfectly pressed suit. He looked elegant and vulnerable, his eyes edging away from contact and set into a face of exquisite unhealthiness. He smoked as he did everything else, consciously, looking at the cigarette as though he didn't quite know what it was for, testing it experimentally.

Half an hour later we were stepping into a club where a young white man holding a trumpet was singing "This Is Love" in an innocent voice—innocent but angular, before an audience of just two tables, both silent, hands bright under lamps, faces lost in the filtered shade. The smoky, hard taste of whisky sank an upside-down question mark of warmth that plumbed my chest and swirled around inside my stomach. I was getting drunk. Lou's face sparkled with sweat; a few points of moisture as definite as the dots on dice had broken out just above his nose. His dark jacket sleeves were pulled back to reveal heavy white shirt cuffs cuffing hands as cleanly as the gauze fits around a thoroughbred's slender shanks. He sipped cigarettes, he sipped drinks with lips newly thinned by the opulent melancholy of the music. Nothing happened. There's no payoff to this story and I repeat it only because the snapshot of Lou, so lost and so remote, impeccable despite the chaos in his apartment, still speaks to me with the force of an event (my plots are all scrapbooks).

That night as we lay in bed, Lou's room lurched here and there as though the camera were hand-held by a skater. He told me how he'd played jazz trumpet when he was nineteen. "I fell in love with our vocalist, a Negro woman a few years older than me, and when she became pregnant, my parents paid her off to go away somewhere. So I've got a twelve-year-old son wandering around—"

"You're sure it's a son?"

Lou looked bewildered, then irritated. "I'm not sure of anything, but I dream of a boy the nights when I'm able to dream of anything."

I asked him what happened to him after that.

"I'd become addicted to heroin and my parents put me in an expensive psychiatric hospital, the one where the movie stars go. My brother was already there."

"What a wild family!" I exclaimed, although my burst of enthusiasm made the whole room dip nauseatingly. I propped up on two pillows that had lost their cases and I prayed for solid ground.

"Yes," Lou said witheringly, "quite *wild*. My brother

committed suicide soon after my arrival. He was living in a halfway house after five years of expert professional treatment." A small black toad of a laugh hopped through his lips.

"Oh, Lou," I said, "I'm sorry," and I wanted to touch him, but I was afraid his body would be cold.

"But the *wildness* of my tale is just starting," Lou insisted.

He told me of a family reunion shortly before his brother's suicide, when both boys had been on leave from the hospital and the whole family had celebrated by going to the Lyric Opera. They sat together in the family box, but during the second act they, the brothers, started fighting. Everyone including the parents was dead drunk, a knife flashed out of a pocket, Lou was spurting blood, his mother was shrieking above the soprano, ushers and then the police were coming through the door, the orchestra was breaking up and bleeping into silence, the audience was in an uproar, and the houselights came up.

"That's when I got this," Lou said, pointing to his stomach scar. "Not from my brother. I lost so much blood I passed out, and when I woke up I was in Methodist Central. A stupid cunt of a nurse had left me with a thermometer in my mouth, she'd gone out of the room—can you imagine, you never do that with a patient in a coma—and I knew it could be the basis for a really stiff malpractice suit, so I just chewed it up very slowly and swallowed it, all the broken glass and the mercury too, and I knew I'd either die, which was cool, or wake up rich enough to leave my parents for good. I woke up. They'd sliced me open and removed several feet of gut, that's why I have to eat so often now, otherwise the food goes right through me—"

"But you *don't* eat!" I wailed. "That's precisely—"

Lou silenced me by laying his open hand over my mouth; then he played a little tune on my lips with his fingers. "But I hadn't counted on my habit, which was becoming so expensive that before I got the settlement money I had to rob my father's house, which triggered some goddam new alarm he'd installed since I'd split, so I was nabbed, the fuzz found the tracks on my arms, it was all pretty *bogue* so the only way out of a sentence was to go back to the same bughouse."

I don't know how aware Lou was of the sexual longing he awakened in me, but as he told me his story, he kept hitching me tighter and tighter in his embrace. Or he used me as a guitar to strum or a flute to pipe, something inert but expressive he could play. "Then my brother killed himself—he was seeing a woman in town and only visiting the hospital every afternoon, and the woman, a local girl, couldn't take him anymore, he was too crazy for her, so he O.D.ed, maybe he wasn't even intending to die, just shake her up."

Although I wanted to comfort him, or suggest through gestures that he, at least, was safe from such a fate, safe in my arms, I knew there was no room for me in this story.

"That was when I fell in love with Charlie, the pianist you met, he'd been a child prodigy, he'd played with the Cleveland and the New York Philharmonic, and then when he was a teenager, my age, he couldn't take the responsibility and he, too, picked up a habit, he got busted. Well, we were both musicians and junkies, except he was a real musician. We used to lie out by the pool and sun and doze, and I'd look at his powerful arms and shoulders 'driving the music to sleep under silence, darker and more elegant than roses,' that's the end of a poem I wrote about him."

He laughed and sat up. "You know, Bunny, there's nothing more romantic than a concert pianist, especially one who won't play. He plays for me now, but only at home, he's got a Steinway grand, and you should hear him tear through the Rachmaninoff Third, your hair would stand on end."

Suddenly my own life seemed shabbily devoid of incident. I longed for the courage to do something reckless and the years in which to regret it.

The only light was coming from a horrible fluorescent tube in the bathroom, which made our bodies appear larval and brought out muddy circles under Lou's eyes. If I leaned my head back on the pillow I was looking at the cityscape upside down. The revolving searchlight at the top of the Drake tower beamed through low, tumbling clouds, as though a circus trainer were gliding a whip under the plunging bodies of horses in a lather. Here and there, windows of distant apartments still burned.

Lou left his curtains open and we awakened at noon, naked in a hemorrhage of sunlight under the gaze of office workers in the next building, so close we could see a typist take off her glasses and massage the bridge of her nose.

In the afternoons we'd sometimes go to the beach, but Lou came up with so many problems and fears and objections that usually we didn't get out before evening. Since he was supposed to eat six small meals a day, after he toyed with one, he'd order a second, ignoring both.

I showed him a story I was working on, which I hoped to sell to *Esquire* or *The New Yorker* for a great deal of money, which would free me of my parents. "But your prose is so mindless," Lou said. "As in this sentence, when you say, 'I had no thought in my head,' I mean, you don't stop to think at all, do you, Bunny, you just babble. And then the way you dote on your characters. I can't bear that sort of doting. And this chandelier. The only reason you bother to put it in the story is so that it can come crashing down at the end, which is an absurdly cheap touch. But the worst is the doting, this lip-smacking satisfaction you take in all these dreadful middle-class bores with their *problems*, as though having a problem were an automatic bid for sympathy instead of an invitation to impatience or contempt."

His words stung me. Every criticism seemed irrefutable if previously unsuspected. It was true I loved my characters, to whom I'd distributed the various voices and vices of my friends. It was true I wrote in a trance and never revised; my mother had told me I was a genius. A genius doesn't grope, learn, rework, or even work. And it was true I wrote to be adored—by my mother first of all, and then by Lou or whomever I was with. Yes, I wanted fame, and when the heat of vision, fired by Drambuie, was on me in my white room, I felt I was already famous. But there was another reason to write: to redeem the sin of my life by turning it into the virtue of art.

Until now, I'd showed my stories only to appreciative readers. Other young writers would ply me with compliments and in exchange I'd praise their work. The usual inspiration for my fiction was the "powerful" television drama with its cozy view of character, its melodramatic plot, and its message. To show that this was literature, however, one threw in a symbol or two, preferably something from the Passion of Christ, and a poetic haze of phrase condensed from our best Southern writers. An epiphany was clapped on to lots and lots of hard-hitting dialogue, which was easy to write, although one pretended otherwise. The characters were all suitably defeated and sensitive.

Lou had too refined an ear and too great a horror of the obvious to like my inflated playlets. He was also too unhappy and anxious to take an interest in other people's lives. He ended up with a small canon of books about himself—John Rechy's *City of Night*, which was just appearing chapter by chapter in magazines, the few isolated scraps of William Burroughs he could find in print, Jean Genet's *Our Lady of the Flowers*. In these books he saw his own darkness reflected. He appreciated that in them there was no trace of

American optimism. He also liked that these pages were devoted to "sexy fairies" and that every page could cost the reader some come.

For Lou, who'd never known a conventional family, bourgeois life seemed remote—remotely risible when he was out gunning for squares, remotely appealing when he was fed up with the disorder of his own life. "Oh, Bunny," he said to me late one night, hugging me and smelling of that strong odor of people who swallow too many vitamin pills in daily remorse for nightly bad habits, "I'm so sick of sick faggots and drunk old queens. I'm so sick of men! I don't think I can bear the feel of one more man's beard. Here I am, a thirty-year-old man, I should be founding my own sweet little family, but I'm still bouncing around the bars, being probed by fingers, mauled, stuffed with cock, and I wake up every morning hung over, hemorrhoids aflame, crotch hairs plastered down with someone else's come." Astounded pause, widening eyes, horrified shout: "And my face raw with beard-burn!" He shuddered, even stroked my face, from which I willed the noxious hairs to retract. Then he launched into rhapsodic praise of marriage in terms so banal, so painfully silly, that I kept looking for the ironic smile that might make some sense of his ranting. I'd liked Lou's willingness to live a life of homosexual crime, but now he was talking himself into respectability.

I listened and nodded and felt obliged to go along with him. I had to scramble all the chromosomes of my beliefs to match his gene by gene. From my psychoanalysis and from my more private self-doubts—my certainty that the basic things in me were all wrong—I'd picked up the habit of mistrusting my instincts.

But as the weeks with Lou went by, something in me rebelled against him. I wanted my own way. If I put my will aside temporarily, I did so to learn from Lou, for never before had I met someone who was so much an artist and so little an intellectual. If I gave a story an overly ingenious title, he'd say, "But a title should simply name what's going on, like a good picture caption. *Family Portrait* is a good title, as is *Early Death*." Slow smile. "Of course Faulkner titles are the best. *Light in August*. Did you know *light* is an old word for 'pregnant'?"

Lou hated "college-boy" advertising slogans, clever take-offs on Shakespeare or the Bible ("The spirits are willing but the flesh is weak" for a hangover pill). "No, the dumber the better. *Shrink hemorrhoids* is still classic," he told me with deep serenity in the way he said "classic."

Lou's eerie aestheticism—based on his conviction that he possessed a perfect ear and an irreproachable sense of decorum—took on anything and everything. He had an aesthetic of religion (Catholic orthodoxy over corny Protestant cultism), an aesthetic of psychoanalysis (Freud, not that seedy Jung), an aesthetic of drugs (the deadly nightshade of heroin rather than the "loco weed" of marijuana; "Pot's for people who want to *feel funny*, like those cows that get high on loco weed and run into electric fences").

One night toward the end of August I was sleeping upstairs in my mother's apartment. I'd waited for his call all evening and I'd called him several times without success.

Now Lou wanted to see me. He breathed noisily and said with a thick tongue, "Bunny, I need—" and then the receiver must have fallen out of his grasp, since I could hear him still mumbling to himself. I hurried downstairs in the elevator. I rang his doorbell again and again, and even knocked, but I didn't want to create a scene. His neighbors had already complained to the management.

At last he opened the door. A centimeter of cigarette smoked in his hand. Behind him in shoals of faint light, the

wreck of his furniture was heaped up. He walked with the
floating gait of someone moved by tides, not the will.

"Lou, honey, what's wrong?" I asked him. I followed him
into the bedroom. His black cat was gorging itself on an overturned carton of chop suey Lou must have ordered in. I
watched the cat swallow lump after lump of glutinous vege-
tables pooling on the carpet. Its working throat was reflected
by the mirror that had fallen off the hook. The mirror had
cracked in half but stayed upright. Glasses of rum and Coke
stood empty or half full on every flat surface. The impression
was of a middle-class apartment where a tribe of bums had
been squatting for weeks. The fluorescent tube in the bathroom and the television screen, empty picture rolling, provided the only light.

"Bunny," he said as he collapsed on the unmade bed,
"you've got to get me—" static on the line, but for a moment
I thought he actually said, "a high colonic irrigation."

At last I realized he *had* said a "high colonic irrigation,"
whatever that meant. In pained snatches he explained that
when he shot up (heroin? he didn't say), his digestive tract
would sometimes "stall" as a result of his having lost so many
yards of gut. The only way to restore peristalsis was to find
someone with the archaic equipment necessary (small smile)
for this disagreeable therapy (still smaller).

It was one in the morning, but in a controlled panic I
strummed the Yellow Pages. The first two numbers didn't
respond but the third yielded a sleazy male voice filtered
through Lord Calvert and Kools, a minor Mafia voice.

Fortunately Gerald, the doorman, had gone off duty and
the lobby was unattended. It was drizzling. Lou was as hard
to get into a taxi as a colt—he was all stiff legs, melting torso,
and sharp elbows. He smelled funny and I was afraid the
driver might complain, but no, we moved through the unpeo-
pled streets in silence. The windshield wipers beat out a slow

two-quarter rhythm, the first stroke on the G below middle C, the second an octave above, played over brushes on cymbals: the rain sizzling under our tires.

The irrigationist's office was in the Loop between two movie theaters and above a taffy-candy apple stand. Wearing a dirty white nylon uniform half-snapped up the back, he let us in through the smoked-glass door. He showed us through a dim room. We walked on dirty linoleum imbued with the smell of Lysol and cigarettes. Lou's wobbly legs didn't surprise the man. We went into a smaller room dominated by a raised surgical table and gleaming aluminum tubes coming out of a grotty tile wall over a sink.

Whining like a sleepy child, Lou undressed and crawled onto the table, his practiced rump rising automatically in the air. Pedantically I explained to the irrigationist that Lou's peristaltic motion had stopped, that for some reason hospitals no longer possessed the necessary equipment, that—

"Sure, sure." The man's yellow-toothed chuckle and the familiarity with which he patted Lou's butt tipped me off. Lou had been here before. The man extinguished his cigarette and set to work. Lou looked up at him with eyes swimming around a fixed point of longing. This man had—or could do—something Lou wanted. The man put on clear plastic gloves.

He lubricated the tip of a tube with KY and inserted it into Lou's rectum. Lou arched his back, tilting his ass still higher. The miserable room, the weirdness of this transaction, the gurgling and flushing water, the burning lateness of the hour—all chilled me. I'd fallen off the edge of the world. My hero was a pervert, eyelids drooping shut from heroin, inner arm blue with bruises, and now he was cooing like a baby and had curled on his side and was staring up at his savior, his tormentor.

SIX

▪ ▪ ▪ ▪ ▪ ▪ ▪

Gerald, the doorman, had of course figured it all out. Every free moment he was studying the floor indicator above the elevator. Since there were only four apartments on each floor and he knew who was at home, by a simple process he'd deduced that I was coming down from my mother's to Lou's all the time.

When she returned from Munich, my mother told me she was worried because I had taken up with a friend ten years older, a notorious homosexual and drug addict whose family, though once nice, could by no means be considered nice now.

"Honey," she said, looking at me from brown eyes as sweet as mine but far more intense, "what's going to happen to you? All your fine gifts of mind will be destroyed, your reputation and character."

I knew she was right, and I considered her small warm hand in mine to be an intolerable reproach. I jumped up from the couch and started pacing. "I know what I'm doing."

"Don't bite my head off," she said, clouding over. "Anyhow, honey, I don't think you do know. You've compromised me, and I have to live in this building. Besides, you wasted the summer. You didn't earn any money for school. You look pale and unhealthy; you didn't even have good, wholesome fun with kids in your own age bracket."

She was so short that when she settled back in her seat, her feet didn't quite touch the floor. Although she was trying to generate calm (her head was lifted back to a noble angle suitable for framing), her face seemed to be filling up, turning darker with emotion. She was being flooded by it. "You're a special person, a quality person. I don't know why you have to throw yourself away on cheap people. We've never been cheap in our family. I work so hard, and your father, well, he may have horrible faults but he's always been honorable. He's observed the divorce agreement to the letter, you can't take that away from him. But maybe we overestimated you; after all, we never had you properly tested, we don't even know for sure you're so bright."

The minute the terrible possibility of my having merely normal intelligence presented itself, my mother's bruise of a face took on a nasty expression. She lifted the tailored jacket of her suit away from her body and let it relax in new, more satisfied folds. "I don't know where these urges in you come from—perhaps from your father's mother's side. My family is completely normal on both sides. My own father, bless his heart, had a real romance with his sweetheart, my mother, and my mother's father sired twelve children, nothing wrong there, nothing homo there or—ha!" and she let out a cry of delight at the recollection, "no *morphrodites,* for that's what they called homosexuals down South. No morphrodites in our bloodlines!" The merriness of the memory gave way as her smile faded to the seriousness of the eugenicist claim and implied moral lesson. Once again she picked here and there at the sticky fabric of her jacket. In her eyes, clothes were an infallible sign of character; when listing people's merits, she often cited their wardrobes. Perhaps she was fussing with her apparel by way of demonstrating her imperviousness to my moral contagion.

"You disgust me," I shouted. She pointed her jaw out, it went white, and her mouth looked as stitched and definite as the seam on a baseball. "Don't you realize I know I'm neurotic, that I'm a brilliant person saddled with a terrible disease, that I'm working day and night feverishly to cure myself, and that anything you can say against me I've already analyzed in depth with Dr. O'Reilly?"

For an instant I was terrified she'd ask me for an example of this wisdom; I couldn't remember a thing. I felt that I was a fake, an amnesiac, improvising my life moment by moment, and that nothing stuck to me, least of all insight. Even the essays I had written at Eton looked completely unfamiliar to me now and revealed a general intelligence as well as quite particular information I'd since lost. Every night I was shorn of the experiences I'd gained during the day.

Over the summer I'd read nothing save a history of eighteenth-century philosophy, and even that had scarcely registered since my mind had always been boiling with Lou (where was he? when would he call me next?). But one thought that had sunk in was Hume's oddly Buddhist notion that there is no self. We're only one discrete state of consciousness succeeding another, and our so-called memories are just deceptions invented now . . . and now . . . and now.

In my case, amnesia, the wet sponge trailing the chalk marks, did away even with the serviceable illusion of continuity. I felt entirely in thrall to the present, which made my suffering all the more acute, since I could never put my pain in perspective except through humor; for me, clowning had taken the place of memory.

"We're shelling out all this money to O'Reilly," my mother was saying, "but you don't seem to be getting any better. I blame your father. Every boy needs a male model."

Indeed, I thought. I imagined Bobby Phalen, Lou's favorite pinup, as *my* male model.

"I had to be both father and mother to you. But now what? Now you're an adult and what's done is done. You seem to be getting worse. You're so nervous and, frankly, more and more effeminate. By the way, I've read of some interesting hormone treatments for your problem they're experimenting with in England; they implant female hormones in your leg through a simple operation and—"

"*Female?*"

"Yes, because estrogens neutralize your sex drive altogether; they neuter you and soon you're free to lead a normal life." Her right hand made a small rounded motion in the air when she said the word *normal*. I could see the pure technology of the hormone pack appealed to her practical side.

"Don't be ridiculous," I said, but a sudden chill grasped me, exactly as though my lungs were being squeezed by cold hands. My mother went on to ask if I thought I should be put in a psychiatric hospital—and the hands squeezed tighter. It occurred to me that this woman, who was as familiar and shameful to me as my own body, could take it into her head to lock me up. After all, I wasn't disobliging her in a mild, acceptable way, choosing chemistry rather than physics. No, to her I was a sort of criminal; I'd chosen crime, sex crime.

I wanted to be heterosexual, or so I told myself. As a budding writer, I knew I'd never be able to give a convincing account of marriage, birth, parental love, conjugal intimacy, the spicy anguish of adultery—none of the great occasions— until I'd rid myself of this malady which was so narrowing. O'Reilly had warned me that homosexuality would condemn me to an embalmed adolescence, that I'd never grow out of a stale narcissism.

And yet something wild and free in me didn't want to give in to them, the big baggy grown-ups. No, if I were perfectly honest (and I couldn't be, I lacked the necessary confidence), I'd have to admit that there was a world run by women and feminized men (not effeminate but feminized men) that I wanted to escape, the world of mild suburban couples, his and her necks equally thick and creased, their white hair similarly cropped. The hard hot penis I grabbed for under the toilet-stall partition or the slow wink of a drag queen looking back at me over her ratty fox neckpiece just before she turned the corner—these glimpses piqued my craving for freedom, despite my yearning after respectability.

I felt I owed nothing to anyone. My only job was to dodge out of the crossfire. Homosexuality did not constitute a society, just a malady, although unlike many other maladies it was a shameful one—a venereal disease. Could one be loyal to syphilis?

And yet syphilis was not a desire one pursued; once contracted, it left nothing else to be done. But a homosexual could be condemned precisely because he persisted in *practicing* his vice. If I despised homosexuals, I distrusted everyone else. Of course heterosexuals had to be placated and amused. When I was with them, I memorized their reticences and enthusiasms, the subjects they would guffaw over and those they ignored, embarrassed. But I felt not at all attached to any other human being.

This distrust was confirmed when I returned to school by a series of arrests of homosexuals in the toilets. A professor of engineering, and the administrator in charge of "in-plant feeding" (the cafeteria), and four students were nabbed. Their names but not their pictures were published in the town and school newspapers. I knew one of the students, Jeremy, a tall fat boy with red cheeks, redder lips, ears as neat and protuberant as the handles on a pre-Columbian jar, and a gross soprano voice which he'd suddenly unsheathe, dazzling and flexible as a saw in sunlight. He'd be in his stall, a clucking, roosting hen, and suddenly that falsetto, loud and upsetting, would flash forth.

"It was entrapment," he told me. "There was a guy—I should have suspected something. His *shoes*, no queen would be caught dead in such clodhoppers, spoil her frock, her line, don't you know. He showed me this big old thing hard, I mean it was *hard*, you can't fake that, she was an excited *gal*, and then, don't you know, the next thing somehow I felt myself being drawn against my will, and before you could say *wunderbar!* I was bending over this bratwurst when he opened his palm and there, Fräulein Ding, *there*—" and Jeremy drew a deep breath, raised his hand, pursed his lips like an overly animated children's entertainer creating suspense "—*there* was a cop's badge."

"How horrible! What did you do?"

"At first I just drew myself up and thought, If I act like a perfect lady nothing truly untoward will happen to me. I lifted an eyebrow, threw my scarf around my neck, and turned to march out head high, but the next thing I knew he'd slapped this rather gauche ID bracelet around my wrist which cunningly enough was attached to a matching bracelet on *his* wrist. For a moment I thought we were going *steady*."

Jeremy was given a seven-year suspended sentence, provided he reported every month to his parole officer and saw a state-appointed psychotherapist three times a week. He who'd always been so flamboyant, who could make us believe his shabby knitted scarf was a marabou boa, turned wren-brown, his big, fleshy body no longer a diva's girth but now a heavy penance to be concealed. He stopped vocalizing in the corridors, he cropped his hair ("I've entered my sensible lesbian period," he solemnly explained), and he even started dutifully escorting a girl to the movies.

Even though I was terrified of being arrested, I couldn't stop going to the toilets. Now when someone suspicious-looking came in, the toilets would flush in a chorus of panic and, just by standing there a second too long, the stranger could clear the house. When someone would dare to sink to his knees in the next stall I'd greedily suck him without hesitation. I'd plunge his cock as fast and as deep into me as possible.

I knew I had to leave Dr. O'Reilly. Annie Schroeder had dug a kitchen knife into her heart. She'd been hospitalized, released, and she'd stabbed herself a second time. Now she was in a maximum-security ward. O'Reilly himself was deteriorating quickly, more and more often falling asleep during my hours, forgetting my name, mumbling incomprehensibly. I knew I had to leave him, but even my body rebelled against such a rebellion. I fell sick with a high fever, then I danced one night at a fraternity party in a shoe so tight that three days later my left foot was abscessed and I had to be hospitalized. The foot became painfully swollen and had to be lanced. Afterward it was placed inside a sort of aluminum dog kennel that protected it from the touch of sheet and blanket.

For some reason, a graduate student in psychotherapy came by my bed. Outside, the first snow of the year was falling. The therapist, whose forehead was flushed and scaling, wore a tweed jacket and smelled of sweet tobacco. His mouth shot up on one side in an *accent aigu* of irony.

We didn't speak very directly. I was sharing the room with someone who was asleep, to be sure, but he might have been faking it. I said that I thought I was resisting breaking off with Dr. O'Reilly. "At least that's what I assume. I don't *feel* anything, naturally, since I've somatized the anxiety."

He wasn't smoking, but he touched his lip with his pipe as though he needed the feel of the cold amber mouthpiece to release his thoughts or words. "But why are you going to a shrink at all?"

"I want to change."

"Change what?"

"My object choice."

He looked me intently in the eye, and now I could see that he, too, must be homosexual. "But people don't really change," he said. "It's useless to try. It's more a question of adjusting, of learning to play the hand you've been dealt."

"Oh no," I said, angry. "I *am* changing, I *must* change. I'd kill myself if I thought I was stuck with these cards, which frankly are lousy—and you know it."

His face folded shut, and he left after exchanging a few of the necessary banalities. I felt triumphant.

I couldn't get well. I stayed in the infirmary, first with one ailment, then another. I watched the snow fall. My foot healed, but I broke out in hives. The hives subsided, and I was wracked with diarrhea. My roommates came and went. One of them, who was in traction, turned the conversation one evening to girls, then more generally to sex, finally to men. I watched his erection grow under the sheet. My own pressed against my stomach like a ruler on a board, hour after hour through the slow routines of the hospital. After lights out, I hobbled over to his bed and sucked his cock, which was nearly black and looked like a horse's, the same abundant foreskin.

Finally I realized I'd never get well until I saw O'Reilly and settled things. One of my fraternity brothers, a guy with perfect teeth and the knack of appreciating everything, drove me and waited while I looked out at the snow filling O'Reilly's garden and gathering like a rabbit muff over the folded hands of the gilt Kamakura Buddha.

O'Reilly nodded simply, picked at a scab on his face, and said, "Yes, I agree, you're right, our work isn't going well. It's best you find someone else."

And it was all over. His outrages against me, his unfulfilled promise to cure me—all the grievances I'd been hoarding were canceled like debts voided by a new government. He didn't owe me anything, nor I him, and on the trip back I was lonely and bruised, and I envied my friend his broad shoulders, his steady hand on the wheel, his manliness, which was so pungent I could smell it, although I couldn't make use of it. A few weeks later O'Reilly had a breakdown and was sent to the same hospital where his beloved Annie was already a patient.

When I got well, I went to the union pool and stood under the showers. I'd become pale and scrawny after two months of being in the hospital.

I met a man. He was in the shower across from me, tall, older, smooth-skinned, his face more olive than his body. I'd never seen him before. He smiled at me. His smile relaxed me, as though I'd just been restored to the human race.

In the locker room the man smiled at me again, not in the usual furtive way (seductive, hostile, afraid) but just as though we were already friends. He had wonderful green eyes and an engaging smile, although one tooth was a delicate biscuit brown. His shoulders reflected the overhead light. When he turned I could see that his buttocks registered in sinewy detail every motion he made; they weren't piled high like stiff mounds of whipped cream, the way teenage boys' butts looked. No, his hips were narrow and fluent.

No one else was around in the locker room, although two or three voices boomed from the pool. The smell of chlorine was giving me a headache.

We started talking, and everything I said made him nod and smile. I thought he might be laughing at me. What puzzled me was why someone so handsome would show an interest in me. As he dressed, I could see he had beautiful clothes, and that intimidated me, too.

He invited me to come to his apartment for a cup of tea. It was already dark out. A cold wind was blowing steadily, sifting snow. The afternoon had been warm enough to melt the snow on the sidewalk, but now it had frozen white as milk glass. I felt a small secret pride in being with someone so handsome. His carefully combed hair froze stiff. His salient cheekbones shone and caught the passing lights. The intimacy between us seemed as sudden and transitionless as in a dream. When we reached a dark side street, he put my mittenless hand in his pocket and held it without saying anything.

His apartment was big and underfurnished, as though a flood had scattered the contents of a single room over several. He sat me on a straight-back chair stranded in the middle of a carpetless wood floor, but when he stepped back and saw me marooned there he laughed and invited me into his bedroom. His name, he said, was Fred. His window cast a yellow trapezoid on the pure blue snow outside. The wind had traced in snow the black bark of the tree below. A soft tango was playing on the radio. He switched off the light. The snow looked fluffier, almost as though it had risen slightly.

We sprawled side by side, athwart the bed, fully dressed, our wet shoes on the floor, staring at the ceiling. Fred's voice and the tango explored the folds of my brain like a deadly parasite, whose progress can't be detected except after it slowly starts to unsnap higher functions. In the center of the ceiling a pressed metal rosette had lost detail under each new layer of paint. Fred's voice made my ear glow, or was it the cold? He told me that he'd just been released from a mental hospital.

"I was in for a year. That's why I don't want to sleep with you right away. I'm very tender, just like a crayfish between shells." We both laughed at the image. Our remarks slowed and scattered; a composer wouldn't have had an easy time scoring them.

My feet were warming up. Fred seemed really perfect because he needed me. I had a function to serve. Ordinarily I couldn't imagine what use I could be to anyone. I asked him what he was studying. He said he was finishing a degree in English. "I'm writing on Herrick, on his 'Corinna's Going a-Maying,' which is odd to think of in the snow."

A long sighing silence, the sigh of contentment. "What does 'green-gown' mean?" I asked.

"A 'green-gown' is a tumble in the grass. I suppose it's like a birthday suit." And we both laughed together. "But surely you already knew that. You *had* to know it in order to ask," and we both laughed harder. I liked the way our laughs sounded, although I still cringed at the sound of my speaking voice. I couldn't lower it. Physically I could, but psychologically it felt presumptuous, as though it were arrogant to sound like a man instead of a boy.

He told me his story. When I glanced over at him, his Adam's apple was as prominent as his chin and nose. The idea that his voice resided in this box intrigued me. I wanted to touch it.

I told him I needed to sleep with him because my insecurities were sexual.

"But then you might not see me again. And that could be a little . . . risky for me." He said he thought gay men lost interest after they did the "deed of darkness." I said I wasn't a generic gay man.

"I certainly don't want to be in the absurd position of rejecting you," he said, "because to me you're a wonderfully romantic young man, so tense. *Intense.* That's the word." And he opened the wet papaya pulp of his kiss to me. We kissed and undressed. The sheets smelled freshly ironed and felt as flimsy as rose petals. We kept stopping to talk, which at first vaguely irritated me, who thought sex was a crime to be committed as quickly as possible. Perhaps I'd been conditioned by the toilets. But then the *realness* of what we were doing touched me. I was here in a bed with cool sheets we were heating up, and each part of my body he stroked released some new thought in him and feeling in me. The heroics of sexual frenzy had been replaced by this voice, confiding secrets to me in the dark, lit by reflections off the deep lovely miles of snow outside.

And yet the next day I didn't phone him. And the day after I couldn't, and the third day confirmed my silence, and I couldn't understand why I'd betrayed Fred, betrayed myself. It seemed after all that I was just another gay man who lost interest after the deed of darkness.

Maria called me from Chicago to tell me that Paul had killed himself—Paul, the painter I had so much admired when I was at Eton and who'd told me, "Someday you'll have more freedom than you'll want." Maria had heard the story from Paul's girlfriend, who'd found Maria's phone number in Paul's address book. Apparently Paul had moved to the Brooklyn suburb of Sheepshead Bay, where he'd rented the attic in someone's old wooden house. He'd painted a bit but grown so despondent that he'd thrown himself off the Staten Island ferry. There was talk of organizing a memorial show of his work at the Eton museum.

The friends I'd chosen seemed to be going crazy or dying or getting arrested or succumbing to drugs. The self-destruction all around me scared me. Maria cried over the phone. I knew she and I must take care of each other. Paul had once told me that art should be a consolation for life, not a reflection of its ugliness. Until now I'd seen my own writing as nothing but a polygraph test, but now the suffering I witnessed led me to reconsider my work. Since I was a Freudian,

I told myself that wish fulfillment should join the repetition-compulsion as a motive for making art. According to Freud, people repeated the most painful events of their past in order to gain mastery over them—my fiction until now had seemed born out of just such an urge. But now the fresh colors of a wished-for world, a utopia in which kindness reigned, called to me. The puritan in me was afraid to falsify this vale of tears by rendering it as Happy Valley, but Lou had said truth must be sacrificed to beauty, which made Freudian sense if *truth* means repetition and *beauty* our fondest wishes in search of fulfillment.

I hitchhiked the three hundred miles to Chicago and stayed with Maria. Again we set sail every night, flying the colors of art and love. Again we drank wine and played *Manon Lescaut*, an opera in which the jumbled text scarcely justifies the pell-mell duets and ecstatic high notes—a disparity that resembled our love, Maria's and mine, so reticent though ardent. Half playfully, we flirted with the idea of marrying.

"Would I have to change my name?" she said.

"I'd change mine to yours."

We carried home bags of groceries, went for a ride in the suburbs, snuggled up to watch television. Maria enjoyed the world, the world's charms, without paying the world's price. She simply refused to see our homosexuality or age difference as a problem. She wouldn't discuss it. She started with the idea that bohemians were exempt from the ordinary rules.

We went to a lesbian bar together. Maria entered the Volley Ball arrayed in black: a black trench coat over black jeans and a man's black shirt. Her delicate white skin looked as raunchy as Elvis Presley's flickering image on television. We watched the women dancing together while three old Negro men in the band, faces petrified into indifference, tooted and banged. A butch entered squiring a blonde whore tottering along on spike heels under dairy whip hair, her chubby hand rising again and again to tuck a stray wisp back into the creamy dome. On the wall was a sign, flyblown and fading, that read: "Hard Times Party Tonight." Maria explained that the sign suggested a costume party and was a dodge around the law that forbade women to wear more than three articles of men's dress—jeans, boots, and a T-shirt, say. A few businessmen, whose fantasies ran to lesbian couples, sat around the bar, eyes glued to the dance floor. A bouncer kept them away from the women—look but don't touch! The one toilet was unavailable for a whole half hour at a stretch. Two women had barricaded themselves inside and were necking. Most of the women addressed each other with names drawn from children's books ("Piglet," "Eeyore," and "Pooh" were favorites) or by men's nicknames ("Andy" and "Tony" seemed popular).

Maria's apartment smelled of oil paint and turpentine. Her father had carved a grandfather clock for her in his basement shop at home. The Salvation Army couch Maria had upholstered in crisp blue-and-white bed ticking. She would sit on a high stool, dressed in a white smock, a cigarette burning in her hand like incense before an idol.

I posed for her, but she said I wasn't a good model. She spent most of her time modeling in clay two nude female figures whose linking arms and legs formed the oval frame of a mirror.

She clung to me when I left. She said, "You've spoiled me with your visit. How can I go back to my spinster's life?"

"I'll write you every day and get back down here in a week or two, three at the most."

I wanted to marry Maria and avoid the solitude and suffering everyone had told me homosexuality would bring. I thought marriage would define my nebulous feelings toward her; if I were married, I'd be a husband.

Yet something kept me from answering her letters. I resolved every morning to write her; but every night I went to bed without having mailed off a letter. Her letters dropped regularly into my box. Then two weeks of silence. Then this letter: "Dumpling, you haven't written or called in a month, an insulting silence I can only assume is intended as a rejection. No lover would act the way you have. I accuse you of gross neglect.

"It's just as well, anyway. Boys really don't thrill me. Last week I met a fabulous dyke named Maeve at the Volley Ball who looks just like Anthony Quinn and who's bombarded me with champagne and kilos of chocolates. Thank heaven for dykes, or where else would a girl find a little gallantry? Certainly not from you, you naughty neglectful Dumpling."

SEVEN

■   ■   ■   ■   ■   ■   ■

In my senior year of college I was accepted into a graduate program in Chinese at Harvard, but my father was unwilling to keep me on his payroll, and his income was too high for me to qualify for a fellowship.

That summer after graduation I didn't know what to do with myself. I lived with a childhood friend, Tommy, in the basement of his family's house. He found a job as an apprentice bus driver and entered a training program. I was driving a pickup truck in Des Plaines delivering fruit juice and eggs door to door. When I heard middle-class executives, my father's crowd, say they deserved to be highly paid because their jobs involved assuming responsibilities and making decisions, I snorted with impatience. I knew that such exercises of the will were gratifying, whereas driving a truck in the July sun through the Chicago suburbs was no picnic.

Lou told me he was moving to New York. He invited me to come along. Just like that I decided to go, even though I had only two hundred dollars to my name. "I'll send you the busfare back to the Middle West when you strike out," my father told me.

Lou and I stayed in the YMCA on West Sixty-third Street. I spent ten of my precious dollars having my resumé typed and duplicated. I mailed it out to a few places, but that seemed hopeless, or at least abstract.

I had a single suit too heavy for the heat, three wash-and-wear short-sleeved white shirts, a greasy tie, two pairs of black stockings, and one pair of black lace-up shoes badly scuffed on the sides. I had never learned how to groom myself. My mother had ignored the whole issue. In prep school I'd showered because I'd had to, but in college my hygiene and wardrobe had become impressionistic. I was a sleepwalker.

Now I had to look alert, reliable. The job market appeared capricious and cruel, so unlike the meritocracy of school, in which study was duly rewarded with high marks and one level led naturally to the next. The working world seemed so vulgar and simple-minded that I couldn't imagine why we'd been taught so much Confucius, Kant, and Renoir. I had an interview for a trainee position writing copy for a trade magazine in electrical engineering. Of what use now was my course in the music of Bartók?

All day I'd sit hunched over a cup of coffee in the YMCA's basement cafeteria trying to get up my nerve to place a phone call, visit an employment office. By three in the afternoon, headachy and suicidal, I'd return to my room, masturbate, and take a nap. I thought I'd rather die than call a stranger and ask a favor.

Lou's very slickness made me seem all the more bumbling. His room was just as crummy as mine, but he kept his appearance impeccable. He was being sent out on interviews by an executive headhunter. He was considering salaries of forty thousand dollars, whereas starting positions for writer trainees in 1962 paid only five thousand dollars.

August was approaching, and soon everyone would leave town for vacation. "The whole city shuts down," a lady at an agency told me. She asked me questions, listened, bathed us both in her cigarette smoke, coughed a full minute, and finally said, "You're kinda weird, you know, but I like it. I like the whole package. I think I can sell it. Tell me I'm crazy. Yes, I'm crazy. But I think I can sell it."

Lou cruised the corridors of the Y and came back with descriptions of what he'd found: "All these pleasant fellows, the regulars, sitting around in the fake Moorish reception room watching TV and sipping orange soda and scanning the transients checking in. After the late movie on the tube, off to bed, but not before Fred from Toledo stops by for a cup of instant Sanka that Bill from Tampa heats up with his electric coil. They listen to the new Ferrante and Teicher album. You see, Bill's made his room real homey, soft lights and all. Fred gets the great idea they'll spend Thanksgiving together, never too early to plan for these lonely holidays, we'll have turkey dinner at Schrafft's, it's not too expensive and it's very nice, and then we'll take in a show at Radio City. They agree and kiss coldly. Neither gets an erection, so they laugh and say, 'Isn't it silly for us to kiss when we're just sisters?' " I suppose Lou made all that up.

It seemed that outside the Y everyone was living on the streets and no one ever went to bed. Lou and I took the subway to the Village, emerged at Sixth Avenue and Eighth Street, and walked up Greenwich Avenue. Most of the strollers were straight couples, but here and there, flashing past like a parakeet, was a gaudy little queen, a paste clip on a shirt that might have started life as a blouse, her gait complex with extra motions, micro-motions somehow added, as though a mad scientist, after breaking walking down into its components, had had trouble reassembling the elements into a convincing continuity.

"But we all walk that way," Lou said. "We queens are so self-conscious, our little heads so drugged on just the sheer thrill of existing publicly, that we can't even cross a room without simpering and mincing. It's not that we start out wanting to appear effeminate. It's that we use effeminacy after the fact as an alibi for our embarrassment, our florid but somehow ill-timed gestures, the bizarre tilt of our heads, our—" But here his lecture dissolved into a tearful laugh, for Lou loved to assail us in terms that were pushed to such an extreme that even he saw the absurdity.

We were passing below the women's prison on the corner of Eighth and Sixth, just next to the old Jefferson Market Courthouse, and two women on the street were calling up to the metal-shuttered windows. "Lorine, you cheat on me, bitch, I beat yo' black ass, hear? I love ya', honey, save ya' love for mama." Over the motor hum and the tocsin of impatient horns, these women called out to each other, their New York voices penetrating and forlorn.

"Look at them, Bunny, they're so heroic, these dykes, they don't give a shit about all these Village Beatniks and dull-normals, they just want to wail out their love, keep that prison cunt faithful till release, ah!" and Lou pressed a broken hand to his chest as though he were a Saint Sebastian pierced by melancholy, "it's so beautiful, this beautiful poetry of gay life."

On this hot July night the streets were thronged with people. Here a crowd circled a sidewalk artist sketching a solemn young man with waved hair and spotty skin. The sitter was posing as though his profile were about to go on the coin of the realm. He was the only one who couldn't see how the sketch was coming along, this disappointment being patiently prepared for him. There, in the little park across from the Waverly movie theater, an impromptu game of basketball had broken out and bare sweaty black and tan torsos flashed through the dark, reflecting the lights surging up Sixth.

Cars on MacDougal slowly waded through people like buffalo through flooded paddies. The sound of voices, of street musicians, rang off the brick walls of tenements. Above the streetlights shadowy families sat on metal fire escapes. Now we passed an ornate Italian coffee shop, flyblown mirrors hung in gilt frames dimmer than a helmet in a Rembrandt. The eagle atop the espresso machine flew imperiously through a cloud of steam.

No faggots appeared to have strayed over to this side of Sixth Avenue, but once we recrossed it we were back among what Lou called the "Cha-cha queens, hairburners, and glandular cases." A hissing trio like rattled snakes in an agitated basket were hanging out on a stoop, their lips flecked with foam. Another pair were dancing in the water of an open fire hydrant, shirts tied to expose their tummies. Lou was in a delirium: "Bunny, we're home, you can press your ear to the pavement and hear the heartbeat," and even though he made me feel such a prig, my heart did leap at all the possibilities this city offered to meet men. Before, I'd caught only half glimpses of queers, but like a hunter who pursues his deer deep into the night forest, at last I'd come upon a moonlit clearing filled with thousands of moving antlers, all these men.

Lou had the address of a gay restaurant in the Village. When we were led by that majestic personage called the Mater D to our table in the garden, we were studied by other customers, and only after we'd sat down, ordered our oysters Rockefeller (with Pernod sauce on a bed of spinach), and sipped our daiquiris did we relax and look around.

A gay bar, a cruisy toilet—that I understood, but a gay restaurant? The suggestion that gay men, like Negroes, might want to enjoy one another's company astounded me.

The city seemed like a Bring-Your-Own party that had gone on too long. Even children were still playing at mid-

night. A blind woman stood on a corner singing in a quaver-
ing voice the song my mother had sung to me at bedtime when
I was a child: "I'll be seeing you in apple-blossom time." At
stoplights cars shouldered each other out of the way, jockey-
ing to gain a few inches at the starting gate. As we headed
up Park Avenue in a taxi (Lou was treating), we leaned our
heads back and looked up at the illuminated spires streaming
past. At another stoplight a group of Puerto Rican teenagers
dressed in baseball uniforms shouted at each other over the
roof in raucous voices. In Chicago there'd been the Loop, but
it had been virtually deserted after dark; here people seemed
to live in the center city, and I expected to see lines of wash
strung between skyscrapers.

I got a job. I had to wait until the second week of Sep-
tember to start work and I wasn't paid until six weeks after
that, but at least I had a small purchase on this island. Lou
staked me until I received my first check, for he was writing
copy now for a top vodka account in a small agency. We both
moved out of the Y into apartments, he into six rambling
rooms on the Upper West Side, I into a tiny three-room rail-
road flat in the Village, on MacDougal above Houston.

At school I'd already grown used to assuming and shed-
ding disguises. In New York the costume ball continued. At
work I wore a coat and tie and behaved with circumspec-
tion, but in the Village I dressed as a "hipster" (the new
word). Lou had already taught me the hip vocabulary, but
the old jazz hipster was being replaced by the image of someone young, white, innocent, loving, and permissive, someone
who drank wine and smoked pot but avoided heroin, someone
who put into spiritual practice the socialist injunctions
against owning personal property; like the flowers in the
field, this child toiled not.

This evolution in style seemed to me a purely local
phenomenon. I knew that the Detroit and Chicago of my

childhood would never change. They represented the eternal, if distasteful, verities. I was sure that what was happening was only a new eruption of the old bohemian spirit.

I'd found a job as a writer trainee for a national magazine. During the first six months I had to rotate from one department to the next, working first as a researcher in the library, then as an expediter in the mailroom or the production department. At last I was permitted to write a single caption, edited by three different hands before the picture was dropped in the final layout at press time. By the end of the year I had been given my own cubicle and phone and a door that closed. I was still researching and writing the odd caption.

Once a month I'd be invited to a luncheon for twenty people held in a small dining room on the top floor of the building, overlooking all of Manhattan. The older editors would do most of the talking. At my university I'd met professors who, of course, were experts in their field but had no sociable way of talking about this knowledge and knew nothing about anything else. These editors—sharp-featured, capillaries broken from discreet alcoholism—seemed to know everything and to have done everything. They had flown as fighter pilots, one had served as interpreter for MacArthur in Japan, another had traveled with Margaret Bourke-White to the South Pole, or helped expose a city hall scandal, taken a sympathetic look at the Hollywood Ten, researched the profile of Marilyn Monroe at the Actors Studio . . . They mentioned books about the Ballets Russes, the Wright Brothers, Jefferson's slave mistress, Churchill at Malta, and everyone had a wisecrack about the author, an anecdote to relate about once tying one on with him or her in Singapore or Lisbon. One editor knew the best expert to consult on Persian rugs, another spoke of his hopes for the Bermuda Cup, a third named the best greens in Scotland. The current congressional expense-account scandal drew a quick laugh. Mary Leakey's dates for the first hominids were greeted skeptically.

The range of their knowledge was stunning and peculiarly personal, since everything they'd learned they'd picked up on a story. A quick prep and then two thousand words on the endangered statues at Abu Simbel, or two columns on Robert Moses's plan to pave over lower Manhattan. A quick visit to Sidney Janis and some lively copy on this new Pop Art, its star Andy Warhol, the guy who'd said on TV Pop Art isn't satire, it's just a way of liking things.

I could never speak as fast as these editors. The little knowledge I had I wore heavily. It had never occurred to me until now that almost all the news got made and reported by a small elite who'd met each other at a few Ivy League schools.

Although I barely made enough money to squeak by from one check to the next, lived on spaghetti, and purchased my new suit on a revolving credit plan, I scarcely thought about money. On the floor I'd count out ninety-nine pennies for a ticket to the highest balcony at the City Center for the ballet and walk the fifty blocks home; Wilde's idea that the luxuries are necessities, and the necessities luxuries, became my slogan.

Many of my arty, bohemian friends from school had also moved to New York, and we went out together almost every night, usually to sit in a vast room on Bleecker Street. It had been a music hall in the nineteenth century and still possessed a rickety balcony and a ceiling chandelier with etched glass shades to screen the gas jets. No one went up to the balcony or lit the chandelier. The two old ladies with motherly vulgar voices ("What'll it be, hon?") seemed to be looking through us to earlier, more prosperous times. They wore bedroom slippers and nylons rolled below their knees, but above the neck they were impeccable: plucked eyebrows and glowing ruby lips. A few folding screens quarantined off most of the shadowy hall and surrounded half a dozen tables lit by the red neon letters in the window.

There we sat for hours, warmed only by the beer, listening to Barbra Streisand's melancholy record of "Happy Days Are Here Again" and the first Dionne Warwick songs. All around us an adult world was revolving quite indifferent to us; we didn't realize that it existed, much less that it excluded us. Exposed to nothing but the classics and confined to a provincial campus until now, we knew very little about the latest books and artistic trends; the "young" who represented the newest tastes were thirty, not twenty.

A few of the women in our crowd were sleeping their way up into more sophisticated spheres, and if I'd been handsome or socially ambitious I might have done the same.

We were so dazed by the speed with which we were changing that we mistook this virtuosity for insincerity.

My fellow workers had no idea what I did with my evenings. The married men commuted to their families on Long Island; the single women lived cooped up together on the East Side in doorman buildings. Nor did my school friends know that I walked up and down Greenwich Avenue sometimes till three in the morning looking for sex, dressed in "collegiate clothes" I'd never have worn in college.

We were all leftists, of course, although we favored Cuba and China and felt vaguely uneasy about Russia. We'd never examined our socialism, which was composed of sympathy, rebellion, and enthusiasm, no economics, little history, and a total absence of political experience. For us, socialism was primarily social, since everyone we liked was on our side—the poor young (but not the indigent old), foreign peasants (but not bigoted American farmers), the Eastern European proletariat (but not Detroit auto workers), the inspired mad (but not the merely crazy), oppressed Negroes (but not white trash). Homosexuals we would never have thought of as a political entity, or if at all then as decadent sons of the *haute bourgeoisie*, the parasitical element every socialist state had had to execute or expel. I was able to prove my seriousness as a socialist precisely by not even mentioning homosexuals.

One day Maria moved from Chicago and showed up, tearful, on my doorstep with just her black cat Boo-Boo and a box filled with the 1911 *Encyclopaedia Britannica*. She had left Maeve, she said, because Maeve was such a heartbreaker, an intriguer, a Donna Juanna, an Irish drunk, charming and incorrigible.

We sat at my kitchen table, which had a metal top printed to look like grainy wood and a hanging lamp above it cozily dimmed by a shade of gathered brown fabric, left behind by the previous tenant. We drank red wine and ate lasagna and talked and smoked and listened to *Manon Lescaut*.

Maria had given up on Chicago. She'd never go back to its cold winds blasting off the lake, its comfortable, defeated, hard-driven lesbians, its big, underfurnished apartments. She talked with scorn of her affair with Maeve. "It was so humiliating, the broken promises, the tearful reproaches and steamy reconciliations, those drunken fights in bars, midnight phone calls, hurtling back and forth in cars on snow chains. All the hours of gossip with friends, of sympathy from other women—oh, I'm sick of it, sick of it!" She laughed through her tears, her shoulders shaking with sobs or merriment, I couldn't tell which.

My grungy little apartment's three windows gave onto a narrow alley noisy with flapping laundry that by day projected silhouettes like black wings on our yellow shades. The bathroom, the most recent addition, had a tub so small that you washed with your knees around your chin. The sink had been designed for a dirty child. The outer halls, painted with a shiny glaze, smelled of roach spray and were lit by bare bulbs. Our place you entered through the kitchen. On one side was the room I gave Maria that also housed Boo-Boo's bed—the empty *Britannica* box. On the other side was my room, the living room with a couch that pulled out. There I kept my Chinese flashcards in long boxes in anticipation of the day when I'd resume my studies; that day has never come.

Maria had a bright red loden coat that she wore with black Wellington boots and a black scarf. Dressed that way she'd accompany me to the Bleecker Street Tavern and the basement Italian restaurants. She tried to show an interest in New York, and her conversation willed itself toward enthusiasm by the frequent use of such words as "fascinating" and "wonderfully bizarre," but her eyes looked as cold as two holes cut in the ice for fishing.

At night she'd rail against Maeve until a valve would turn and all this spleen would come out as dismal lost love. The phone rang every night, Maeve calling from Chicago. She'd be in a bar, drunk, shouting above the jukebox, or she'd be at home, apparently sober, very jokey and man-to-man with me: "How you guys doing in the Big Apple? I'm thinking of packing my Thunderbird and tooling out that way myself. I know a fellow who works on *Variety* and has promised me a job, want to put Maria on?"

"She's not here I'm afraid. I don't know. Fine. She's fine. Yes, I'll tell her."

Maria followed my end of the conversation, intent on every one of Maeve's gambits. She'd turn red, eyes blazing, then shake her head sadly. After I'd hung up, Maria would say, "I must never see her again. I can't. If I want to sur-

vive." And she'd go back to her homework, learning to like
her new life.

On the street one day I confided to Maria I was dying to buy
the new *Grecian Guild* magazine of boys in posing briefs
but that I was too shy to ask for it from the Italian lady in
the corner newspaper kiosk. Without a pause Maria detoured
over to the lady and said, "I'll have that nice new *Grecian
Guild*, if you please," paid for it, and handed it to me, then
teased me for blushing. I sat in the bathroom late that night,
admiring Bobby Phalen's artfully oiled buttocks, which were
growing leaner and narrower.

Between Maria and me a new kind of intimacy developed, nurtured by her, even defined by her, for I wasn't
worldly enough to understand that a friendship can flourish
only if watered by tact and pruned by diplomatic silences.
With a friend we recognize bounds but within those bounds
respond with candor; with a lover we expect limitless communion but resort to stratagems. Maria recognized the ways
in which I feared sexual intimacy and firmly ended that possibility between us. But she didn't cut the thread of court-
ship, of gallantry, even of romance that lent vitality to our
love. We coined the notion of "passionate friendship" and
we suspected that ours would last a lifetime. If our friendship
was sustained by our past and tapped all the energies of
family reciprocities, its tropism strained toward the future.
At that time I was still too eager for love to appreciate friendship, but even so I imagined I'd spend my life with Maria,
not with Mr. Right. When my mother told me she felt sorry
for me, without a mate to console me or children to sustain
me in my old age, I could only think, I have a mother and
daughter: Maria.

Maria bought me a coffeepot and showed me how to use it. When the toilet got stopped up, she called the plumber. I was afraid to call and didn't mind peeing in the sink or running across the street to the toilet in the Hip Bagel. I'd never had a checking account before; Maria explained how to open one.

Once I'd mastered these new games, I was better at playing them than she. She was less afraid than I of credit, officialdom, or the law because she took them less seriously. I took them so seriously that once I overcame my intimidation I did everything correctly—my "Capricorn nature," as one of my new, hip friends explained.

Maria was so discreet that I dreaded she'd find out I was talking about us both to strangers, for she shared her feelings with no one but me, yet gave her ideas away to everyone. My case was the opposite: I showered my feelings on everyone, trying to defuse them by firing them again and again, whereas my thoughts—about literature, sex, society—I confided to Maria alone.

Of course Maria's feelings for me I never doubted. I knew she loved me. For me, her womanness was always a strangeness, the idea that she belonged to another sex, which for me constituted virtually another species; but we managed to communicate across this ocean of gender. When we set sail during our midnight conversations, our ages were quietly dropped overboard as useless ballast. In our domestic dealings, however, we played the difference up. This emphasis gave a humorous gloss to what Maria wanted to do in any event—tidy up the place. More subtly, it reduced our embarrassment about existing side by side in such close quarters: She became a comically vexed, secretly indulgent older sister and I the lovable but slovenly kid brother always daydreaming over a book.

The instant we stepped out into the snow, she in her bright red loden coat, I in—what? I don't remember and scarcely knew then—our ages shifted again. I became the serious young husband bespectacled and dignified, she the wife in need of protection, as though my edge of a few weeks in New York had somehow made me a native.

Having an actual woman at my side preempted my fantasy of being a woman, a fantasy that was as shameful as it was deep. One day, while browsing at the Gotham Book Mart, I stumbled on a book by the first sex-change, written in the 1930s. I slumped to the floor and read the whole book straight through, sweating in my overcoat. I read until the sunlight began to fade. My face burned with horrified recognition of this tale of a Dutch painter who felt he must at all costs liberate the dryad locked inside his male cortex. Here were the photographs of the *before* and *after* handwriting (vigorous downstrokes turned to rounded curves) and the *before* and *after* paintings (Mondrian to Marie Laurencin) and *before* and *after* bodies (Van Dyke and glinting pince-nez to a nearly erased face peeping out from under a cloche hat, the tottering thin body supported in the wintry garden of the clinic by a German nurse). The post-op artist insisted on having not only his sex changed on his documents (a whim that the game Dutch officials were willing to oblige) but also his rebirthday (refused). In the painter's eyes, a lengthening pendulous age, not mere pudenda, had been the culprit; he had considered the surgery to be a renaissance.

When he met his mother afterward, he could scarcely remember her. He chose as a husband an old friend of the family who'd agreed to marry him once he'd become a she. Her desire to have a child sent her back to have a second operation, from which she never recovered. The shorter and shorter journal entries, the indefinitely extended vacation of the performing surgeon, the patient's horrible pain—all led to the suspension dots of the conclusion, three bloody drops on a snowy page.

I was summoned to my army physical. With all these pale, tattooed boys I stripped and bent over, dressed and filled out forms. Here and there in the crowd I heard an arresting accent or saw eyes flashing with defiance; these anomalies were assembled at the end of the day in the psychiatrist's office. He was almost deaf. Perhaps to be spiteful he'd moved his desk out of his office into the center of the waiting room. I heard each deviant shout the details of his problem. I had checked the box "homosexual tendencies" (the army recognized nothing more definite), but the doctor pretended he couldn't see why I'd been referred to him.

"Here, here!" I shouted, pointing.

"Where? What? Oh. Homosexual. Tendencies. Have you tried psychiatric treatment?"

"Yes," I shouted.

"And?"

"Useless. No. Good."

"Are you the active partner or the passive partner?"

I'd never thought in these terms before. Did "active" mean the one who sucked (the "girl") or the one who fucked (the "boy")? I couldn't sort it out but I decided "passive" sounded less curable.

"What?"

Face crimson I shouted, "Passive!"

I was medically disqualified from the army. The idea that my place would be taken by someone else, perhaps even a gay man too nervous to admit to his "tendencies," didn't trouble me in the least. A belief in morality is based on a belief in the group. I distrusted everyone. Hawthorne's dim view of human nature confirmed mine, although I did not believe in Original Sin, only sin, far too common to be original. Of course I pretended to entertain normal scruples; I didn't want people to look down on me.

Maria found a job in textbook publishing and moved to her own apartment on the Upper West Side. The smell of cat urine slowly faded, and only cat's hairs on the one pair of slacks I never wore (too snug, for some reason) and the clawed ravening of the upholstery up the back of a chair remained as reminders of her presence—those and the improvements (the electric can opener in a kitchen with only two plates, the coffeepot, the framed drawing of me reading).

For a while after she left I lived with a Russian ballet dancer who, when we met at a party, had been all muscled ass, starry smile, and scraps of Pushkin but who, upon moving in, was seldom out of a stained "hapi coat" mini-dressing gown from Tokyo and a wide-mesh hairnet. He detested everything American, told depressing stories of backstage pettiness, and longed to return to the Eastern Bloc, though Budapest this time. Accordingly, I had to drill him in Hungarian vocabulary every night. He lived on nothing but potatoes sprinkled with cumin seeds and scorned my wastefulness (dinners out, cab rides). He was saving every penny for a one-way ticket to Budapest. From time to time he'd let me into his bed, but the hairnet and hapi coat had turned him from a young prince into a sort of untidy Minnie Mouse with big thighs of mushroom pallor.

Then he was gone in a fury (I'd giddily torn the *entire* paper seal off the top of a jar of instant coffee rather than leaving *half* on as a leveler for the teaspoon). I drifted into a busy, dissatisfied life of amateur office work by day and professional cruising by night. The gay bars were being closed down because the mayor was cleaning up the city in anticipation of the World's Fair. One day a new bar would open up way west, south of Canal, in a no-man's-land, and we'd all rush down there, jungle tomtoms having given us the address and hours. But three days later the police raided the bar. We ran up the back stairs, leapt from roof to roof, and clattered down a neighbor's fire exit into a night panicky with silently revolving red lights and the muffled racket of messages radioed to the squad car.

Then a place opened off Times Square, near the Peppermint Lounge where the Twist had started, and we were up there dancing at the back on a small floor behind a Spanish metal grille strung with Christmas tree lights that began to twinkle the minute a suspected plainclothesman walked in; that was our signal to break apart. But that bar was closed down, too.

Subway toilets, last cleaned and stocked with paper towels on the eve of World War I, were sudden descents into the filthy, thrilling tropics. On the way home from the office, my stomach sour from coffee, frustration, and boredom, I'd sway against strangers and read the subway ads for the tenth time.

Because a novel—these words—is shared experience, a clumsy but sometimes funny conversation between two people in which one of them is doing all the talking, it will always be tighter and more luminous than that object called living. There is something so insipid about living that to do it at all requires heroism or stupidity, probably both. Living is all those days and years, the rushes; memory edits them; this page is the final print, music added. But for an instant imagine the process reversed, go with me back through the years, then *be* me, me all alone as I submit to the weight, the atmospheric pressure of youth, for when I was young I was exhausted by always bumping up against this big lummox I didn't really know, myself. It was as though I'd been forced into solitary confinement with a stranger who had unaccountable tastes, aversions, rhythms.

Come with me, then, up the concrete steps to the toilet door, place a dime in the box, turn the chrome handle, open the door a crack, and slip in.

You'll be surprised by how many silent men are standing around. This businessman has rested his expensive leather briefcase on the filthy sink and is leaning against a tile wall. On the floor a bum, reeking of sweet red wine, is sleeping it off, snoring loudly, a sound that draws a red line under the conspicuous silence. Both stalls, one doorless, the other with its door half open, house men sitting right on the porcelain (the seats have long since been stolen). Both occupants have dropped their pants to the damp floor but are leaning forward to conceal their erections. The mood of the room is a cheap alloy of tension and boredom. A train clatters in, you can hear the doors open and shut, then shoes ringing on the pavement in the cavernous station.

And then you lean against the wall and, enduring seconds that pulse in your ear, stretch out your hand toward the crotch of the man beside you. Your action triggers vitality all around you. In a second this raw country boy at the urinal with the rosy forearms and red knuckles, the sickle of a vein superimposed on the hammer of his hand, has turned toward the room, brandishing a big red penis. An instant later everyone has converged on him, the men in the stalls emerge, one is kissing him, the second licking his testicles, a third man the penis, and another is standing beside him, arm around his waist, as though to lend him courage and companionship. The businessman with the expensive briefcase has planted his face between the farmboy's buttocks in total disregard of his expensive trousers, which are getting damp and dirty on the floor, wet with backed-up sewage. He's lapping and lapping; I can see his eyes drifting peacefully from side to side, dreamily independent of the suckling action.

Then the man sucking the cock comes up for air and you take his place, fitting yourself around a tumescence still warm and tasting of the other guy's spit. You look up as someone else unbuttons the country boy's shirt, revealing a hairless chest marbled by blue veins and decorated like a piece of wedding cake with two candle sockets in pink frosting—the erect nipples.

Now everyone is at work on him at once, breath in his ear, lips on his lips, mouths on his balls, cock, and ass, that arm around his waist, as though he really is a bride and this the last-minute flurry of seamstresses fitting him into his gown.

When he comes, he lets out a cry. His body stiffens and he leans back. You swallow gratefully the surprisingly meager but sweet semen, and the boy's ecstasy sets off his bridal attendants, who shoot and shout in a chorus around him. The drunk is still snoring.

In two seconds you've buttoned up, wrapped your raincoat around you, and rushed out into the flood of passengers flowing up the stairs and rivuleting into the night. Your hair is rumpled, your face flushed, and your hand still smells of the country boy. At the subway entrance you catch sight of the businessman just behind you. Without thinking, you glance at his trousers, not too bad, he looks at your wet knees the same moment, and you and he exchange the tiniest smile of wintry complicity.

A beautiful young woman at the office to whom I'd confided the secret of my sexuality (she'd sworn never to betray my confidence) looked at me now with compassion during coffee breaks, held my hand, and treated me as though I had leukemia. From her scattered remarks I grasped that she thought homosexuality was a sadness, a wound, more a poetic disposition than a perverse activity. What would she have thought if she'd seen me on my knees in a subterranean slice of jungle inserted under the leafless, treeless forest of gray Manhattan?

During lunch hour, in the cruisy toilet at the old Whitney Museum (when it was still next door to the Modern), I saw a painting student I'd met at the Eton art academy. He frowned at me and said, "I scarcely recognized you, you've become so fat—what a shame to ruin your looks when you're still so young. How old are you?"

"Twenty-three."

"Well, you look horrible, at least thirty; you should enjoy what's left of your youth."

A week later I mentioned to Maria that my new suit bought on time from Rogers Peet must be made of an inferior fabric since it was already wearing thin just below my crotch.

"That's because you've gotten so chubby, Dumpling, that your legs rub together when you walk."

Until now I'd always eaten just as much as I liked whenever it suited me and I'd always been slender. Although I'd hated gym class and gladly avoided exercise, normal campus comings and goings had sufficed to burn off the huge quantities of food I devoured. Of course, at my fraternity house we'd been given roast beef; now I was too poor to eat anything but spaghetti.

The calamity of having gone to fat shocked me, first because I hadn't noticed it, second because it seemed irreversible. I couldn't imagine dieting. A grim fatalism settled over me that was too anxious to be called resignation. Every morning I'd stand on the toilet to inspect my body in the only mirror in the apartment, the tiny one above the sink, but I could never tell if I was thinner or fatter. I refused to buy a scale and enter the realm of fact; I preferred to conjure my fictions, bloat in despair, dwindle in joy, stay constant to that mild anxiety Freud had termed "boredom."

And then there was something stubborn in me that didn't want to lose weight to attract a man. If the right man came along, he'd be able to see my virtues magically. Once he kissed me, the frog would turn into a prince. I had become a trick question, a heavy disguise, but behind the disobliging exterior was the welcoming child I would always be. Of course, what I'd forgotten was that a lover was not Parsifal and I was not the Grail; the medievalism of my imagination was not sufficiently up-to-date to recognize that the lover was a shopper and I a product.

On cold winter nights, lit like a pumpkin from within by the flame of liquor, I'd cruise the corner of Christopher and a back street called Gay (any chance of commemorating a plaque there now to my hungry ghost?). I'd memorize the shop windows and run around the corner to the neighborhood bar for another drink.

It was the most venerable gay bar in town, its greasy ceiling caked with an inch of accumulated dust, its photos of sporting and theatrical celebrities strangely irrelevant to its clientele. The owners were nervous that their bar, too, would be closed by the police and they instituted curious rules: no more than three men could stand in a conversational group, women were given free drinks, and mixed couples were warmly welcomed whereas the doorman sent away one out of every two single men. On some evenings he'd insist that everyone turn his back to the bar and face the windows and street, as though we were in a display, merely pretending to drink and laugh while actually modeling the new line of hopsack pants or wheat jeans, saddle shoes or penny loafers, and surfer haircuts. I'd had my slightly curly hair relaxed by the same dangerous chemical blacks used to "conk" their hair at that time; once it was properly limp it hung over my eyes in a languid swag.

My fatness abolished the space between my mother and me. She was a thousand miles away in Chicago, but the distance between us was fingernail thin. Like her, I juggled an inner melancholy and surface cheer. Like her, I was always on stage in a role calculated to please. The strangers I wanted to win over were all men—indifferent men whose fierce desires for each other crackled just above my head.

I remembered when I was a boy, after my mother was divorced. It was my eighth birthday. She thought we should celebrate it in an Italian restaurant on Rush Street. She liked to go there because she could meet men at the bar. We split a dish of green noodles and she drank Chianti. She kept smiling at a man at the bar. When my birthday cake was brought in, it created an excuse for the man to come over to our table. My mother was quick to offer him a piece of cake, and he bought her another small straw-covered bottle of Chianti. They arranged to meet later. For a while, she went out with him, but one day he stopped returning her calls.

"It's because I'm too fat," she said. "I don't eat much. I eat like a bird. It's my metabolism. Some people are cursed with a slow metabolism. I have to eat. If I don't eat, I get weak and can't work. God knows I have few enough pleasures. Eating is a consolation. But I eat like a bird. You see what I eat. Do I eat too much?"

"No," I said, "very little."

Now I was just like her. On some days I'd think of my fat as manly, the potbelly of the laborers I'd worked among. But most of the time fat feminized me, turned me into a pink, quivering Rubens with breasts that jiggled when I ran down steps.

I complained to Lou. He was tonic and pitiless. He said, "It's easy to be anything you want. You must want to be fat.

It's a form of loyalty to your mother. Or maybe you're merely afraid of being queer. It's logical. There are no fat gay boys. You're fat. Therefore you're not gay. Certainly the fat keeps you from having gay sex."

I thought bitterly of his stomach, which had been half removed and permitted him to eat constantly and stay skinny.

Lou lived by extremes. After the debacle of his last days in Chicago, here in New York he'd found a high-paying job, joined a gym, bought a luxurious wardrobe of dark cashmere suits. He worked twelve to fourteen hours a day at his office and weekends as well. His West Side apartment he filled with comfortable, anonymous furniture and blowups of his heroes, Ezra Pound, Bobby Phalen, and Cassius Clay. He had no plants, which would have required watering. He suspended his graceful blue bicycle from the ceiling when he wasn't riding it. He did a thorough housecleaning every Thursday night to prepare for a solid weekend of tricking. He liked the black and Puerto Rican neighbors, the cheerful music, the kids playing on the stairs, the fiesta in the streets, the smell of saffron in the halls—saffron or its cheaper substitute, Bimol.

Lou had met a tiny peroxided blond kid named Misty who he had move in with him. "Oh, Bunny," he said, touching my hand as we ate at a Broadway coffee shop. "It was here, right here, that I met him one night."

"At three in the morning."

"Four. The bars had closed. I hadn't scored and, anyway, I couldn't feature another night with a grown-up, some accountant from Jersey City with a screw-on collar pin who wants to sixty-nine because he thinks it's *fair*!" Horrified laugh. He'd been leaning across the sticky Formica table, scrutinizing me, his face in mine, but now he slammed back and disturbed the man behind him. "So, discouraged and

rather tipsy"—a grimace to indicate his disgust with himself—
"I came in here, ordered my mournful *stack* and two burned
sausages, and looked in the corner and saw a divinity, a
little blond god or goddess smiling at me. I could focus on
him only by closing one eye, and I was so ashamed of myself
I wanted to head home and hide. I'd fallen so low I was completely bitter and paranoid and really thought he and his
little drag friends, all so chic and desirable, had decided to
pick on me as a comically woebegone specimen. But finally
this little goddess—I really wasn't sure what sex she was,
she'd been sewn into white jeans with green thread, she had
an Hermès scarf tied to her shoulder bag—anyway, she
came over and I bought her a cup of coffee and now she's
moved in, I can't believe my luck, a perfect little boy-girl
all my own, he makes me dinner just like a little wife and goes
to sleep listening to rock 'n' roll from the radio under
the pillow, our whole nights are afloat on a sea of rock-'n'-roll
wisdom."

I had dinner several times with Lou and Misty, but Lou
never participated in the conversation. He preferred to watch
me interview Misty. Then he'd watch Misty respond at tedi-
ous, childlike, mendacious length—I say "watch" us because
he sat at some distance from us, as though we were actors
having a quick runthrough and whispering our lines. His
pleasure at having such a fabulous creature in his house was
increased when he gazed at Misty from a distance.

When summer came, we three went to Riis Park together, taking the subway all the way to the end of the line,
then switching to a bus that let us off at the big Brooklyn public beach.

One section was gay, and there, late in the long hot afternoon, these cute Puerto Rican guys would start dancing to a
portable radio or even a stack of the latest 45s.

Beers would pass from hand to hand, a circle gathered,

the late sun stared into its own reflection, the smell of sea-weed blended with the cooking smells drifting over from the takeout stands along the boardwalk, the smell of franks and steamer clams. Gay boys sat and combed each other's hair or scampered into the nearly becalmed surf as someone's mother, a Mrs. Meyer, "spritzed" herself by flicking drops over her shoulders from diamonded old fingers.

Someone had set up a white tent in the sand, not the usual boy-scout sort but a noble tent right out of a medieval movie, and three black drags kept going in and out of it to change clothes. Misty was in raptures over a Dionne War-wick look-alike. The dance gathered momentum. We were too zonked from the heat and beer and the sun's stare to stroll over, but we lay on our sides and watched the virtuoso turns each soloist took, daring the next dancer to greater intricacies. I closed my eyes. I listened to the rhythmic clapping of the tribe. When I looked again, the red-haired Puerto Rican boy on the next towel over, wearing a swimsuit that said "Made in USA," had finally stopped doing sit-ups and seemed to be sleeping.

I felt far from the private beach of my childhood in front of our Michigan summer cottage. Now I was at once thrilled to be among so many poor people and afraid I had become one of them. Of course, I wanted to sleep with them, a good many of them, and they were strong and brown and at home on this beach and in this city, whereas I was a white foreigner.

Simultaneously, in another corner of my mind I felt a queasiness about being here with so many tacky queens, these drags with the plucked eyebrows and bass voices, with the silver toenails and immense feet—chagrined and attracted and afraid.

Lou had no such hesitations. He maintained his high-paying job and knew how to pitch an account to the president of a corporation, just as in group-therapy sessions he knew how to cite Freud's distinction between mourning and melancholia. But leaving aside these concessions to the middle class, he'd moved into a marginal neighborhood and even had Misty's initials tattooed on his shoulders in a blue-and-red heart.

On the train back to town, the subway came up above-ground to pass over a long low stretch on trestles. The eight-o'clock sunlight fell on a girl standing at the head of the car. Her blonde hair caught in the wind pouring in through an open window, danced around her like the energy at the heart of the sun. I rested my head on Lou's tattooed shoulder and half dozed. Some of the gay boys were still playing records, and two were jitterbugging. I longed for a Coke. As my eyes fluttered open and shut with delicious sleepiness, our train passed above an inland marsh and the girl turned slowly, idly around a pole while her hair transformed the solid silver cylinder into goldest filigree.

EIGHT

■   ■   ■   ■   ■   ■   ■

For a year I lived as a fat
man. Sometimes I'd be picked up by an older man or a black
man. Both categories seemed more indulgent than the white
guys my age, who struggled to be as thin and boyish as possible and who saw only each other. Once an attractive couple
picked me up. They wanted me to take turns servicing them
as they embraced. I felt like a home appliance one seldom
buys but rents when needed, something like a rug shampooer.
Yet I was disappointed when they failed to invite me back.

When depressed after a long fruitless search, I'd buy
a midnight sack of groceries at the deli: English muffins,
chocolate bars (the big expensive European kind), pepperoni,
donuts, and I'd head guiltily home.

In November Lou took me in hand. He sent me to a diet
doctor who saw me once a week and prescribed steak, salad,
white wine, and amphetamines. In those days students might
take a Dexedrine to pull an all-nighter, but the drug was little
used, although Dr. O'Reilly had of course sworn by it.

The weight melted off me. In eight weeks I lost forty
pounds and became slender. At the same time Lou insisted I

start coming with him to the gym. As a teenager I'd been hit in the head by a baseball; I was always the only one to get vertigo when climbing a rope and a severe burn when sliding down it; I was a perpetual malingerer, despite regularly falling in love with my gym teacher. Now I became nauseated after doing just a few leg lifts and had to sit with my head between my knees. The locker room sent me into a fit of shyness.

But a weightlifting gym for adults is a democratic place. People do what they can, given their size, age, and strength. No loudmouth giant with a T-shirt he's ripped open to fit into will refuse to help even the weakest wimp lift barbells out of a rack. My gym had been the exclusive province of straight Italian guys, all talking football or joking about eating out pussy. But every month more and more gay men joined, at first prissy but soon enough outspoken. A chorus boy with a trick knee who'd been forced to retire at twenty-eight was the first to get really big at our gym. Like the Italians, he was working out three hours a day, six days a week, and running to the deli and bringing back whole barbecued chickens he'd wash down with quarts of milk drunk right out of the carton. He even experimented with drinking bull's blood and had a passing case of gout. When he hit two hundred and thirty pounds, he felt he was imposing enough to turn the radio on Saturday afternoons from rock to the Metropolitan Opera. And in his teeth-drilling high voice he started debating the merits of cocksucking versus pussy eating. The Italian guys didn't care. They thought it was funny. They'd grown up in the Village.

Slowly my body took shape in the gym mirror. Stomach muscles emerged. A chest, biceps, triceps, lats—the whole kit. The gym instructor measured my arms (which grew) and my waist (which shrank). The diet pills gave me a jaw-clenching intensity. If I started looking up something in the

Yellow Pages at eight in the evening, I'd still be reading the columns of names at four in the morning, docilely obeying the cross-references (see appliances; see sanitary engineering). If I lay my head on the pillow I'd dip just below the waterline, but I was like a fish kept in a net bag and dragged through the waves buffeted by the speed. I wrote with the attentiveness of a manuscript illuminator, but after hundreds of hours I'd produced only a gnomic one-act about a pair of lovers, in some scenes played by two men, in others by a man and a woman. I had this idea that my play would demonstrate that the dynamics of love are always the same, no matter which sexes are involved.

And then I met Sean.

He rang my bell one day because he was looking for the Russian dancer who'd lived with me. I invited him in for a cup of coffee. He shed his coat and sat down. He didn't say anything but seemed expectant and bursting with contained energy. He drummed his fingers on the tabletop.

He was six feet tall and had white blond hair that covered darker layers as though his head were a hay mow. He had a hearty manner irrelevant to his surroundings, for I was murmuring in my usual vague, ironic way, whereas he was replying with loud, strangely definite emphases almost as though he'd been paid to exclaim in a commercial. He gave the impression of having been scrubbed very clean. Even his cheeks glowed ruddily. I thought he wouldn't smell of anything if I sniffed his body. He laughed loudly when I said something sort of amusing, but his restless eyes roamed over my little kitchen as though he found nothing worthy of his attention. He leaned forward when he spoke. He seemed to be one of those people so anxious that they don't listen to anyone else and only worry about their own next statement.

He appeared to be Polish, or my idea of Polish. The

back of his head was flat, as though a Polish grandmother had molded it that way so he wouldn't roll out of his cradle. His eyes were too small to be handsome, but his skin was so taut that there was only a single fold under his eyes and not a hint of darkness. The pure skin ran right up to the edge of the pale lashes and framed the sort of pale blue eyes that in a flash photo come out pink as a rabbit's. His skin reminded me that the French word for complexion is *carnation*.

When he strode about my little kitchen he kicked his legs straight out. He happened to mention his father was a billfold distributor in Ohio, and I realized that although he was talking books and ideas, his way of talking was a traveling salesman's—insistent, unstoppable. If I stopped him and took exception, he had an easygoing way of shrugging, laughing at himself, and trying a new tack, as if to say, "Since you didn't fall for that one, try this one on for size." When I spoke at any length, he frowned. He winced with concentration, just as though he were a nutcracker and my words a giant nut.

I processed everything he said in several different ways.

Mainly I was afraid of him. I'd never had anyone so handsome so near me before. Of course I had, but the experience was powerful enough to seem unique. This guy— but have I neglected to say he was luminously attractive, even at first glance, not like a model, for he wasn't that fine, his nose had something odd about it, perhaps it was, yes, too thick, the same thickness from the top to the tip, but all the same he stunned me. I was afraid of him because I wanted him. I didn't like the suspense. Because I wasn't a handsome boy, I couldn't enjoy the luxury of knowing that eventually he'd come around and that meanwhile the game was fun. For me, the game was intolerable.

And yet, just as he was leaving he stood by the door in

his dark blue military overcoat and he touched my hand with his, held it simply, normally, and asked me if I wanted to grab a bite to eat later. I said why not.

Then he was gone. I put my lips where his had been on the coffee cup. I felt elated, because that was all I'd ever wanted, to be loved, and nobody ever had. I questioned my sincerity. Why was I falling for someone so handsome? Then I thought, Why not? Beauty is something noble, like an old name, and I'll keep on seeing it in him even after he's lost it. I thought it was natural that he'd be willing to confide his beauty to my intelligence (now that he was gone and I was less afraid, I esteemed my mind more highly). As he'd held my hand, an appreciative smile had even flickered over his dark red lips.

Sean and I went out to a Village coffee shop on Sheridan Square. The snow had melted, and it was raining. We sat in a window booth and watched all the couples hurrying past, battling with their umbrellas in the wind. For us, the feeling was very cozy, being inside. It wasn't bad for the passersby, either. They were mostly couples on dates who seemed to be enjoying their struggle with the wind; nothing is more urban than a rainstorm. One after another these smiling, wet, fresh-faced couples, laughing and shaking their heads in mock annoyance, came running to stand under our awning. We couldn't hear them through the glass.

It turned out that Sean had met the Russian dancer through Lou, whom he'd encountered at the Carmine Street public pool.

"I think Lou is so intelligent. He's really the most intelligent person I've ever known," Sean said with a curious agitation, as though something were at stake. Then, to cover his embarrassment, he sang three deep notes to himself, "Oom pah pah." After a short silence he said, "I don't know why he dropped me."

"Maybe you were too butch for him. Have you met Misty?"

"I bore Lou. I called him Monday and he sounded like he was falling asleep. I waited three days for him to call me— he said he would. Oom pah pah."

I received an odd sensation when it dawned on me that this deep voice, with its overly clear, penetrating salesman's diction, was telling the truth and conveying an emotion. "He's been very busy this week," I said.

"Don't."

"You seem to be afraid of me," I said, suddenly intuitive. Until this second, when he'd disclosed his feelings about Lou, I hadn't imagined he might be insecure.

"I am."

"Why?"

"Lou told me you were very intelligent."

"But you're far more intelligent than I. You read books in several languages; you know all about the pastoral tradition and the medieval allegory." To my way of looking at things, of course, knowledge wasn't intelligence. I believed in that pure, radiant isotope called "general intelligence," something so abstract that any concrete knowledge would only diminish it.

"Strange you could admit that so easily," Sean said. While we spoke I couldn't forget his beauty, which seemed eucharistic. "Aren't you ever insecure?" he asked.

"I can't endure suspense," I said.

"What are you talking about?"

"Well, once I'm into a friendship I'm really very relaxed and—well, I'm a good friend, I think. But in the beginning, when you don't know whether the other person likes you or not . . . "

"Oh, I see." Sean smeared the ring his cup had made on the table. He said very softly, "I like you very much. Dee-dee-dee dum."

I wanted to tell him right away that I didn't even expect that much. I was so afraid of appearing greedy. And I knew I had the capacity to wait. I recognized that he was too good for me. I was sure medieval knights knew they were unworthy of their lady, and that's why they welcomed trials, proofs, labors.

The idea that he might like me radically revised my version of who we were. I was suddenly one of those funny, nutty, brainy guys welcomed precisely because he relieves the heavenly tedium of excessive beauty. Or we were buddies, and our camaraderie erased the difference between us; who could judge the looks of a childhood friend? Who would want to? Or he thought I was the brain, he the slow learner . . . No matter which scenario the next few minutes or years would confirm, at least I was *in* all of them.

I walked him back to his door. The rain had stopped, but big white clouds still circulated across the night sky, reflecting the city lights, clouds lit up like internal organs about to be studied to locate the fatal, microscopic flaw.

Our shoulders bumped as we walked along. I guess Sean wasn't so tall after all; just my imagination had made him big. Bumping shoulders turned us into chums, and we stole little, embarrassed smiles at each other and looked at our feet. Falling in love is slightly embarrassing because love is a conspicuous and weighty thing. It is a marvel. I felt a bit like a hunter who's captured a unicorn and parades it through the town streets, but the crowds were discreet enough not to stare.

Marilyn Monroe had died and President Kennedy had been shot, and everyone talked and talked about them in those days as though they'd actually known them. People would argue about whether Marilyn had been "modest" or not, but the argument was only semantic trash, never a question of affection, because we were all friendly toward our martyrs. In the dry cleaner's on my corner someone had hung up a woven portrait of Kennedy, but the artist had misjudged the perspective, so that his eyes crossed. It was a camp, but it expressed my reverence. It was the same way I felt toward Sean. I didn't know him, but I felt a perfect right to have opinions about him; he'd become "my" Sean, just as she was "my" Marilyn.

In his little apartment, so similar to mine if less crowded and cleaner, I kissed him. He said, "That's nice." His skin had a burnt-almond taste and smell; his skin seemed to be a tissue of the brain, so directly did it record his feelings. It began to color.

He gently, so gently extricated himself from my embrace. Right away I felt fat again. "Hope you understand," he said, "but I think we should wait until we know each other better."

The next night Sean made me spaghetti. As I watched him, I grew more porous as he became increasingly impermeable. He wore a blue apron over his crisply creased khakis; this dark suggestion of a skirt contrasted with his high buttocks in their military drab. I still hadn't seen him naked. Since I was seated and he was standing, moving about, I thought about his body. I wondered if that expressive skin continued below his neck—whether his chest could blush, his loins pale. And I wondered what his penis looked like, how big it was.

At this time I read James Baldwin's *Giovanni's Room,* in which Giovanni stops being attractive the moment he abandons his heterosexuality. Against this absolutism of heterosexuality, few merits held up. A large penis or a muscular body or lots of money had some appeal, but they were fraudulent when they belonged to another queer. We would piously list all the great dead fags of history, but if someone mentioned a living conductor or pianist, we'd say contemptuously, "Who, *her*?" as though "her" (or "huh" in New Yorkese) homosexuality were instantly disqualifying. Still more damaging to a man's celebrity was the claim that one had actually slept with him. A New York queen would blow on what he pretended were freshly painted nails and say, "Who? *huh*? *Had* huh."

I had not yet "had" Sean, and I wanted to forestall that inevitable disappointment. Although everyone at the time congratulated me on my new body, contact lenses, and surfer hairstyle, I now wonder whether my transformation wasn't a capitulation to a dangerous commodity psychology. Of course, it's better to be handsome than ugly, but I never came to feel good about myself. I had the mole between my shoulder blades burned off, every night I did facial isometrics, I trimmed the hairs around my scrotum to throw my penis into relief and make it look larger, but melancholy self-regard continued to alternate with a generalized guilt as the background to all my feelings.

After dinner Sean talked to me about Catullus. He struggled to express himself. Like me, he was a Midwesterner, someone without a ready way of discussing ideas. If the New York style was nonchalance toward the topic and aggressiveness toward the listener, our Midwestern way was to assume the listener was neutral and to burrow relentlessly into the question. Sean was serious, very serious, and when he spoke he winced.

He led me to his bed. He undressed me and lit a candle and put it beside a mirror on the floor. I looked at myself in the mirror. I was perfect now except for the white silk stitches along my side, the stretch marks where I'd been fat. My vision of us, of Sean and me, was so large that it belittled our gestures or any moment we lived through as though our proper medium was myth, not history. We couldn't stop smiling at each other.

I was so happy. Gratitude and love burned in my heart. I felt Sean was a superior being who was lifting me up and placing me on a throne beside him. Perhaps because I'd never lived with a happy couple, I had no notion of domestic love; dailiness even threatened what I knew about, which was ecstasy. I was ecstatic now, but the feeling wasn't a crisis, rather a slow turning in the amber crosslight. Just as music is invisible but suggests motion, in the same way our muscles generated a sort of music we could see in the candlelight.

His shoulders were broad, too broad given his slender torso, as though a man were climbing up out of the adolescent. We looked down at ourselves in the mirror, not as one might watch pornography starring oneself but to confirm the happy fiction that we were in each other's arms. The commotion of happiness ringing in my head was so loud I could scarcely hear what was happening.

Such moments in a whole long life are neither as rare as one fears at first nor as frequent as later one hopes.

His penis was crooked when erect. It was big and veered off to one side.

The next day I said, "Lou says it's wrong to see each day as a separate beginning. It's wrong to divide time up into days and weeks. He says you should live as though time is one unbroken flow."

"Is that right?" Again that look of anxiety, that wincing look of concentration.

"Yes, and I have no business saying this now, after I've

just met you, but I feel that you're going to turn my life into something like that. Today, all day at the office, I was so full of expectation."

Sean nodded. We ate our salad out of a battered saucepan, sharing Sean's only fork.

"Tell me about Lou," Sean said.

What a fool I am, I thought. "Oh, he's terrific; I love him very much."

"Were you and he ever lovers?"

"Yes."

"When?"

"About a hundred years ago. The best friends are old lovers, don't you think?"

"I don't know. I never had a lover."

"I can't believe that."

"Well," Sean said, "I had an affair with this guy Ted. But we're not friends now. He drove me nuts. He's a professional broken heart. Moons around all the time, threatens suicide, calls me up when he's drunk." Sean leapt up and opened the refrigerator. Staring into it he said, "I guess that's what I think. That's what my friend Julio says. It sounds right."

"You don't know?"

He sank back down. "I don't know anything. Tell me anything and I'll believe it. And *that's* not even true."

"Who's Julio?"

"Oh, this great guy I met through Ted. You'll meet him. He's a famous dress designer."

All evening long I questioned Sean about every detail of his life. I memorized each name. I wanted to know all of Sean's history right away.

Every word he uttered either raised or dashed my hopes. "I'm very tired tonight"—bad, he wants to get rid of me. "But who needs sleep? It's more important to talk to you and" (radiant smile) "more fun"—good, very, very good. "I should study some Latin"—bad. "Can you read while I work? I don't want you to go. I like you here" (pats the couch deliberately, looking me in the eye)—good. Excellent.

Every night for weeks we got together, sometimes at my place, sometimes at his. We didn't have sex very often, but Sean liked me to stay over. He liked to hug me in the bed at night. He liked my mind and would force me to give opinions, which wasn't my way. I wanted to write fiction precisely because I could only see things dramatically, not politically or abstractly. I assumed he liked my sweetness, but once I became sarcastic with a book salesman who had never heard of Ronald Firbank. The salesman kept saying, over and over again, "Is that the *suspense* writer? He's the *suspense* guy, right?" I said something nasty and haughty. On the street again Sean chortled and said he liked that; he even referred to the incident several times later. "Gosh, you can be an arrogant bastard, can't you?" His admiration confused me. I thought it was so unfair that he would push me into being an angry man when I just wanted to be his tender sidekick.

On a Saturday evening Sean tried to study, but after ten the heat in his apartment went off and we decided to go out for a walk. He had told me about the warehouse district south of Canal. I'd never been down there. By day it was crowded with trucks and workers and by night it was deserted, as best I could tell. But he loved it. He liked architecture and spoke about the cast-iron buildings. He knew what New York had looked like at the time of the Civil War, and as we strolled through block after block of dark, dirty unlit warehouses, he re-created the past. We walked down a rainy street lit by a single overhead lamp swaying on a high wire. Its light glimmered across the shiny hackles of the wet, black pavement.

I was afraid of Sean and wanted to make light of him. I made fun of his piety before old buildings when I phoned

Lou, but Lou just said, "Sounds like you're falling in love." I visited Maria and Boo-Boo in their garden apartment on the Upper West Side, but I was restless during dinner, couldn't concentrate on the conversation, and kept pacing. Sounding rather strident to my own ears, I made fun of Sean, telling Maria that he lacked all sense of irony and thought Catullus's poem on the death of Lesbia's sparrow was *serious*, of all things.

"Dumpling," Maria said, "that's the tenth time you've brought up that boy tonight. It sounds like you've got it bad. And the death of a bird *is* serious."

One night as we were lying in bed, Sean said that that afternoon he had used a public toilet and walked in on an orgy.

"Oh, how awful," I said.

"What are they doing there?" he asked.

"What do you mean?"

"Of course I know they're there for sex, but how can they do it? It's really subhuman."

"Totally subhuman," I said.

NINE

■ ■ ■ ■ ■ ■ ■

Lou called me one day and said, "Bunny, I want to get married."

"To a woman?"

"Misty has moved out. He had a chance to go to Miami with a drag act in some sleazebag hotel. I don't want to be alone anymore. I want to settle down, and boys are too unreliable. But the real reason is that I want to make more money. I've been looking at the guys who break the five-figure barrier in the ad biz and they're all married."

"It's not just that easy," I said, "marriage."

"Sure it is. My shrink says you should always act ahead of your feelings. Do now what you know you'll be doing six months from now—what's best for you. But the real question is, how do you get married?"

"First you meet a woman," I said. With Lou I was never certain as to how plain I should make things. "Then you date her. Then you ask her to get married."

Long silence. Low voice: "How sweet . . ."

I promised to take him to a party of "straight people," kids from my school living in New York. Everyone drank gimlets and the hostess hired an oyster shucker to come up from Baltimore with crates and crates of oysters. The most famous person at the party was the jazz composer Charles Mingus, who was in a fat, paranoid phase. Even so, he talked to us all in his intense, original way. He turned off the music and asked us to listen to the layers of silence. He insisted that total silence didn't exist and that he could even score all the hums and swishes of the city night. Then the music came back on (it was "My Guy") and the hostess and I grabbed large wooden ladles from Mexico and held them in front of us like penises and danced our famous spoon dance—you had to be there. We were very drunk.

I introduced Lou to Ava, a girl I'd known for years. I'd first met her at Eton; she'd gone to our sister school.

A week later Lou called me. "Bunny, Ava and I—hold on," he clunked the receiver down and mumbled, "baby, give me a banana. Not that one, it's too brown. If you're going out, get me Pall Malls. . . . Hello?"

"Yes, what are you up to?"

"Marriage! Ava's going to be my wife."

"Oh, Lou, I'm so happy for both of you."

"Well, you know, you introduced us. We wanted you to be the first to know. Baby, pick up a carton of Cokes, too. Oh, my life is changing. The lonely times are over. Ava's going to be my wife and cook beautiful food and bear my children. Bye, baby. There goes my wife. My *wife*! I'm going to be her king. Do you know that wise old saying, 'A man's house is his castle'?"

"That's great, just great, I'm so happy for you."

"Yeah, isn't it? I finally got out of that shitty gay life."

Yet it didn't seem so shitty just now. We maintained, of course, the premise that we were sick, that our experience was limited, that we were missing out on the good things of life, and that our old age would be lonely. Worse, we anticipated a steady effeminization with the years. I knew I'd end up a seventy-year-old waiter, hair peroxided, camping with my gay customers and eyeing with hatred all the women customers I didn't already know and share beauty secrets with, a wizened old bird lined from excessive dieting and unwilling to go out at night for fear of hoodlums.

But just now that seemed a long way off. With Sean, of course, I pretended to be very studious and serious and even unfamiliar with gay life, but on nights when I was free I went out cruising.

After the World's Fair cleanup, gay bars started opening again, every month a new one. The Village gay life, which until now had collected along Greenwich Avenue, began to seep slowly down Christopher Street. Spring came, and boys were sitting on stoops almost all the way down to the Hudson.

Every day I'd arrive at work later and later. We were supposed to be there at ten, but I never arrived before eleven. No one said anything. I had my captions to write, then whole paragraphs, but the company was so overstaffed that we were given two weeks to write a hundred lines. We typed on lined paper that gave the exact character count, but it didn't matter, since every textblock was rewritten by all those idle editors over us. I closed my door and fell asleep on my desk, called all my friends, took two-hour lunches, had my shoes shined by a man who went from floor to floor with his kit and who once even offered to bump off anyone I wanted for two hundred dollars.

I lived for my nights. I'd rush home and fall asleep in my clothes. Hours later I'd awaken, eat cottage cheese out of the carton and a whole tomato, then I'd dress for cruising and head out into the night.

The appeal of gay life for me was that it provided so many *glancing* contacts with other men. At the gym I was becoming an old hand, and now I was the one to show the new guys how to work the lat machine or do heavy squats without injuring the back, but I never knew their names. At the bar I would buy drinks for "friends" and they for me, but again we seldom knew each other's names. If at the time we'd been called on to make a comment about this anonymity, we would have said it was "sad" or "pathetic," but a second later we would have been smiling and feeling that surge of popularity as we walked down Christopher greeting one guy after another, adding another detail to the mental dossier we were compiling on each acquaintance (Oh, Blondy is with Spare Parts—I wonder if Spare Parts is keeping him. No one's ever figured out till now how Blondy can afford so many new cashmere crewnecks on a dental hygienist's salary. Oh, and there's Mike the Barber with his ratpack. I wonder if Mike will say hi to me when he's with that glam bunch—he did!).

On Saturday afternoon while I was working out, a handsome stranger in a bomber jacket came in, walked slowly, arrogantly through the gym and locker room, came right up to me, shook my hand, introduced himself, asked me to pull up my T-shirt, which I stupidly did. He rubbed the back of his hand on my new washboard abs and said, "Nice. You'll do. Here. Call me." And he left. And I called the number on his printed trick card and went over, but the good part was just having been chosen like that at the gym.

Sean looked sad and I said so. He smiled and stood. He swayed slightly and leaned on my shoulder as he passed me on the way to the window. He climbed out on the fire escape and pissed into the dark.

"Did I say something wrong?" I called to him.

He stepped back in and said, "It's just—"

"What?"

Sean shrugged. "Oh, nothing."

"I'm strong. Don't worry about hurting me."

"I just don't see why you're interested in me. All your

friends sound like they're so smart—I know Lou is. Besides, you've read a lot and you're older."

"Why do you think I'm interested in you then?"

"I don't know." He put his glass on the floor and smiled, but with an uneasy, baffled look in his eye, as though he were about to be hit.

I came over and sat beside him and put an arm around his shoulders.

He cleared his throat. "Do you think I'm intelligent?"

"Of course."

"That guy Ted? He told me I was dense."

"Ted knew you were hung up on being intelligent, so he said you were dense. It was a way of holding you."

"Tell me your honest evaluation of me."

"I am being honest. Obviously you're very intelligent."

"I don't believe you."

"You get good grades, don't you?"

"That doesn't mean anything."

"Do you know what your I.Q. is?"

"No."

"Of course, I don't see any difference it makes anyway. I recognize that you're smart, but that's not why I like you."

"Then why do you?"

"Because you're handsome and strong and natural."

"I don't even know what that means—natural. You're handsome, and just as strong as I am."

"I don't think I'm good-looking."

Sean stood and pulled me up into his arms. He held my head in his hands, looked at me a long time, and kissed me. We went into the bedroom. The sheets were cold.

It was late April, but tonight was strangely cool. I had spent a quarter of my weekly paycheck to buy a gardenia plant for Sean. Its buds would obviously never open; one blossom was already brown, but the remaining three cast off their intoxicating perfume, so heavy as to be distracting. It was almost as though I had two lovers in the room, the man and the flower, but I've always been someone who needed a distraction to concentrate, music I must tune out in order to focus my thoughts.

Now it seemed as though our conversation was continuing. Kisses that with other men were only empty forms now filled with content. Sexual acts served as shades of meaning, a darkening or lightening of the voice.

Afterward I said, "You have such wonderful hands. They're so warm and gentle. I could spend my whole life sleeping in your hands." As I said those words, I felt the tension in my body knitting. I did want to sleep in Sean's hands. I pictured the fingers and thumbs cradling me as I lay in the hollow of the cupped hands. I said, "I mean it, my whole life."

He smiled, his lips looking even redder than usual, Médoc red. He pulled me into his arms and pointed at our reflection in the mirror. It was really happening.

As we went into the kitchen, where the shower stall stood, raised high and narrow as a sentry box, Sean said, "Do you think I look gay?"

"No, of course not."

"Why not?"

"Because gay types are stiff. They make a beeline down the street with their arms clamped to their sides and their legs as close together as possible."

We stepped into the shower, pulled the tan plastic curtain shut, and looked each other in the eye.

Blue flames from the stove burners provided the only light in the room, two soft penumbras glowing on the tan curtain, picking out a wet lower lip, the curve of Sean's chest, the shiny back of his hand in motion. He washed me all over, turned me around, scrubbed me with a fiber mitten.

Then we embraced and the water discovered a new body

for me to lave and love, as though we'd been immortalized in marble. Since my love preferred static myth to changing history, eternity to time, marble suited me perfectly—a marble fountain, the static figures fixed in an eternal embrace but the water providing the illusion of movement.

A week later I was sitting at my desk thinking of Sean. An acquaintance who worked down the hall had stopped in to confide in me about her new boyfriend, and I'd wanted half a dozen times to say, "Yes, that's right. That's just the way it is with me and my guy." But I didn't dare. I knew I had to hide my sexuality from most people, even though I was so proud of Sean, so pleased when we walked down the street bumping shoulders. I couldn't remember exactly why we had to be ashamed.

"Hello, Bunny? This is Lou." There was a pause over the phone, and my visitor mimed a farewell kiss and left me, pulling my door shut behind her.

"Lou! How are you? How was your trip to Chicago?"

" . . . "

"Did you meet Ava's parents?" Silence. "They must have met yours, huh? A big family pow-wow?" Silence. I decided I would keep fooling around until I hit paydirt. "It must have been gruesome." Despite the silence, I flew blind into: "I don't know why you went out there. Seeing your own parents is bad enough . . . " But what if the trip was a success? I let a long therapeutic silence spread itself out between us.

Lou whistled. "That's Miles Davis's 'Funny Valentine.' "

"Oh?"

"My . . . funny . . . val . . . "

Starting all over again, I said softly, with exactly the endearing, breathy, formal but tender lilt Lou could give the phrase, as though he'd just coined it, "How nice to hear your voice."

"Thank you, Bunny. . . . They were terrible people."

"Ava's parents?"

"Do you know what her mother said to me?"

"No, what?"

"She asked me if there were any other children. 'Are there any siblings?' I said I had a brother who'd committed suicide. She said, 'I don't know whether I can accept that.'"

"How appalling."

"I'm not sure I can accept her daughter as my wife."

"How was the trip otherwise?"

"Fine except I went blind in one eye, got so doubled over with anxiety I couldn't eat or walk, was knocked over by a taxi after I heard my drunken father lecture me about what perverted creatures out of hell my brother and I had been as children."

"Oh no! Always such a mistake to leave New York."

"Ava, can I have some nice soup?" Ava made some remark and Lou muttered, "Ava's soup burned. This apartment is a dump. We haven't had heat in a month. Stupid spic super. Today I was held at the office and then I was half an hour late for my shrink. So I rushed over on my bike and had my hour, now fifteen minutes, and then I asked the nigger elevator operator if I could use the john in the building but—"

"Do you have to use those pejorative—" I said.

"Don't give me that sobsister shit: Kike analysts, nigger elevator men, spic supers. . . . You know we talk this liberal bullshit, but do we ever stop to wonder why these germs have been considered inferior for centuries? Anyway. I got out on the street, and the front wheel from my bike had been stolen."

"But this is like a—"

"It's *not* a nightmare, baby. It's New York City. That's what it is. So I hailed about forty cabs. They'd slow down but then see the bike and take off. If you rode a bike you'd recognize how interesting it is that we take the most criminal element of our society, license them as cabdrivers, and set them loose behind ten thousand wheels on our city streets. And *not one* of them can speak English."

He sighed. "Well, I walked, I *walked* all the way across town, and by this time I had to shit so bad I went down into the IND, finally located a dime, and what do I find in the john: there are two toilets and roosting on each of them is a big grinning fairy!" Lou paused after the lightning exclamation and waited for the thunder of his own revulsion to roll over him. "Ugh! I could strangle every fucking fairy. You know how we used to deplore efforts to clean up Times Square? Well, turns out the cops are right, fairies *are* subhuman, they *are* going to pervert our children. An adult man works hard for a living and tries to provide for his family in his little apartment—no wonder he wants to bash every lush-life pansy in the teeth, the grinning chortling *gargoyles* right off the roof of Notre Dame! Nobody would let me take a crap. I went back to the street, unlocked my wreck of a bike from the street lamp, and wheeled it home, like one of Beckett's tramps.

"I had given up all hope of getting back to the office—they may fire me—and I had almost made it to my building when I shit in my pants. I couldn't use the elevator; I wasn't fit to ride with normal people. I walked up the four flights and took off my three-hundred-dollar Meledandri suit and washed it out with soap and water, and then took a shower. You wanted to know how I was."

"Oh, Lou," I said, "I don't know what to say."

"Why did I get diarrhea?"

"Couldn't it have been just an accident?"

"Come on, Bunny. You've been in therapy."

Just as I was beginning to speculate, Lou whispered into the phone, "Bunny, you're the one. I don't want to marry Ava. I see what a mistake I've made. Will you wait for me?"

"What do you mean?"

"You're the real love of my life. Do you love that boy?"

"Who?"

"What's-his-name."

"Sean? I think so."

"And you don't love me anymore?"

"Lou, you're my best friend."

"Really?"

"Yes."

"I never had a friend. I don't like what's-his-name."

"Why not?"

"I'm jealous. You're *my* lover. He's taken you away from me."

"He hasn't taken me away. I'm your friend. I love you."

"Do you?"

"Yes."

"Baby, I can't talk anymore. Ava's calling me to supper. Goodbye."

"Take care. Goodbye."

"Goodbye. You're wonderful."

TEN

Sean didn't want to be gay, and waking up beside me was too much evidence for him that he was becoming homosexual. I suggested that we start therapy together and go straight together—slowly, I hoped. Through Ava I found a psychotherapist named Dale who specialized in a treatment based on the idea that everyone at all times was playing a game.

Sean and I were placed in separate groups in which all the other members were heterosexual. A group met once a week with Dale in her office, and one other evening without her in the apartment of a member. Unhappy marriages, celibacy, impotence, adultery, alcoholism, divorce, career frustration, the coldness of men and the hysteria of women, bankruptcy, friendships riddled by spite and envy—we watched the painful surfacing of all these problems. Like a team of midwives, we encouraged the birth of each memory.

What came harder was the shrink's theory that we must re-create among ourselves the hostilities that had divided but perpetuated our families. Listening to each other's stories was no problem; that called on the familiar American skills of shocking confession and compassionate audition. But it was trickier to point a finger at a fellow member, a housewife from Scarsdale, and shout, "You're trying to guilt-trip us by playing Poor Me."

We usually sought the origins of our pain in the unresolved conflicts of childhood. Those of us who had bad memories had to keep rereading the same old tea leaves. I was let off lightly. Since I was a homosexual, everyone knew what caused my disease (absent father and overprotective mother), so no one poked about for further explanations.

My only enemy was Simon, a recent Russian immigrant in his sixties. He'd entered therapy to convince his wife that he was making an effort to curb his rages, but he still beat her regularly. He'd even knocked out a tooth. As a Russian, Simon wasn't used to the American way of coddling people. He hated our welfare system, detested out-of-work blacks and thought they should all be sent back to Africa. He thought sexual perversion should be punished by castration or lobotomy, but he was convinced by the other group members that I was making an honest effort to go straight. In his mind the cure was simple. I should go out with girls, buy them candy, strike them, no doubt, finally marry them. Whenever I started spinning my analytic gossamer, he'd say, "But wot about de goils? I wanna hear about de goils."

I embraced Dale's system with passion and rigor. I thought about the games people play not only during my sessions but also at work. In my own modest way, I even set up shop as a therapist for a few of my fellow employees. We were all so idle—and so frustrated from the company's duplication (or negation) of our efforts—that we had the time and spleen conducive to auto-analysis.

In therapy I became so expert in spotting covert games that Dale herself would sometimes ask me for my opinion. Once in a great while someone would notice that I had said nothing about myself for ages, but I was too valuable an ally to alienate. In my mind I was earning chips I'd be able to cash in one wonderful day when I would need everyone's attention and sympathy.

One night over supper with Maria I yawned and said, "Of course Maeve was just playing Yes, But."

"What do you mean?" Maria asked.

"That's one of the games people play," and I went on to explain it with majestic confidence.

Maria put her knife and fork down and grew silent. Without raising her eyes she said, "When I met you, you had one of the sharpest, most open, most skeptical minds I'd ever encountered. Now you've become the dullest sort of bigot. You see absolutely every last thing through those ridiculous therapeutic glasses. You're as smug as a Catholic convert or an American Marxist without enjoying the intellectual range and depth of either system."

"Why do you find my therapy so threatening, Maria?" I asked, already trying to label the game she was playing.

"You're my best friend, Dumpling, but I don't think I can continue this friendship if you don't change. I can't bear to see the wreck you've made of your mind. It's all because you can't accept being gay, which isn't such a big deal. You're still white, a man, handsome, charming, from a well-to-do family, intelligent—everything's been handed to you, but you—"

Keep collecting injustices, I thought, naming one of the games members sometimes played.

Maria's case interested me. I noticed how she was slowly giving up her pro-Russian stand in favor of feminism. Women's rights. I asked her what earthly rights women lacked. They could already vote, divorce, work. Maria became so angry with me that she had to swallow an extra high-blood-pressure pill. Her voice shaking, she told me how women earned half of what men made for the same work but how they were usually refused the better jobs. "The woman problem is a poverty problem," she said. "You joke around about whether to say *Miss* or *Ms.*, but the real issue is poverty. Most of the poor families in America are headed by single women, usually black."

We ordered brandies. She said, "Do you remember how we used to smile at Buddy and Betts, those two old dykes at Solitaire? We used to think it was so amusing the way Betts played the *malade imaginaire*. I just got a letter from the colony director telling me that Betts's malady was hunger. The poor old things didn't have any money, and Buddy got too old to be the sheriff. They never did have much money. Then Buddy started drinking. Last winter they both froze to death." Maria's eyes filled with tears. "Those lovable old eccentrics were starving. The real woman question is poverty."

When I'd first met Maria, she'd held in contempt everything she was—middle-class, American, artistic—in favor of a remote ideal, a Soviet Union we knew next to nothing about except that it stood for principles we considered progressive: respect for labor, division of wealth, equal opportunity for women, atheism, science. In recent years, however, we'd read more and more accounts about Russia that had disillusioned and finally appalled us.

Simultaneously, Maria had become aware that women were oppressed in every country regardless of national policies or economics. She became angry with me when I suggested that her own lesbianism made her especially sensitive to women's indignities. "Why do you have to search for a personal reason for political convictions that can be established through rational arguments? It's so demeaning."

Maria's feminism may have been objective, as she insisted, but nevertheless it provided subjective benefits to her.

Because she was now defending what she was, a woman, her politics elicited pride not guilt, affirmation not chagrin. She began to paint again. Art was no longer a badge of privilege, but a quiet, deft way of making things, as one might make a new window box. She painted, listening to *Der Rosenkavalier*, as she had that first day I'd ever seen her, so many years ago, waltzing around her studio at the Eton art academy, her eyes closed.

By chance I knew a young woman who was in Sean's group. I badgered her to break the rule of secrecy and tell me what he was saying about me. She and I were seated in a cozy, dirty booth in a coffee shop on upper Broadway.

"But he's really sick," she said. "He paces up and down and talks about feeling flames leaping along his arms— 'bizarre somatic delusions' is what Dale calls them. He tries so hard to detect a heterosexual urge in himself he even pretends he's getting excited over Dale, who could be his mother and has ankles thicker than his waist."

"I know it's going to hurt," I said, "but what does he say about me?"

"He's never even mentioned you." She was polite enough to add, rather feebly, "That's the sickest thing of all."

Under pressure from the group to date girls, Sean told me the sexual part of our relationship was over. He looked so pitiful, so *flayed*, that I didn't object. I thought that a real person in my position would have said, "Fuck you. So long," and walked out for good. But I felt sorry for Sean. The report of his behavior in group made me fear he was far more disturbed than I'd imagined.

I also felt sorry for myself. I had stopped my compulsive toilet cruising since I'd met Sean. His sexual acceptance of me, paradoxically, had given me the courage to seduce other young men and take them home. In our mythology, a proper trick was more respectable than a tearoom quickie. A trick committed enough of his time to you to come home with you, mount your stairs, mount you, expose all his body, not just his penis, share a cigarette, and go through the usually empty but respectful ceremony of exchanging phone numbers.

If Sean left me, I'd be consigned back to the toilets, to my grubby, sleepwalking, streetwalking life. Since he'd been the first break in my bad luck, I assumed he'd be the last.

When we were together, I thought of nothing but strategy. I refused to give Sean reassurances, hoping he'd come back to me pleading for them.

But what I hadn't taken into account was how small a part I played in Sean's life. If he thought of me at all, he must have seen me as a nice guy though sometimes a pain in the ass, always coming on. But he was contemplating the flames dancing on his flesh, flashing on his money worries and school, brooding about going straight. He grew thinner and thinner, and Dale had to feed him with a spoon during their sessions, which had become daily, or he wouldn't eat at all.

Then she put him in St. Vincent's, in the psycho ward. He ran up and down the halls, knocking down nurses and patients, and had to be heavily medicated and put into restraints. He cried when he wasn't sleeping. Dale turned his case over to a doctor on the ward, who promptly went on vacation.

Lou, an old hand at being in bughouses, visited Sean with me. "Listen, Sean, you've got to talk to anyone and everyone around the clock," he said. "Start your own group therapy in the TV room. Psychoanalyze your roommate. Talk the psych-grad student's ear off. That's the only way to get well and get out. There's a bed shortage and it's costing the city money; they don't want you in here a second longer than necessary. There's no conspiracy."

"Is that right?" Sean asked tonelessly, his lips cracked from the dehydrating sedatives.

I cried in group, but Simon froze my tears by asking, "What about de goils?"

Eventually Sean, bloated from suffering and pills and completely silent, was shipped home to his parents in the Midwest.

I wondered how much I'd been responsible for his break-down. The worst thing had been my inability to remember that he was weak. For an instant I would grasp he was fragile, but a second later I'd resent his intransigence, his casting me back out into the darkness.

I missed Sean so much I started to fester with it. I'd lie in bed and cry *it* and turn in *it* until I'd soiled myself with *it*. Everything, feebly, spoke *it*, even the neighbor's laundry palpitating shadows on my blinds. "Woke up this morning, blues around the bed. Sat down to eat, blues in my bread," said the song, and I sang it. I'd played a game, pretending to fall in love, but now the game had tricked me; I was caught.

I started hyperventilating, although it felt as though I was getting too little air, not too much. Pins and needles started in my hands and feet and spread upward. If the numbness reached my heart, I thought, I would die. I carried a brown paper bag and breathed into it on the subway as a way of cutting down on the amount of oxygen. My hands would jerk and fly around all on their own, and if I was in public I'd cover by pretending to pat my hair.

When the weather became warm, I lay on a towel in the park in hopes of getting a tan. I basted myself in suffering. If Sean had stopped loving me, I was unlovable. My memory would wander back to his apartment, to the blue gas jets by which we'd showered, to the salad we'd eaten out of a sauce-pan, to our mortally young faces in the candlelit mirror—but then I'd slap myself awake as you must treat someone who's swallowed too many sedatives.

In the park on my towel I searched for something to

like. If I could find one thing in the whole world to like, I could start again. I saw a cop on a horse riding toward me and I thought, looking up at this centaur, admiring the shiny flanks and gleaming leather boots, hearing now the creak of the tack, here's something beautiful, something I can like. The cop rode up, looked down and said, "Get your shirt on, this isn't a beach. You're breaking the law."

Sean wrote me twice. Flat notes, and each sentence I saw as a safe compromise between several dangerous ways of saying things. The joke was that the great love of my life was a man who knew nothing about me and next to nothing about himself.

Suffering does make us more sensitive until it crushes us completely. I started to write about Sean, and the writing, like a searchlight sweeping wildly, almost caught my fugitive feelings. A close call, but another failure, for I was so afraid of being sentimental or self-indulgent, of not distancing myself through the appropriate irony and understatement and objectivity, that I wrote about myself in the third person. I invented a stand-in for myself but with ten points less intelligence. Yet how could I like myself or ask the reader to take seriously a love between two men? A plea for tolerance was the best I might have come up with, but I was too proud to plead for anything.

On early summer nights in the city I drifted down Christopher Street to a new dance place, the Stonewall, which had the hottest jukebox. The clientele was a bit tacky, all those black and brown boys and drags who'd attracted me at Riis Park, but they were the best dancers, the sharpest dressers, the most generous lovers. Many of my old friends didn't interest me much because they wouldn't let me talk about Sean anymore. Only Maria and Lou indulged me.

For me, the Stonewall was a place where I could watch

people in the inner, darker room, sit along the wall and feel at once alone and comforted. I liked to watch a giant black man who'd twirl and slice the air dangerously with his outflung arms and pointed toes, a flailing death machine of a ballerina. I was so glad I'd bothered to acquire a nice body, since it gave me something to offer every night to a different man—the graying high-school principal, the Puerto Rican hairburner, the death machine. I went to bed with anyone who wanted me.

One night I talked with a woman who explained to me she'd had her sex changed. "My husband doesn't even suspect I was once a guy. We live in a huge housing development. We even have our own shopping center, can you believe. One day at the mall I saw another post-op also passing. She's never told her old man neither. Anyway, we're best girlfriends, we watch the soaps together. But sometimes I get lonely for gay guys. You gay guys do know how to have fun."

A man I'd met at a bar invited me to the house he'd rented in Cherry Grove on Fire Island. The house had a name, "The Wicked Witch's Ding-Dong," and the instant we arrived my host put on a silk caftan and mixed cocktails in the blender out of crème de menthe and milk. He made a cognac icebox pie with a graham cracker crust and started his famous key lime chicken basted in rum, but then he began to drink those cocktails with the neighbors, Bill and "Dot." We all sat on the small front porch, while the others evaluated each passing number. "She buys her polka-dot schmattes at F.A.O. Schwarz." "That one told me she's got an inner beauty, but she could die with the secret." "Here's Edwina— she lost her husband to that slut over on Tuna," naming a boardwalk in the next community, the far classier Pines, where most of the renters were still heterosexuals.

On and on they went, dishing every passerby. My host, drunk and belligerent by now, told me that the usual thing was for a guest to bring a quart of J&B scotch for the weekend. Shamefaced, I scuttled down to the liquor store and rushed back the requisite tribute.

The burned chicken was served at midnight, but we were all too smashed to do anything except toy with the cinders. We went dancing at the disco, where by local law every group of men had to include at least one woman. At last I escaped to the Meat Rack, that stretch of scrub pines and sassafras bushes that lay between the ocean and the bay.

I was so sad about losing Sean that I felt my life was over. In the mirror, we'd looked into our reflections as though we were contemplating an allegory whose symbolism had been lost but that was still replete with meaning, a serenade on the grass that may speak of sacred and profane love or of the Platonic love of wisdom or of Meleager's love of Atalanta— but love in any case, some strong form of love.

In the dunes I felt sacralized by suffering. If as a child I'd known my whole long life was going to be so painful, I'd never have consented to go on leading it. At each step I had looked forward to more freedom. Paul had told me someday that I'd have too much freedom, and he was right. At least, I had too much free time. I had wanted to have fun with other gay men and to make my own money. Now I'd done that and I'd made my body beautiful, or so people told me; but I loved Sean and he wasn't even part of my life anymore. My suffering had humbled me, and his had extracted something vital out of me. I worked out every evening at the gym, wishing I could start a conversation with another man, but I lacked the confidence or necessary hope. I snatched up every issue of the *Post*, which was running a series on love, on how to give it and receive it, and I read every word.

Sean seemed like a sickness I'd contracted, a sickness

such as malaria that you never get over and that gives you a
spell of chills during the least expected moments. Because I
had always doubted the authenticity of my feelings, I was
shocked at the virulence of my love. Now I could only wander
around the world, charismatic with suffering, handing myself
over to whoever would have me, just as a Buddhist monk
must eat whatever is placed in his begging bowl, even if it is
meat, even poisoned meat (the very dish that had killed the
Buddha). In the pines under the moon, listening to the surf—
which was invisible, since it was on the other side of the
dunes, crashing slowly and voluminously—I felt the shock
of each wave in the ground under my moccasins and moved,
a mendicant, eating whatever was given me. I ate all the men
and didn't mind or even really notice. I cried while I sucked
one cock because it was bent to one side, just as Sean's had
been.

I came back to the city and my sad serenity vanished.
At night I'd be about to drift off to sleep when I'd sit straight
up, gasping for air. The magazine I worked for published
an editorial on homosexuality for no particular reason. It
denounced the "chic new trend toward treating homosexuality as though it were a *different* way rather than a *lesser*
way." The essay deplored homosexuals' "glibly self-justifying
references to the ancients." It actually said, "We must blush
for fifth-century Athens." In conclusion, the essay read: "Let's
face the sour music: homosexuality is not a sophisticated
or naughty aberration but a pathetic malady. We must make
certain that in this era of drugs, free sex, and sloppy liberal
rhetoric the Homintern, that conspiracy of bitter inverts who
already have a stranglehold over the theater, fashion, and fiction, does not pervert the lives of decent people by glamoriz-
ing vice, neutering the female body, and making the fine old
art of being a mature man or woman look dull—or as *they*
would say, campy."

When I cried in group therapy about Sean, about the helplessness I felt now, Simon said, "I wanna hear about de goils."

A rage I couldn't control boiled up inside me. The other men in the group had to pull me off Simon. I knocked his chair over and was sitting on him, choking him with both hands and shouting, over and over, "Don't you *ever*, don't you *ever*—" but I didn't know how to finish the sentence.

I'd always regarded my sister as the norm. She had managed to marry, have children, settle in the suburbs and lead a respectable life. I saw her only occasionally when I was home for the holidays, and then she'd shyly press her three children forward. One Christmas Eve she and I stayed awake all night trying to sort out the parts of a tricycle to be assembled according to instructions written in English by a Japanese. I never talked to her about my real feelings or my real life, but I assumed I knew everything about hers.

Then she announced that she wanted to visit me in New York. She'd be coming without her husband but with the neighbor lady, Peg. Since by now I was making a decent living, I bought a new sofa bed for them.

My sister was in love with Peg. Awkward, bespectacled, ashamed, my sister gazed at the handsome Peg with adoration and recounted to me by the hour the sad saga of Peg's life (brutal parents, elderly husband, delinquent children, unfulfilled artistic ambitions). It was obvious to me that Peg didn't love my sister but enjoyed all the attention, something her husband wasn't providing.

The two women never stopped drinking. First thing in the morning they'd stir up a batch of bloody marys, declaring that they were on vacation and determined to whoop it up. I discovered that my sister no longer thought I was a weirdo but someone who'd had the courage to lead a free life. She seemed strangely gratified that I found Peg beautiful—my sister apparently was as obsessed with physical beauty as I. I think she also was hoping that somehow, mysteriously, things would work out between Peg and her in my presence.

I was shocked. I called Maria and said, "I had closed the books on my sister. She was the mother of three and the PTA member. Do you think she's really a lesbian? Or is she just copying me?"

Maria laughed. "Didn't you tell me she was always getting crushes on other girls? She never dated men and she married the first guy who asked her."

My sister and Maria spent a long boozy evening in New York together after Peg flew home early. "Your sister is a riot," Maria reported. "She is so extraordinarily frank—frank to the point of shocking even jaded old me. But she has no sense whatsoever of her rights as a woman. She's terribly confused. She says the worst things about herself, thinking she's being honest. She hates her husband, she never stops drinking and she's absolutely desperate about Peg, but funny at the same time. It sounds like the suburbs are a lesbian hotbed. Tomorrow night we're going to a dyke bar; your sister has already bought boots and trousers."

Another night my sister made me accompany her to a black-and-tan lesbian dance place where a lesbian band was playing. There we were, me in a coat and tie, she in her suburban pleated gray skirt and shoulder-strap bag (we'd been to the theater), trying to get past the bouncer, although we looked like a provincial husband and wife who'd strayed to the wrong door. "But we're gay!" we kept protesting, laughing. "We look square but we're a hundred percent gay." Then I added, "This is my sister and she's trying to come out and she's afraid to come in here alone." That did the trick.

I'd never felt so close to my sister before. I was no

longer the younger brother but the older mentor, despite my misgivings. We sat in a corner, studied the dancers, and, hypnotized, watched a standing woman comb her seated girl-friend's hair with an Afro pick, slowly, hair by hair. The face was as rigid as a Benin bronze and the hair was caught in a lavender and gold crosslight. I asked my sister how she could give up the security of marriage.

"There's nothing secure about suffering," she said. "Dick is frustrated and wounded. He wants to have sex all the time; I never knew people could be so horny, and I can't bear for him to touch me. I sit near the window for hours hoping to catch a glimpse of Peg. I invent excuses for going over there. I'm sort of the ringleader for the whole neighbor-hood, all the women admire me; but I create activities just to involve Peg and have another excuse for being with her. The kids—I love my kids, but they make me nervous, and I suppose I sometimes snap at them because I think that with-out them I could leave Dick."

I feared my sister would suffer for years to come. Al-though her coming out meant that I'd lost my sole hostage to normality, at the same time her homosexuality exonerated me. There was something—genetic or psychological—in our family that had made us both gay. I asked her if she'd told our father. I wanted her to share my culpability in his eyes. But she wept and pleaded with me not to give her away. I understood that just as I was married to our mother, she was married to our father.

Maria would stop off in Chicago now to see my mother and sister on her way home to Iowa. When I was growing up, my mother had had a horror of evenings out with the girls and had frequently said, with a smile, "I like *men*." But now, without ever renouncing that theoretical preference, she grew closer and closer to Maria. And my sister, bewildered by the tough lesbian world she saw at the bars (she and Maria went back to the Volley Ball in Chicago), found in Maria someone she could emulate.

I did not travel.

I didn't experience the melancholy of tramp steamers or of mornings waking up cold in tents.

I stayed on in New York.

I went out a lot and I had new adventures, but I never forgot Sean. At last he wrote me that he'd found a lumberjack for a lover and they'd opened a dude ranch in Arizona. He said I'd been "too gay" for him. I lived too much in the "ghetto." But I hadn't caused his breakdown. His suffering had been due to money pressures, intellectual self-doubt, and the "usual" coming-out anxieties. What he liked about his lumberjack, he said, was that no one would ever guess he was gay, not in a million years.

A million years passed.

Lou called me one day. "Wanna turn a trick? I've got a double for us. Two johns from Akron in a midtown hotel room."

He gave me the address and I joined him.

Lou had been sober for the last few months. Ava had left him, not because of the boys, but because of the drugs and booze. He'd passed out in the corridor of his building. Neighbors (he didn't know which) had dragged him into his apartment and left an Alcoholics Anonymous leaflet on his chest. He joined that day. His sponsor in A.A., an eighty-year-old crime novelist, told him that she thought shrinks were for shit. She said it was obvious to her that despite whatever psychological problems might have triggered his drinking (such as growing up in a totally alcoholic family), the disease was now self-perpetuating and created the problems it pretended to solve. When Lou told her that he was afraid sobriety would make him a square, she suggested he add a new vice to his life, one irrelevant to drink, but totally unacceptable.

Lou had turned to prostitution. Although he was now earning over a hundred thousand dollars a year in advertising and was in his late thirties, he could still look like a dumb teenage drifter. After a full day of pitching a campaign, he'd change into a T-shirt and jeans right out of the dryer and a corny cowboy hat of the sort never seen west of Jersey. Then he'd stand, skinny and forlorn on Third Avenue and Fifty-first, and be picked up by married men in cars.

I met him at the hotel just off Times Square. Our customers were already drunk and playing a tape of Beethoven's Fifth they'd doctored with trippy insertions of Joni Mitchell's talkative ballads. Lou and I knew who Joni Mitchell was, but we pretended we'd never heard of Beethoven. Our clients winked at each other over our heads.

I had to put on a leather harness, stick a swan feather up my john's ass, and call him "Pretty Peacock" as he strutted proudly about, cocking his head from side to side like a bird while wanking off in an all-too-human way. Fifty bucks for me and seventy for Lou who, after all, had organized the party.

Afterward Lou and I drifted down toward the Village. We didn't despise our johns. In fact, I was flattered that I'd been able to sell it at my advanced age (I was twenty-nine). I felt for now at last as though I were one of those tough guys I'd admired at Riis Park and here at the Stonewall.

The night was hot. We gay guys had taken over all of Christopher Street; even the shops were gay. Although the bars were owned by the Mafia, we somehow thought of them as ours. Just as this street, this one street in a city of ten thousand streets, felt like ours.

Of course, stories of police violence still circulated.

In the Stonewall the dance floor had been taken over by Latins. I had a friend, Hector Ramirez, a kindergarten teacher who, because he lived with his parents in the Bronx, borrowed my apartment every afternoon after school to rehearse new dance steps with another Latin twenty-two-year-old, similarly mustached and dressed in carefully ironed beige cotton shirts over guinea T-shirts and highwaisted pleated pants held up by a thin black crocodile belt. They were here tonight, twirling out of a tight clench, hips on small pistons, faces illegibly cool. Another friend, the death machine, came up to me and rested his size-twelve black hands on my shoulders and stared into my eyes with a mad gleam: " . . . is dead."

"Who?" I shouted over the music.

"Judy. Judy Garland."

Then the music went off, and the bar was full of cops, the bright lights came on, and we were all ordered out onto the street, everyone except the police working there. I suppose the police expected us to run away into the night, as we'd always done before, but we stood across the street on the sidewalk of the small triangular park. Inside the metal palisades rose the dignified, smaller-than-lifesize statue of the Civil War officer General Sheridan.

Our group drew a still larger crowd. The cops hustled half of the bartenders into a squad car and drove off, leaving several policemen behind, barricaded inside the Stonewall with the remaining staff. Everyone booed the cops, just as though they were committing a shameful act. We kept exchanging peripheral glances, excited and afraid. I had an urge to be responsible and disperse the crowd peacefully, send everyone home. After all, what were we protesting? Our right to our "pathetic malady"?

But in spite of myself a wild exhilaration swept over

me, the gleeful counterpart to the rage that had made me choke Simon. Lou was already helping several black men pull up a parking meter. They twisted it until the metal pipe snapped. By accident, the dial cracked open and dimes scattered over the pavement. Everyone laughed and swooped down to snatch up the largesse; the piñata had been struck open at this growing party. Two white, middle-class men in Lacoste shirts came up to me shaking their heads in disapproval. "This could set our cause back for decades," one of them said. "I'm not against demonstrations, but peaceful ones by responsible people in coats and ties, not these trashy violent drag queens."

I nodded in sober, sorrowing agreement. But a moment later I pushed closer to see what Lou was doing. Someone beside me called out, "Gay is good," in imitation of the new slogan, "Black is beautiful," and we all laughed and pressed closer toward the door. The traffic on Christopher had come to a standstill.

Lou, a black grease mark on his T-shirt, was standing beside me, holding my hand, chanting, "Gay is good." We were all chanting it, knowing how ridiculous we were being in this parody of a real demonstration but feeling giddily confident anyway. Now someone said, "We're the Pink Panthers," and that made us laugh again. Then I caught myself foolishly imagining that gays might someday constitute a community rather than a diagnosis.

"This could be the first funny revolution," Lou said. "Aren't these guys great, Bunny? Lily Law should never have messed with us on the day *Judy* died. Look, they've turned the parking meter into a battering ram."

The double wooden doors to the Stonewall cracked open. I could hear the cops inside shouting over their walkie-talkies. One of them stepped out with a raised hand to calm the crowd, but everyone booed him and started shoving and he retreated back into Fort Disco.

The city trash cans were overflowing with paper cups, greasy napkins, discarded newspapers. A new group of gays rushed up, emptied a can into the splintered-open doorway, doused it with lighter fluid, and lit it. A cloud of black smoke billowed up. "They've gone too far," I said.

A black maria came around the corner of Seventh Avenue and up Christopher the wrong way. The cops cleared the sidewalk, formed a cordon, and rushed the remaining bartenders into the van past the smoldering garbage, but the crowd booed even louder. Once the van had driven off, the cops pushed us slowly back from the bar entrance.

Down the street, some of our men turned over a parked Volkswagen. The cops rushed down to it while behind them another car was overturned. Its windows shattered and fell out. Now everyone was singing the civil rights song, "We Shall Overcome."

The riot squad was called in. It marched like a Roman army behind shields down Christopher from the women's prison, which was loud with catcalls and the clatter of metal drinking cups against steel bars. The squad, clubs flying, drove the gay men down Christopher, but everyone doubled back through Gay Street and emerged behind the squad in a chorus line, dancing the can-can. "Yoo-hoo, yoo-hoo," they called.

Lou and I stayed out all night, whooping like kids, huddling in groups to plan tomorrow's strategy, heckling the army of cops who were closing off all of Sheridan Square as a riot zone and refusing to let cars or pedestrians pass through it.

I stayed over at Lou's. We hugged each other in bed like brothers, but we were too excited to sleep. We rushed down to buy the morning papers to see how the Stonewall Uprising had been described. "It's really our Bastille Day," Lou said. But we couldn't find a single mention in the press of the turning point of our lives.

A NOTE ON THE TYPE

This book was set on the Linotype in Old Style No. 7. This face is largely based on a series originally cut by the Bruce Foundry in the early 1870s, and that face, in its turn, appears to have followed in all essentials the details of a face designed and cut some years before by the celebrated Edinburgh type founders Miller and Richard. Old Style No. 7, composed in a page, gives a subdued color and an even texture that make it easily and comfortably read.

Composed by Maryland Linotype Composition Company, Inc., Baltimore, Maryland

Printed and bound by R. R. Donnelley, Harrisonburg, Virginia

Typography and binding design by Marysarah Quinn